MW01178027

Where Dreams Have Gone

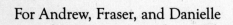
For Andrew, Fraser, and Danielle

Where Dreams Have Gone

Norma Harrs

Simon & Pierre
Toronto • Oxford

Copyright © Norma Harrs 1997

All rights reserved. No part of this publication may be reproduced, stored in a retrieval system, or transmitted in any form or by any means, electronic, mechanical, photocopying, recording, or otherwise (except for brief passages for purposes of review) without the prior permission of Simon & Pierre Publishing Company Ltd. Permission to photocopy should be requested from the Canadian Reprography Collective.

Simon & Pierre
A Member of the Dundurn Group

Publisher: Anthony Hawke
Editor: Liedewy Hawke
Designer: Scott Reid
Printer: Webcom
Front Cover Painting: Shelagh Miller

Canadian Cataloguing in Publication Data

Harrs, Norma, 1936-
        Where dreams have gone

ISBN 0-88924-276-3

I. Title

PS8565.A663W47 1997   C813'.54   C97-930053-3
PR9199.3.H37W47 1997

1 2 3 4 5 BJ 01 00 99 98 97

THE CANADA COUNCIL | LE CONSEIL DES ARTS
FOR THE ARTS | DU CANADA
SINCE 1957 | DEPUIS 1957

We acknowledge the support of the Canada Council for the Arts for our publishing program. We also acknowledge the support of the Ontario Arts Council and the Book Publishing Industry Development Program of the Department of Canadian Heritage.

Care has been taken to trace the ownership of copyright material used in this book. The author and the publisher welcome any information enabling them to rectify any references or credit in subsequent editions.

Printed and bound in Canada.

 Printed on recycled paper.

Simon & Pierre
8 Market Street
Second Floor
Toronto, Ontario, Canada
M5E 1M6

Simon & Pierre
73 Lime Walk
Headington, Oxford
England
OX3 7AD

Simon & Pierre
250 Sonwil Drive
Buffalo, NY
U.S.A. 14225

Contents

I would like to thank Liedewy Hawke, my wonderful editor, for her painstaking work and her unfailing good humour. Also thanks to Tony Hawke for his continued faith and encouragement. And special thanks to my talented sister Shelagh Miller for the cover painting.

You Can Never Trust an Alsatian

Robin lay on her bed and stared at the tributary of tiny cracks in the ceiling plaster. At night time they became places and faces. Today, they were what they were. Her anger reduced them to mere grotty signs of wear and tear.

She'd been banished to her room because she had chanted "Trish loves Duggie Foster!" just as Duggie was walking his big Alsatian past their house. Trish had been on the front step with her, looking to see if the postman had brought any mail, and it had been done to annoy her more than anything else. She hadn't intended for him to hear.

The trouble was nobody in the house had any sense of humour. The very idea of Trish loving Duggie Foster was absurd. He was a tax accountant who lived four houses down and who wore suits even to walk his dog. She'd never seen Duggie rumpled or untidy-looking. In her imagination she even saw him going to bed in his eternal navy blue suit. He was the kind of dink to wear rubber gloves to pee. Robin detested Duggie Foster.

He wasn't detested by everyone. Robin's mother was always going on about what a good catch he'd be, at the same time giving meaningful glances to Trish. Trish was twenty and expected to be on the look-out for a man.

Men, to Trish's mother, were a breed of fish that could be reeled in on a line. If he was a "catch," in Robin's mind he was a "bottom feeder"!

He was rich, that much she knew. What she also knew was that Duggie fancied Trish. Then everybody liked Trish, and she, in turn, never slighted any man who was smitten with her.

If there was anything her parents considered questionable about Duggie, it was his dog. Her father hated Rinty with a vengeance. Rinty ran after his car on the street, barking like crazy. He said more than once that the dog should be muzzled. Her mother said Alsatians were notoriously unpredictable.

Duggie walked him twice a day, regular as clockwork and always past their house, never in the other direction. Duggie himself wasn't bad looking, except for his nostrils which flared, so that you could see inside of his nose and all the nose hair. It was somehow an indecent sight. He was also far too smug and self-assured.

To Robin's mind he seemed like an old man. He'd lived with his mother for as long as Robin could remember. He was part of the street. As familiar a sight as Mrs. Foster, his mother, a wee pixie of a woman with a collection of hats that put the Queen Mother's assortment to shame. Mrs. Foster didn't wear the hats, the hats wore Mrs. Foster.

"For God's sake would you look at the chamber pot she has on today," Robin's mother would marvel from the window. "Gallagher the butcher will wet himself when he sees that one." She might make fun of the hats, but Robin sensed her mother envied their flamboyance. Against her own serviceable and modest velours, Mrs. Foster's were garden-party grand and hinted of other visits besides trips to the butcher.

Shortly after the episode on the front steps and Robin's banishment to her bedroom without her dinner, Duggie started dropping by to call on Trish. Rinty was tied up to the front gate and lay malevolent and nervous across the path, waiting for his master to come out. He barked at everything that moved. Her mother hid behind the curtains and waited for Duggie to take him away. She wouldn't have ventured out to save her life. "I've heard about those Alsatians," she said to Duggie. "They're police dogs, trained to attack people."

"Isn't he a wee lamb," Duggie tried to reassure her over the sound of Rinty's hysterical barks.

Duggie's visits were awful. He fawned all over her mother as though she was the one he was interested in, and her mother lapped it all up. Trish was guardedly coy.

What if Trish actually liked him? The thought made her want to vomit. All she could think about were those nostrils up close. She half hoped her father would have something negative to say on the subject of Duggie, but he never said a word. Duggie was full of talk about his business and her father seemed happy to talk over his tax problems with someone.

The conversations were dead boring, with Duggie bragging on and on about the money he could save people. Even Trish's eyelids began to close. When he saw that, he switched to talk of Rinty, his one other real interest in life, and then they were entertained with equally dull tales of Rinty's escapades.

Things began to take a serious turn when he started to drop by on Sunday afternoons looking for Trish to go for a walk with him up the Lagan. Formerly Trish and Robin did the walk together. Now Robin was no longer welcome.

Duggie's attraction grew when he bought a spiffy-looking dark blue Jaguar. He invited the whole family out for a spin. Sulkily, Robin refused the offer. Her mother was totally captivated, and Trish was thrilled to be driven around town in the Jag. Robin felt a kind of desperation when Trish kept going on about him, *Duggie says this* and *Duggie says that*. She couldn't visualize her darling Trish married to this robot and having to visit them both and listen to Duggie and his deadly lectures.

Robin was bound and determined that she would never marry. Long ago, to be precise the day that she and her best friend Jill had found out how babies were really born, they'd both decided to be spinsters. They would buy a house together and live on a diet of Mars bars, swearing that vegetables would never cross the doorstep of the house. Now, at a mature twelve years of age, especially since the new boy had moved into Number 94, she was less sure about her vow.

Meanwhile there was the problem of Trish and Duggie. Then came the dreadful day when Trish came home with an enormous engagement ring on her finger. The diamond was so big she could hardly get her gloves on. Even Robin was silenced by its magnificence. The house was suddenly filled with people come to look. Trish became oddly silent when people said nice things about Duggie and asked where they were going to live.

"Where *are* you going to live, dear?" her mother asked when everyone had gone home.

"We can't exactly leave Mrs. Foster. Duggie says she has to be with us. He says there's nothing wrong with their house." Trish's pretty mouth was now down-turned and her eyes avoided Robin's.

"You'll have to buy hats like his mother's," Robin said, lifting an apple off the table and taking a huge bite.

"Don't be such an eejit!" Trish flounced out of the room, ran up the stairs and slammed the bedroom door.

"Sometimes you're too much," her mother said, turning on Robin.

Robin studied the bite marks on her apple. "I suppose you'll make me go with the first person who comes along? Sell me to the first bidder."

"If you don't go and do your homework now, you're up for sale!"

When Robin went to the bedroom she shared with Trish, Trish was lying on the bed, staring up at the ceiling. Robin jumped on the other bed and took up the same pose. She was still eating her apple noisily.

"It *is* a nice ring," she said finally.

Trish didn't reply and Robin turned to look at her. There were tears streaking down her cheeks.

"What's wrong?"

"I don't know."

"Yes you do," Robin accused.

"It was all your fault anyway," Trish said.

"How was it my fault?"

"You and your '*Trish loves Duggie Foster.*' How do you think he got the idea?"

The reality of what Trish was saying suddenly struck home. Was she about to be responsible for her sister making the worst mistake of her life?

"Just tell him you don't want to marry him."

"I can't do that," she wailed. "Everyone's seen the ring."

"So what?"

"Oh, God, you're impossible. You understand nothing." Trish leapt off the bed and slammed out of the bedroom.

Robin felt odd, sort of queasy. Was it even dimly possible she might be responsible for the whole mess? She sat up and swung her legs over the side of the bed. If so, then it was up to her to do something about it. She had no idea just what, but she knew she had to think of something.

The following week nothing changed. Trish seemed resigned to her fate. She started to complain about Duggie's obsession with the dog. Whenever they planned to do something together, it seemed the dog always came first. The dog had to be walked or taken to the vet. She usually went with him when he walked the dog, and stood for ages in the park at the top of the street. Duggie would spend eons of time exercising Rinty while Trish waited patiently for it to be over. Robin always saw them there when she walked through the park to the street behind where her friend Jill lived.

One night when she was coming back from Jill's place, Duggie was there alone, throwing the stick back and forward for the dog. He threw the stick vaguely in Robin's direction and as a joke she picked it up. She began barking and ran back to Duggie. The dog chased after her, snapping at her heels. In her effort to avoid the dog's anger, she ran full tilt into Duggie.

"Careful, little sister!" He put his arms around her to steady her and kept a friendly arm around her shoulders. She looked down at the dog with terror and up into Duggie's pink nostrils. She was trapped between two nightmares.

"Go on! Give it to him. He won't hurt you."

She released the stick and the dog took it in his jaws and bounded off.

"There." Duggie patted her on the bum, keeping his hand there for just an instant longer than she thought was necessary. "Want to stay and play with the dog?"

"Not on your life!" She knew her response was too fast and also quite rude, but it came out before she could stop herself.

He shrugged. "Suit yourself."

When she got home, her mother and Trish were sitting hunched over the coffee table. Her mother had a large sheet of paper in front of her and Trish was leafing through a notebook. It appeared they were making up a guest list for the wedding. Robin's father sat buried behind his newspaper. Robin slumped on the sofa and watched the two of them engrossed in their list.

"Are you really going to marry that pervert?" Robin said suddenly.

Trish and her mother looked up as though electrified. Her father dropped the newspaper and took his spectacles off his nose. Robin had no idea why the words had come out. But now that they had, the die was cast.

"What are you talking about?" Trish demanded.

Her father put up a silencing hand. Robin shrugged. "Well, are you?"

"What are you saying?" her father asked solemnly.

Her mother stood up. A slight tremor had come into her hand. The paper she was holding shook a little, as though ruffled by a breeze. Robin bit her lip. She knew she'd gone too far, but there was no going back.

"I just think he's not very nice, that's all."

Trish stood up. "That isn't what you said. You called him a 'pervert.' You just don't go around calling people perverts."

"Trish, why don't you go to your room and your mother and I will handle things," her father said.

"What things? I'm not a baby. Let her say what she has to say."

All eyes turned to Robin again. "Well! We're waiting," Trish said.

Robin closed her eyes with the faint hope that when she opened them again they would all have gone and everything would be wiped out. She opened them, but even squinting didn't alter the collage. Her father had his sternest expression in place.

"He put a hand on my bottom," she said, looking from one face to the other and allowing what she'd said to properly sink in.

"That damned bastard!" Her father scrunched up the newspaper and threw it on his chair. Her mother let out a painful moan, and Trish did nothing, just stared at her in disbelief.

"I'll kill him." Her father moved to the door.

"She's a little liar. She's jealous," Trish spat out.

Her father paused at the door.

"Jealous of Duggie Foster? I'd rather marry his mother." Robin crossed her arms and looked defiant.

"George, come back!" her mother directed to her father. "What exactly do you think you're going to do?"

"Kill him," her father said.

Trish flopped into a chair. "Brilliant!" she said with disdain. "The world's greatest little liar will have her father's death on her conscience when he gets the electric chair for killing Duggie Foster."

"They hardly ever give the death penalty any more," Robin said complacently.

"You realize the seriousness of what you've just said?" Her father looked fit to explode.

"Well, I guess he was just trying to be friendly," Robin shrugged, "… but he did pat my bottom."

"So now he patted your bottom. For pete's sake, Robin!" Trish threw her hands up in the air. "You just about accused him of child molestation. Sometimes you're a total maniac. He's never even laid a hand on me and she accuses him of this."

Everyone stared at Trish in amazement. "What do you mean he's never laid a hand on you?" her mother rounded on Trish.

Trish's face went scarlet. "Well, he respects me."

Her father stood transfixed, his eyes bulging. "You've gone out with him for six months and he's never touched you?"

"Well, he's put his arm around me … that kind of thing."

Her mother and father exchanged a look of deep concern.

"I don't understand you. What do you want me to say? He raped me or something? Is that what you want?"

No attempt was made to go back to the wedding list. Everyone sat in silence for the longest time. At one point her mother and father went into the dining room and shut the door.

Trish smiled suddenly at Robin. "You really are dastardly. How did I ever get a sister like you?"

When their parents came back, Robin was banished to her room. She was glad to be out of the mess. Up in the bedroom, she went through the drawer where Trish kept her jumpers. Pulling her own off over her head, she began to try them on, posing in front of the mirror and imagining what she would look like if she had some real chest to fill them out. It was a nuisance having a sister so much older. Often she'd wanted to ask her parents why there had been no children in between, but it was always hard to get around to the topic.

The following morning at breakfast nothing was said, but Trish sat there and the ring had disappeared from her finger. Robin had no idea what time Trish had come to bed, but obviously the family conference had somehow dealt with the problem of the engagement.

Duggie didn't come past their house any more when he

walked the dog. Robin could only assume he went the other way, the long way around, to the park. When he saw her in the street he nodded curtly, but there was nothing to indicate that her father or mother had told him of her accusation.

Six months later, her father ran over Rinty in his car and killed him, right in front of their house. The way he told it, the dog had just run out. Nobody saw the accident, but many of the neighbours came pouring onto the street. Duggie came running and went almost mad with grief. He yelled and screamed and even cried. At one point he accused her father of killing Rinty deliberately.

"The damned dog was always running out at me. You should have kept him tied up. It's not my fault if he runs under the wheels of the car."

"You hated him!" Duggie yelled.

They all stood mesmerized, watching Duggie's performance. Her father didn't say another word. Trish kept well back, standing right by the side of the front door, out of Duggie's sightline.

In bed that night, Robin finally asked, "What happened when you gave the ring back?"

"Nothing." Trish rolled over on the side facing Robin. "He just took it."

"You mean he didn't yell and scream and carry on like he did tonight?"

"No!"

"I guess he really did like that dog best."

Harmony Connections

Reena wasn't sure when things began to turn sour. In fact, the housework had been neglected since the first day she started "Harmony Connections," but she hadn't really noticed. Actually she'd noticed very little until the moment Jacko peed on her leg as she stood at the phone.

She ignored the dampness at first, thinking it was from Carly who maybe had a wet diaper, but this time there were no little arms wrapped around her leg, just a whoosh of warm wet and then the puddling in her shoe. It was real annoying – she was just talking to her best customer to date, a geologist new to Sudbury who travelled all over the place in his job and complained that it never gave him time to meet women. He was going to be in Sudbury for a while and wanted to know if she could arrange something for him. She was deep into the conversation when she felt the warm wetness on her foot.

Jacko stood off from her, sheepish, tail between his legs. Screwy little runt. It was his revenge for not getting out enough, but the snowdrifts were four feet deep outside, so it was pretty useless trying to walk him. She made a little square clearing outside the back door and shoved him out every hour or two to widdle. His stream of pee etched through the snow like a laser and now had made a kind of mini, yellow, icy skating rink that he skidded on whenever she dropped him outside. It had been several hours since his last outing.

It was Lorne's idea in the first place to have a dog. Naturally! He was gone about 265 days a year, selling packaging across the country. He'd no idea what it was like to have to look after both a baby and a dog.

Lorne had been gone for ten days and there had been nobody to shovel the walk. There was only a tiny track the mailman had made for himself. Teed off, he'd knocked on her door and complained. She told him she'd been sick, and when he stared at the tangle of her hair, she knew he'd believed her.

It was nice when Lorne was gone travelling because she didn't have to do anything she didn't want to: not comb her hair, not tidy up the place, not cook proper meals, not do anything in fact except answer the phone and sort out her files. After a while the untidiness of the place would get to her, but first of all she relished the chaos.

If anyone had told her before she married Lorne that she would ever be like this, she would have laughed in their face. She'd never been a messy person, but living with Lorne had brought out some kind of demon in her. It was the demon of disobedience more than anything else. Lorne was a stickler for everything in its place. He almost got sick seein' as much as a picture hanging a quarter of an inch crooked.

Carly screamed from the other room. Covering the phone with her hand, she moved with the receiver to the door of the living room, her foot squelching in her shoe.

God Almighty! Carly had her hand stuck in the VCR slot.

"Excuse me just a minute," she apologized to her client. Burying the phone in a pile of dirty laundry that sat on the table and praying that he wouldn't hear the wild screams, she went to the child's rescue. "I told you not to touch that."

With Carly stuck under her arm she went back to the phone. If the geologist had noticed anything, he didn't say. He thought her rates were reasonable, and she assured him that she had several girls who would be just perfect for him. She felt like saying, "Take me!" A long trail of yellow spittle from Carly's mouth was tracking onto the front of Reena's sweater, but it made no difference. There were traces of a variety of meals already there.

She hung up the phone. It was all so unsatisfactory. He assured her he would send the money, but his voice had sounded uncertain. She shook Carly and the child smiled at her, mistaking the gentle shaking for play.

"You little bugger!" She set the child down abruptly. The VCR had been fixed twice already and Lorne had screamed his head off ... said she should have been watching. He was happy enough when the cheques from her clients arrived.

Lorne thought she should be some sorta super woman, cooking up gourmet meals, cleaning the house, and running the business at the same time. She'd read all about burn-out in Chatelaine. There was no way she was gonna go dashin' off to no shrink to talk it all out. She had her way of managing, and if Lorne didn't like it, he didn't have to see it. Trouble was his mum ... old bitch ... was always on the phone. "*Just checking, dear!*" She'd landed in on her more than once and done her usual sniff, as though somethin' was bothering her nose.

The dining-room table that she had to use as a desk was piled sky high now with files and dirty laundry. Lorne was always nagging her about a proper filing system, wanting to buy her a computer, but she knew she could manage fine without one. She had all her customers filed away in her head anyway. Even the couple of information forms Jacko had chewed up she had rewritten. Having a photographic memory helped for a start.

She was filling in her new client's name on one of her forms when her best friend Deborah called. Deb checked in once in a while to see if anyone eligible had signed up. It was on the tip of her tongue to tell her about the geologist, but suddenly she decided to keep him to herself.

Deb was desperate to have children. Sometimes Reena wondered why she didn't just get a turkey baster and take her chances, for God knows she labelled every man Reena had tried to get her a date with as a "loser." Trouble was Deb wanted the brains of Einstein for her child and the body of Schwarzenegger, when she looked like a cross between a jelly-filled donut and a bag of potatoes herself.

It was interesting about Deb. Reena had a pile of women on her files who were far from losers, nice women, attractive women, even beautiful women, but not one of them had Deb's amazing self-confidence. Deb never talked about diets or improving her figure. She told Reena often enough that she'd come by her figure honestly. Her father a smidgin more statuesque than Danny de Vito, and her mother, on the same eye level, were a hundred pounds overweight.

"I took one look at them when I was about ten and knew that I could wish all I liked, I was gonna be what I was gonna be. You don't get race horses out of shetland ponies." She made the pronouncement with no bitterness.

Deb was the best person Reena had ever known. She seldom wanted things she couldn't have. Wanting a child of her own was the only exception, but Reena could understand that. She'd never seen anyone who loved children more than Deb. She doted on Carly, and sometimes when Reena watched her with Carly, she felt like a total failure by comparison.

Deb worked at a Daycare, earning a pittance, but she did the job because she loved it. She almost begged to baby-sit Carly, and Carly in turn loved her. At times Reena felt a twinge of jealousy as the kid always chose to go to Deb when she hurt herself.

Carly tugged at her skirt as she cross-filed her geologist. She ringed his name with a red pencil, making a mental note to repair the chipped and peeling nail polish on her forefinger. She sat looking at the name: John Tucker. He said on the phone he'd been all over the world in his job. She imagined what it would be like to travel. It was something she'd always wanted to do.

Carly's face squished into her knee and she saw the snot from the child's nose tracking down her jeans. She didn't bother to wipe it up. It was a non-stop job wiping up. The doctor had said some kind of allergy. She whined now and Reena lifted her and carried her to the window. The child's arm stretched out towards the outside and she began to cry.

"No, it's too cold. We don't go out today!"

She was only eighteen months, but she seemed to know exactly what Reena said to her. She began to wail, a long protracted howl. The phone rang again, and quickly Reena went to the kitchen cupboard and got a cookie. She put it into the child's hand. The crying stoppped immediately.

"Harmony Connections," Reena said brightly.

Her geologist's money arrived by Friday, along with a photograph that went way beyond Reena's expectations. He was gorgeous. He was all togged up in a real outdoorsy kinda way with a red check shirt, blue jeans, and great heavy work boots. He was kinda squatting down on a rock, holding something in his hand and smiling at the camera.

Whatta hunka hunka man.

With Carly tucked under one arm, Reena dialled his number.

She felt a slight thrill when she heard his voice again.

"Thank you for the cheque," she said into the phone. "I was wondering when we could set up a meeting?"

"You have someone already?"

"That's not quite the procedure." Reena adopted her most businesslike voice. "I always like to vet my clients personally," she lied. Until the moment of saying it, she hadn't even thought of this.

The words just sprang out of her mouth. She had meant to tell him that she would be sending him the usual forms to fill out.

"I should come to your office?" he asked.

Her office! What a joke. Her eyes caught the bin where she piled Carly's used diapers and ran across to the hump of papers that Carly had scrunched and left on the floor.

"No. I think I would like to meet you somewhere for a coffee, if that would be all right with you?"

Again there was a pause. "Right! Fine with me."

"The mail is the pits," she said quickly. "It's sometimes better to kill two birds with one stone. Bring the forms. See you in person."

"I could fax any information to you that you might need," he said quickly.

"No!" Shit. She felt a rush of panic. "My fax is down right at the moment," she lied. "The fact is the office is being renovated and everything's a mess here." *That for sure was no lie.* "We've been growing so quickly, we've had to add on."

God forbid he should ever decide to check the address.

"Fine. When do you want to meet?"

"Friday. Would Friday be all right?"

"Sure."

Lorne wasn't due back until Saturday, so that would be no problem. Deb would cover for her.

They set up the time and the place, and Reena hung up the phone and then swung Carly around to face her.

"Well, babe. Your mum has a date."

The child, catching her mother's mood, laughed happily.

The next thing to do was to go through her wardrobe and decide what to wear. A suit seemed too formal. A dress too casual. What to tell Deb was a problem. She could lie and say she was going to visit friends, but Deb knew all her friends, and they usually did things real casual, no dressing up. She could say she was going to a baby shower, but she would have to make up a whole new person. Ever since she'd known Deb they had shared everything. To suddenly produce a friend that Deb didn't know, needed too much work and too much lying. She decided to tell her the truth. Tell her there was a new man on her roster and she wasn't quite sure about him. Felt that she needed to check him out before she foisted him on some unsuspecting woman.

"Must be a dish," Deb said with a grin.

"No! Anything but. He just sounded strange. Better to take a look."

"So where are you going?"

"Traders."

"For a coffee?"

"Sure. Why not?"

"An' whatever else evolves."

"What you take me for?" Reena said blushing.

"Ye're checkin' him out for me, right?"

"Right! Nothing but the best for a good pal."

"All his life this guy's been looking for a woman of substance. I can see it now. Svelte turns him off. He wants somethin' he can getta hold of. Tell him I have handles all over. Real good love handles."

Reena tried to kiss Carly as she was being held in Deb's arms. The kid turned away and pushed her face into Deb's shoulder. Reena felt a twinge of real guilt. It was as if the kid knew, but that was a ridiculous thought.

She was just about out the door when her mum called. Deb held the phone out to her. She knew she couldn't handle that. Her mum had a kind of sixth sense about lying. She made frantic gestures towards Deb, waving her arms and mouthing "No."

"I think she's gone, Mrs. Dutka. She's got a shower." Deb made a face at Reena. "I don't know, I think one of her clients ... Yeh! ... she's sure doin' great ... Yeh ... too bad ... Well, maybe me next ... Right! I'll tell her you called." Deb hung up the phone.

"Yeh, sure she might get me a date. If she wasn't takin' them for herself."

"Aw come on, Deb! I told you. I'm not sure about this one. God, he could be an axe killer. Sometimes your instinct tells you that you have to check things out."

"Sure! Sure! Sometimes a photograph tells you other things, too."

"Deb!"

"Go on! Git, before I change my mind about sittin'. Don't do anything I wouldn't do," Deb called after her. "You look gorgeous by the way."

Reena stumbled down the front path, cursing as she slipped sideways into the snowbank. She dropped the bag with her shoes as she fell. Bloody Sudbury winter! The folder with her file slipped out of her hand and papers fell out into the snow. Gathering them as best she could, she shook them off. In the car she laid the forms out to dry and turned the heater up full blast. The cold air hit her full in the face. She could hear Lorne's voice screaming at her to let the engine warm up. She had her own theory. The sooner you turned it on, the sooner it heated up.

She checked herself in the mirror. She'd given her hair a lighter rinse the night before and she did look good, she decided. Her coat had seen better days, but she'd be dumping that, and she knew she looked good in the pale turquoise blouse.

She drove into the parking garage of the Sherwood Hotel. God, how she hated that garage, pitch black and cold as death. There was an ominous thump as she drove over a grating at the entrance and she felt the wheel peculiar under her hands. She took the first empty stall she could find and got out to examine the car. The front left wheel was flat as a pancake.

"Shit! Shit!" Lorne had told her to have the wheels checked before he left. But then Lorne was always telling her things to do with the friggin' car. Lorne loved his cars more than anything else on the face of the earth.

She stood staring down helplessly at the tire. Just what she needed, especially when it was a million below zero outside. If she didn't have something done to it right away, it would be frozen to the ground by the time she came out.

Changing into her shoes, she dumped her boots in the back

seat. Gathering her file, she slammed the door shut, closing her coat in the door at the same time. As she went to walk away, she almost toppled over, the coat pulling her back to the car. She stared down at the flat tire again as she hauled her coat from the door. *Deal with it right away!* Perhaps she could lay it all on her geologist's shoulders. Men loved stuff like that. The only thing was the damned car. It was a rusted tin can. She hated him to see it. If material things were any gauge of success, the car would tell him she was a flop.

In the entrance of the restaurant, she took her coat off and handed it to the coat girl. She loved the atmosphere in Traders, sort of 1950's. A diner with a difference – a few palm trees here and there and a couple of goldfish swimming in a pond right at the entrance. Thank God they didn't have no lobsters in tanks the way they had when her mum used to go in the fifties. Lobsters in tanks gave her the heebie-jeebies. They reminded her of giant cockroaches.

Then she saw him behind her. He was giving the coat-check girl a more than friendly once-over. She patted her hair in place and turned around, clasping her folder to her breasts.

"You're John Tucker!"

"Right. And you must be Reena Kozak?"

She felt her knees going slightly weak. He was just as good-looking as his photograph had shown him to be, but maybe twenty years older. Not that it mattered. Men didn't go in for having their pictures taken all the time.

The hostess led them to a table. Reena was conscious of her skirt sticking between her legs. Damned static. There'd been no time to fix herself. She must look like a real dog's dinner. No wonder he'd been looking over her head to the girl who took the coats.

They sat down at the table. She found herself staring right away into a big shiny ashtray that distorted her face. Her nose looked as though it stretched from ear to ear, and her forehead and chin receded like they were being pulled back by an elastic band.

Screw that! Concentrate! Concentrate! Business. Business. No time to think about anything else.

"What would you like to drink?" he asked as a waitress

came to the table.

"Coffee's fine!"

"Nothing stronger?"

"No. Thanks anyway." She knew in her mind she would start with a coffee, and then when she was more comfortable, she might have a beer, but it wouldn't look good to accept one now. He ordered a Labatts Blue and leaned back in his chair.

"I'm feeling a bit frazzled. My car wouldn't start, so I had to borrow a friend's," she lied glibly. "Just as I was driving into the parking garage, I got a flat tire."

"Too bad."

"Yeh, it's a real rustbox, I shoulda known." She shrugged. "When the waitress comes back, I'll get her to bring a phone book and call a service-station."

"I can change the tire for you."

"Listen, you're my client. Not a mechanic."

He smiled. "That's okay, for a lady in distress."

She didn't quite like the way he said "lady," as though he might have some doubts. She peered back at her reflection in the ash tray.

"No! I couldn't possibly," she heard herself say.

"Don't worry about it. It'll take a minute."

The waitress arrived at the table, setting Reena's coffee in front of her, and his beer on a little paper doily in front of him.

"Do you have a phone book?" Reena said, looking up at her.

The waitress looked blank. She obviously thought she was bein' asked for some new kind of drink she wasn't familiar with.

"Never mind!" He shook his head at the waitress. "She doesn't want one after all."

"Am I missin' something here?" The waitress looked perplexed.

"Not a thing," he said, giving the waitress a wink. *God, she hated men who flirted with waitresses right in front of your eyes.*

"You get me the girl," he said, squinting at Reena as he lifted the beer to his mouth. "And I'll get you a new tire."

"No problem," she laughed.

"Really? You mean you haven't got a mile-long list of life's losers?"

"Lonely people, but not losers. How come you need to use me?" She placed emphasis on the "you." He could take it how he liked.

"I told you, I move around. Spend most of my time in the bush, or up north."

Was there a slight white line on the finger of his left hand?

"Never been married?"

He shook his head. "Lived with a few, but never taken the plunge."

He was lying and she knew it. She felt uncomfortable suddenly. There was something about his eyes that bothered her. He would screw them up and look at her intently as if he couldn't see properly and then kinda open them wide and turn his attention elsewhere. Like he was boring into her mind and then he found it didn't interest him. The lower part of his face had the bluish tinge of men who had problems keeping their faces clean shaven.

"What kind of girl would you like to meet?"

He took another sip of his beer and grinned lazily at her.

"Like you."

"I'm not available."

"No? Married?"

She nodded.

"Too bad."

The waitress passed him and his eyes followed her legs. No, this guy wasn't fussy. She felt sorry now about the impulse that had made her come here. Maybe when he checked into every town he phoned an agency like hers.

She sorted out her papers. She would take down some details, drink her coffee, and beat it out of here. "Interests?" she asked, digging into her handbag and taking out a pen.

There was a kind of cynical twist to his mouth now. He lifted a nonchalant hand. "Heh, listen, I'm a real flexible guy."

"Do you have any hobbies?"

"Sure." He laughed suddenly, a rather nasty, mean laugh, and a shiver of fear zipped along her spine like an electric shock.

"I'm not sure I can talk about them here."

There had been banter like this before she'd been married. Good fun, flirty kinda stuff that she could do as well as anyone, but usually it came from someone she knew, not from a complete stranger.

She decided to ignore the tone of his voice. "Usually I fill in these blanks." She held out the form to him. "If you really want to meet someone, it's a good idea to take this seriously."

"Sure I wanna meet someone."

She put the form on the table and lifted her coffee cup to her mouth. The coffee was stale and half cold. She glanced around her quickly. Now that her eyes were becoming used to the dimness, she was more aware of the other people in the restaurant. It would be just her luck to see someone she knew.

"Put down 'running,'" he said suddenly.

"You jog?"

"You might call it that."

"Anything else?" She concentrated on filling in the form.

"Country and Western."

"Anything else?"

He shook his head.

"What company do you work for?"

"I freelance."

She bit the end of the pencil, feeling a jagged sliver of wood rough against her mouth. A freelance geologist? Was that possible? Maybe that was how it worked.

"What kind of age do you have in mind?"

He shrugged. "Old, young. I don't give a shit! Just no dogs."

Her stomach turned over. He was striking some sort of memory chord, an unpleasant one. When Lorne had drunk a few beers and was relaxed and watching "Roseanne" or one of the other sit-coms, he made frequent comments about the women who appeared on the show. "Good tits," "tight ass," or he would snarl about Roseanne, "untidy slut," as though he were discussing *things*, not people.

She shoved the paper towards him, "Here, why don't you fill it out!"

"Hell, I can't see in this light." He gave a little indifferent shrug. "It's all shit anyway, isn't it?"

"No, it's not." She was all of a sudden angry. She pushed the coffee cup away from her, gathered the papers and stood up.

"I think this is a waste of time for you."

"Hold your horses!" He pulled himself together and straightened up. "Siddown!" he commanded.

"No thanks."

She turned on her heels and walked with as much dignity as she could manage towards the door.

Fuck! There was the dumb car to deal with now. Maybe she'd just get a taxi home and let Lorne cope with it when he got back the following day. Then she'd have to explain what she was doing and why she'd decided unexpectedly to interview one of her clients. God, it wasn't worth it!

"Do you know if there are any service-stations open?" Reena asked the coat-check girl. "I have a flat tire."

The girl shrugged. "Couldn't say."

Suddenly he was at her elbow. He nodded towards the girl, who immediately brought him his jacket. It was a sorry-looking, fringed, tan suede which had seen better days. In the brighter light of the lobby he looked terribly down-at-heel.

"Show me where your car is!"

"It's all right. I'm gonna grab a cab."

"Fuck! Why do that. I can change the tire in a minute."

She stood indecisive. He moved towards the door. "It's in the parking garage across the street?"

Reena looked back desperately at the girl. She felt like saying something to her, but the girl turned away. Reena stood uncertain on the sidewalk. He looked back at her. "Well, do you want me to fix it or not?"

She wanted to say no, but then she thought again about Lorne. She tailed along behind him as he crossed the road. She was up three levels in the parking garage and it was dark. Suddenly frightened, she had the urge to run. He wasn't even waiting for her. He was charging ahead.

"Which floor?"

"Third," she said in a choked voice. Turning over on her heel, she cursed her shoes. She should have kept her boots on. She should have stayed home. There were a thousand "shoulds," but it was too late now.

He walked up the stairs to the third floor, never saying a word to her, not even turning to look at her. *Jesus! What was she doing in a dark parking garage with a total stranger?*

She felt relief when they reached the car. She didn't care any more about the car's appearance. It suddenly seemed like an old and valued friend. She opened the trunk for him and he bent low, peering in at the pile of junk. God knows the last time she'd cleared it out. There were old shoes, a couple of pairs of kids boots, bats, balls, a roll of old carpet that she'd brought from her mother's and forgotten to take out, and a load of empty pop bottles in cardboard carriers.

"I told you it was a wreck." *Why was she apologizing?* "My friend's a hoarder." He knew of course it was her car. She heard her own voice going on and on.

"Where's the fucking spare?" He peered over her shoulder as she dumped stuff onto the ground.

"Under all this." She pulled back the rotten piece of carpet and exposed the spare. He rooted around, finally pulling it out with difficulty. He doubled over again poking around in the trunk.

"Where's the jack?"

She had no idea where the jack was. She began to shiver. It was icy cold and so dark she could hardly see a thing.

"I can't do nothin' with no jack."

"I dunno, maybe it's in the car."

"For chrissake open the door an' look! I can't stand here all night."

She fumbled for her keys in her handbag and with shaking fingers opened the car door. She pulled up the lock on the back door and straightened. She could see his silhouette, but nothing else. "There's a flashlight in the back somewhere."

She opened the back door of the car and suddenly he gave her a mighty shove and she fell into the back seat. Terror made her scream out, and then his hand was over her mouth and the entire weight of his body was on top of her. He was forcing her head into the seat of the car and she thought she was going to smother.

It was almost a mercy when he twisted her on her back and she could get some air, but then he had her dress up around her neck and was tearing at her pantyhose. Jesus! The hand over her face smelled of rubber. Something sharp was digging into her stomach. This was it, she was about to die. What had that policeman told her once about attempted rape? Just to lie still. It was the fighting that egged them on. She could feel a finger pressing against her teeth. With all the effort she could summon she managed to move her mouth so that his finger slipped in between her teeth and she bit into it with all her force.

That was the last thing she remembered, until she woke up in hospital. She didn't know where she was at first, then she saw her mother's face looming over her and heard her voice.

"Reena, honey! It's me."

She tried to move her mouth and say something, but it felt all tight and odd and didn't respond the way she wanted it to.

Her mother stuck a straw between her lips and propped her head up. She took a drag of water from the glass her mother held.

"What happened?"

Her mother shook her head. "They found you in the parking lot, in the back of the car, unconscious."

"Jesus!" Everything began to come back. Then she started to feel the rest of her body, unfamiliar and aching.

"What day is it?"

"Sunday."

She lay back and tried to take it in. It was Friday night she'd gone out to Traders. What had happened to the day and a half in between?

"Where's Lorne?" Lorne had been due back on the Saturday, that much she remembered.

Her mother looked distinctly uncomfortable. "He was here earlier. He's lookin' after Carly. The police want to talk to you. Do you feel up to it?"

The police. That was just what she needed for her business, the police sticking their noses in.

"No, I don't. I don't want to talk to them."

"Reena! You were raped by some maniac. You can't just let him get away with it."

Raped. The enormity of it began to sink in. She didn't remember anything about the rape, so she could pretend that had never happened. God, he could have had AIDS, anything.

Her mother might have been reading her mind. "They took a blood test."

"And?"

"They don't have the results yet."

"Oh, my God."

Her mother took her hand. "What possessed you to go and meet him? You don't usually do that."

She didn't answer but turned her face towards the pillow. Instantly, she felt the pain of her cheekbone. "Let me have a mirror!"

"Why don't you just rest."

"Get me a mirror!"

Her mother rose reluctantly and fetched her handbag from the window ledge. She came back and sat down. Opening the bag, she took out a small hand mirror. Reena felt total revulsion when she saw the pulp of her face.

"Doctor says you'll be fine. The bruising will go."

"Shit!"

"What did Lorne say?"

Her mother bent her head. "He's mad."

"About me or about the friggin' car havin' a flat tire?"

"Don't be silly!"

"Why isn't he here?"

"I told you he's lookin' after Carly."

"Hell, Deb would do that."

Her mother bit her lip. Reena closed her eyes. She could feel tears oozing out of her eyes and she'd no intention of her mother seeing. She couldn't stand any sympathy at that particular moment. She didn't know whether she passed out or fell asleep, but next time she opened her eyes, a big ugly policeman was standing over her and her mother had gone.

"You fit to talk?"

She closed her eyes again, praying he would go away, but it wasn't to be. She had to go through the story from the beginning. She concentrated on a shaving cut on the policeman's chin as she talked. She was careful what she said about the past. Sure, she sometimes met the clients, both men and women. Vetted them. She didn't know whether he believed her or not. She wondered if maybe Deb had told him the opposite. She wasn't even sure he'd been to the house.

She related it all slowly. When she was finished, he held up a piece of paper. The piece that she'd written the geologist's name and number on. "Is this the guy you met?"

She nodded. Deb must have given them the piece of paper.

"We brought him in for questioning." The policeman folded the piece of paper and stuck it in his pocket.

"You got him already?"

"Yes and no." His eyes looked sideways and there was a pause. "He says you led him on."

She turned her head away in disgust. "Naturally!"

"We don't necessarily believe that." He looked at her not unsympathetically.

"Bully for you!"

"Listen, this guy was bad news from the minute I met him.

I had a cup of coffee. If you ask the waitress, she'll tell you that. All I wanted to do was get away as quickly as possible."

"So you let him con you into fixing your tire?"

"I wanted to call a garage. You can ask the coat-check girl. I asked her about a garage. He kept insisting."

"Right!"

"Listen, why don't you just get out! I don't need this."

"Hold on!"

"I was scared outa my mind, if you must know. The garage was dark. I don't like goin' there with a complete stranger." She jabbed a finger towards her face. "You think I got this because I was pullin' him on top of me?"

She could feel the tears starting up again, and there was no way she wanted to cry in front of this big bully. She tried to bite her lip but immediately felt nothing but pain. Self-pity overwhelmed her. Where the hell was Lorne, or where was Deb? She kept her eyes closed and eventually heard him clunking out.

All she could think about were the lab tests. What if the guy had been infected? She put a hand down to her crotch and felt the area. She felt bruised and sore. God almighty, what had he done to her? She cried until there were no more tears and then she was gone again just as suddenly as the first time, she fell asleep exhausted.

She was in the garage again, only this time it was Lorne with her an' all the time he was goin' on about her being irresponsible. He was throwing things out of the trunk to get at the tire and then he came out with a great big sugar donut in his hand instead of the real wheel. "Now look what they gave you at the garage. What a dumb bitch! This isn't goin' to hold up." Instead of putting it back in the trunk he began to put it on the car. Bits of it kept crumbling off and he began shouting at her. Then, when there was nothing but crumbs by his feet, he began to hit her and she started to yell, "No! No! No!"

She woke up with a start and Deb was there slapping her hand.

"Oh, God! I was havin' this dream, Deb."

"I know, you were yelling."

"Where's Lorne?"

"He's comin'. Your mum's gone to get Carly."

"You're sure he's coming?"

Deb nodded. "Are you all right? You look awful."

Reena began to cry again, disgusted with herself for having so little control.

"What if the guy had HIV, Deb? I can't get that outa my mind."

Deb held her hand tightly and stroked her arm. "It's okay. Everything's going to be all right."

"No, it's not. The guy's sayin' I led him on. What if Lorne hears that?"

"He's not gonna believe that. They all say that."

"Yeh. Tell that to Lorne."

Lorne came later and Deb got up and backed uneasily out of the room.

"I'll wait outside." She gave a small wave to Reena. Reena wanted to call out, "Don't go!" but Deb gave her no chance.

Lorne didn't make any attempt to kiss her, but stood apart from the bed staring down at her with a look on his face that was far too familiar.

"How's Carly?" she found herself breaking the silence.

"She's okay."

Right at that moment, instead of drifting off like she'd been doing all that day, she felt suddenly as though her body lifted off the bed and was looking at them both from a distance. She saw Lorne. Saw him real good. Saw the beer belly like a knot in the lankiness of his body. Saw the meanness in his eyes. No different from the look in the geologist's eyes. Saw everything there in the back of his eyes: the anger at the thought that maybe, just maybe she'd led the guy on. Already she was fast-forwarding in her brain. Seeing how she could tell him the truth. She could see him storming out. Taking Carly. Locking her out of the house. She erased backwards and began again with a clean tape.

"I was stir crazy, Lorne. Snow all week, Carly teething. I had

35

to get out. This guy seemed strange over the phone. I decided to check him out."

"The house was like a shit factory when I got in. What's the matter with you anyway? My mother was dead right about you ..."

Reena opened her eyes again. She couldn't believe what she was hearing. He was more concerned about the condition of the house than he was that she'd been beaten up.

"My mum's in, scrubbin' the place out. You should be real proud of that."

"Are you givin' her the going rate?" It slipped out of Reena before she could stop herself.

"You fuckin' bitch! You have no remorse."

"Maybe if you wanted a cleaning lady, you should have hired one and forgotten about the ring."

"Maybe I should ... a damn sight less trouble." With that he turned on his heel and left. Deb came back into the room.

"You all right?"

Reena nodded. She felt somehow stronger. Her anger had made her stronger.

"What did he say?"

"He didn't give a shit," Reena said. "He only cared that the house was a mess."

"Jesus! Men."

Lorne didn't visit her again in the hospital, but his mother came, bringing with her copies of "Good Housekeeping" and "Family Time," and a package of homemade cabbage rolls. The very smell of the bag made her want to throw up. She'd never had the courage to tell her that she hated cabbage rolls. Reena concentrated on the woman's deformed, arthritic knuckles as she talked on about disappointment. Those knuckles, Reena often thought, represented Mina Kozak's whole mind-set. Twisted.

Reena closed her eyes as her voice went on and on. She should have been an expert on what made for a bad marriage, Reena thought cynically. Her own marriage was one of convenience and nothing else. Bill Kozak was a little machine rather than a man, but luckily a machine who had managed to keep her fat and well-fed. His tool-and-die-making business was a lucrative one, but he was pale and unhealthy from a life in his shop. He seldom expressed an opinion on anything, but when he did, Mina wasted no time cutting him off.

"I'm feeling fine, thanks!" Reena said, interrupting the woman's lecture sarcastically.

Mina Kozak shut her mouth which had hung open in shock for an instant. "I hope you've learned something?" she jumped in again quickly.

"Plenty. Enough to do me for a lifetime."

"So you'll give up this foolish business?"

"What foolish business?"

"This marriage agency."

"Is that what Lorne sent you to do? Talk me out of it?"

"No, Lorne never said a word."

Reena knew she was lying. "Good. For I've no intention of giving it up."

"You'll ruin your marriage."

Reena laughed bitterly. "Mother-in-law, why don't you just take your prying nose out of my marriage and go home and think about your own!"

The woman stood up, furious. "This is all the thanks I get."

"This isn't thanks, believe me."

"Bitch!" She gathered her coat around her shoulders and tried to move off, but it caught in the arm of the chair which she dragged a few feet with her. It made for an untidy and messy exit. It was all Reena could do to stop laughing.

Meanwhile, Reena waited for the lab results. The doctor told her to be patient, it took time. His eyes said, "*Let the bitch suffer!*" Cold eyes. The kind of eyes that blamed her for the mess she was in. She knew it was no good confiding her fears about AIDS to him. He would do nothing to speed up the results.

Lorne didn't show up again and her mother came to tell her he was off on another trip. Deb had taken Carly into the Daycare

Centre with her, and they were taking turns baby-sitting the child at night.

"Good. I don't want dear Mina near her."

"She offered to keep her."

"You told her no bloody way, I hope?"

Her mother nodded.

It was a surprise when after three days they told her she could go home. She called Deb at the Daycare and she came in with Carly to pick her up. Carly turned away from her when she put her arms out, but Deb lifted the little girl towards Reena.

"Go to Mummy!"

Reena buried her face in the child's front. The smell of stale milk was suddenly delicious.

"You want to go to your place or your mum's?" Deb asked.

"My place."

"You sure?"

Reena nodded. The house was completely tidy and smelt unpleasantly of disinfectant. The kind you sometimes smelled in public toilets. Reena opened the note from Lorne she found on the dining room table.

"This is what a good home is supposed to look like. Why don't you think about it for a while? Either you change or I'm out of here and I'll take Carly with me."

Reena passed the note over to Deb. Deb read it and looked up. "The bastard."

"No welcome home! No hope you're better."

The phone rang at that moment. They both stood looking at it.

"Want me to answer it?" Deb asked.

Reena nodded. "If it's a client just tell them I'm busy."

Deb put Carly down and picked up the phone. "Yeh. Just a minute." She held out the phone to Reena. "It's not a client. It's the hospital."

Reena felt her stomach churning. She knew it was the lab-test results. Perhaps it was the doctor to tell her she was HIV positive. She stood frozen.

"Want me to take the message?" Deb asked.

"No! I'll take it." Reluctantly she took the phone from Deb. She didn't put it to her ear right away. Suddenly nothing mattered any more. The fact that Lorne wasn't there, the pain of his brief stupid note, nothing mattered but whether or not she was going to live or die.

Carly came to her and tugged on her jeans. Reena put a hand on the child's head and put the phone to her ear.

"Reena Kozak ... Yes ... Thank you." She hung up the phone. Bending, she lifted Carly and swung her up in the air.

"Deb, how long does it take to have locks on the door changed?"

"Locks?" Deb frowned. "I've no idea. I guess they could do it right away."

"Good. Let's have a look in the yellow pages."

Fertility Goddess

The night Stephen announced the casting, he gave a talk about the play and his aims. Elizabeth wasn't used to looking at the front view of Stephen. He usually sat four rows ahead of her in church. She knew the nape of his neck and the shape of his head intimately. Even the small pustule that exploded on his neck Easter week did nothing to diminish her ardour. Indeed, she had fallen in love with the back of his head before properly seeing him from the front. She knew he was married, but then so were most of her favourite actors, and she permitted herself to be in love with them from a distance.

She had known very little about Stephen until Moira, her best friend, filled her in on the details. Moira lived four doors away from the Blakes. What Moira's mother didn't know about her neighbours, she made it her duty to find out.

"They've been married six years, no kids. She's had all kinds of tests to see why," Moira imparted to Elizabeth. "Course, maybe they don't do it," Moira offered quickly.

"Don't be dumb! All married people do it. Clinics don't give advice on immaculate conception?" Elizabeth wasn't sure why she was insisting that this was true. She would have preferred to be wrong. Certainly, their presence at church offered no clues about their true relationship. There was something very solitary about their side-by-sideness on the church pew. Their shoulders seldom touched.

Elizabeth studied her script intently and tried to avoid looking at Stephen. When she did glance up, he was staring at her. She knew she was blushing. Inexplicably, he had cast her as "the other woman," and everything about their relationship was subtly altered. At sixteen, to be cast in this role seemed strange. June Turner could have played the part, she was certainly the proper age, but he had given June a walk-on. Elizabeth had pictured herself playing the wronged heroine. She thought Stephen understood that, but he chose Wendy Wright for the part, and she was puzzled and uncertain whether to be angry or flattered.

Elizabeth had started the dramatic group the previous year. It had begun more or less as a recreational thing, something that the Reverend McAllister thought might be a good outlet for some of his parishioners. At that time Stephen had promised to help, but until now — until suddenly stepping into the breach to direct *The Echo of Laughter* — the extent of his involvement had been to help with the choice of plays.

Most of the organization had fallen onto Elizabeth's shoulders. Because of that, as a kind of reward for her work, she was more or less allowed her pick of roles. If Stephen knew this, he was obviously pretending ignorance.

Even with all her confusion about the turn of events, she still loved to hear him talk. It was an effort now to feign indifference. He had a way of making his points by turning his palm up and closing his fingers and thumbs together, as though drawing his thoughts from thin air. When he was excited by a topic, he blinked a lot. In bed at night, when she thought about him, as she inevitably did, she imagined running a caressing finger across those eyelids, calming him with a touch.

When Stephen had finished his little speech about the play and people were dispersing, she bustled around tidying up. The Reverend McAllister had given the drama group the right to use the hall attached to the church, but there was a strict set of rules that had to be followed. Most of the responsibility was Elizabeth's. She usually stayed behind until everyone had gone to make sure everything was in order.

Putting the chairs back neatly, she gathered empty glasses from around the room. Taking them to the kitchen, she rinsed them under the tap. She felt as though she were breathing from her throat instead of her lungs. If she inhaled more deeply, she would surely burst into tears of frustration and disappointment.

Usually Moira helped clear up. Tonight, she left the hall with Patrick McCausland without a backward glance. Elizabeth would normally have felt happy for her, for Moira had a crush on Patrick, but this evening she could only think about her own misery.

She busied herself going through the checklist for the hall, and when she came out of the kitchen, everyone had gone except Stephen. He was gathering up his notebooks and papers lying on the desk. Elizabeth stood at the door waiting for him, trying to seem cool and indifferent, trying to steady her legs.

He joined her at the door. "All shipshape?"

She nodded wordlessly.

"Aren't you happy?" he asked, watching her lock the door.

She stuffed the key of the hall deep into the pocket of her coat. If she could have crawled in after it, she would have.

"I would rather have played the part of Laura."

"That milksop! Surely not."

"Milksop?"

"Eternal bloody housewife. You didn't want that for yourself?"

A little twinge of pleasure eased her misery.

"You have too much character for Laura. Maryanne was definitely for you."

"You think so?"

"You're a much better actress than Wendy. You'll be wonderful as Maryanne."

"Thank you!"

"Never take the goody-two-shoes roles, they're not much fun. That goes for life too."

She was unsure whether he was offering some kind of criticism, but she refused to let it affect her mood.

"Here, let me walk you home."

"But it's miles out of your way."

"That's all right. It isn't late."

Her mood swings were always unpredictable these days, but it would have been impossible to predict the wild joy that now possessed her. She felt her confidence expanding. Here, the most wonderful man she'd ever known was treating her as an equal.

"And am I a watered-down version of Maryanne in real life?" she asked when they had walked a while without exchanging a word.

"Watered-down?"

"Yes, Dostoyevsky claims the world is filled with types. We're all characters from plays, but less than the real thing. He says that in *The Idiot*. I just wondered if that is how you saw me as the 'other woman' type?"

"Dostoyevsky, you've read Dostoyevsky?"

"Yes. I love Dostoyevsky."

"You know I teach Russian literature?"

"Really?" She feigned surprise. She knew perfectly well he taught Russian literature at the university. It was the reason why she'd buried herself in Dostoyevsky and Tolstoy for the past year. She didn't need to pretend enthusiasm for the books, though. She had in fact been overwhelmed by her discoveries. Especially by Dostoyevsky's *The Idiot*.

"So, do you?"

"Do I, what?"

It was almost too foolish to repeat.

"Do you think we are all like watered-down characters from plays?"

"Some of us."

She felt more than a little silly, embarrassed to have asked the question, for his answer seemed off-hand — an answer meant for a real *idiot*. But if he were laughing at her, he didn't show it.

"So what did you find so wonderful about the book?" he asked.

She'd rehearsed her answers to this very question in bed at night. They came glibly off her tongue now. Inspired by reality, she even found unfamiliar and to this point unused words to describe her emotions and thoughts. More than once she turned and saw the slight smile on his face. He might be thinking her a fool or admiring her. She had no sense of which, but could only hope he was admiring her.

She didn't want to reach home. She would gladly have lost her way. They were there too soon. He looked up at the lights of the house with what appeared to be regret. She had often lingered with young friends, but this hanging around was something reserved for youth, not married men. He patted her shoulder with an avuncular hand, as though suddenly reminded of his duty and responsibilities.

"You're a lovely, intelligent girl."

Was it condescension? Had she talked too much, too brightly, too superficially?

"Sleep well!"

What irony. She tossed and turned all night. The light touch from his hand on her shoulder had marked her skin, even scorched her flesh to the bone. She felt altered, not just by his attention and words, but by his confidence.

All night, in and out of dreams, she imagined scenarios where he would announce his marriage was over, that he'd fallen in love with her. Then his wife's face would appear and Elizabeth would burn with shame. The images kept coming back. They became more and more vivid, eventually blotting out any guilt feelings.

Her mother and father watched her covertly during the following weeks. They weren't used to the tractable, dreamy individual she had become. They laughed together, calling her starstruck. They put her strange, elevated mood down to her role in the play.

The play had in fact become totally secondary to the drama that was taking place both on and off the stage. At times she pretended stupidity, just to hear him explain things. Sometimes even moving awkwardly, so that he came onstage and put an arm around her shoulders, turning her in another direction and explaining why it was important she should be facing this way or that way.

One night between acts she poured herself a glass of orange juice in the small kitchen and, as she turned, she almost walked into him. His eyes focused on her chest. She almost forgot she was wearing the necklace her Aunt Helen had brought her from Mexico. For a moment she thought he was studying her breasts. She felt her face flush scarlet. He lifted the pendant part of the necklace, his finger brushing against her breast.

"Xilonen ... the Aztec goddess of young corn ..." He looked directly into her eyes, "... a fertility goddess. Did you know that?"

She wished she could have said yes. So often he seemed to assume that she was more than she was, knew more, understood more. She stood frozen, unsure whether to pretend. For an instant she was certain he was going to kiss her. She actually tried to imagine what it would be like to be kissed by a man with a beard. His dark eyes focused on her lips. His lips parted slightly. His head bent down towards her, but before he could do anything, Moira came barging through the door.

Moira, as stage manager, was supposed to be in charge of juice and snacks. She might have sensed something in the air, for she stopped dead at the door. He dropped the pendant, and she swore it made a ringing sound as it clanged against her chest.

"Sorry!" Moira looked from Elizabeth to Stephen and gave a rueful shrug.

The pendant seemed to pulsate on her breast, perhaps it even exuded light. It was as though his hand were still there. She was quivering. If she uttered a word, her emotions would be as visible as the clothes on her back. She knew about cats in heat, dogs in heat, but never knew that humans could be in heat!

Retreating to a corner, she buried herself in *Anna Karenina*. The words on the page meant nothing. She read the same paragraph over and over. Eventually he joined her with a glass of juice in his hand. He stood over her, and she was glad he didn't sit down. She imagined that she exuded a scent not unlike that put out by animals.

He bent down and moved the book so that he could peek at the title.

"Anna Karenina! You like it?"

"I love it."

"Tolstoy used a real-life incident."

"Really?"

"A neighbour killed herself over a lover. It made a deep impression." He stood very still, staring down at her. Elizabeth felt her face flush again.

"Tolstoy was thirty-two when he married. His wife was only eighteen." He delivered this piece of information apropos of nothing, then looked away immediately as though he'd embarrassed himself.

Elizabeth didn't want rehearsals ever to end. As opening night approached, she felt no joy, knowing it would all be over soon. No more Stephen. Back to watching the nape of his neck on Sundays in church. It occurred to her that she was totally unaware of what else was happening around her. All she knew was that when she was onstage, she came to life for him and nobody else. She had no idea how the play was going or how good the cast were.

Opening night came and the play was a great success. Her mother and father were lavish in their praise. Stephen hugged everyone. Everyone except her. She moved from group to group in a daze. Her sisters pounded her on the back. Her cousin told her she was born to play "the other woman." Elizabeth tracked Stephen's progress from person to person. It was as though he avoided her. She felt unbelievably hurt.

Joan, his wife, came over. She smiled and said, "Very good!" She looked smug and happy.

In bed that night Elizabeth cried as though her heart would break. Stephen hadn't said a word. That was the only thing that had any meaning. He hadn't said a word to her.

Like an automaton she went through the motions of the play the following night. Stephen was nowhere in sight — that was the way it was to be. Life would go on. It would go on without Stephen. All the mundane and boring everyday things in her life would take over again. There would be nothing to look forward to any more. Stripping her face of the stage make-up, she endured Moira's chatter, wishing Moira would just leave. Some people came to say how wonderful they had all been; she accepted their praise half-heartedly. Moira said she would stay behind to help close up. Elizabeth told her to go since Patrick was hanging around waiting for her. Moira was filled with her own happiness, she was too occupied to notice Elizabeth's mood.

She was locking the doors of the hall when Stephen stepped out of the shadows. Her heart skipped a beat from fear, but then she recognized who it was.

"Sorry, I didn't mean to frighten you. It's only me," he spoke reassuringly. I'll walk you home."

"There's no need."

"I'd like to." He walked beside her. "It went well tonight."

"You were there?"

"Yes. You were wonderful."

"Thank you!" Just three little words and he had managed to erase the ache that had filled her body since the night before.

They walked silently, footsteps matching perfectly. Did it always have to be like this between people — this swing between dissonance and complete understanding? They were approaching the park gates, a short cut for her whenever she was accompanied, a path she would never dare take on her own. He moved to take the long route in front of the university.

"Shouldn't we go through here?" She stood questioningly at the gates.

He paused and then, with a shrug, led the way through the gates. "I want to apologize," he said eventually.

"What for?"

"Everything."

"I don't know what you mean." She had never lied so blatantly before, but how could she say that she knew perfectly what he meant.

"I couldn't go near you the other night. Not in front of Joan."

"I know."

"I'm sorry."

His hand caught hers in the darkness. She felt intense happiness. More than she'd felt in her whole life. With the lights of the city disappearing behind the ancient oaks and elms that framed the park, a starry, beautiful midnight blue universe floated above their heads. She put her head back and stared up at the lights.

"Cassiopeia ... Orion ... the North Star ..." She pointed upward as she spoke. She knew perfectly well he wasn't looking at the sky but at her.

"Yes," he said quietly.

"Isn't it wonderful?" She looked at him. They were very close to each other and it would have been so easy to move into his arms. She looked back up again at the sky. "It's nice to recognize them, isn't it?"

"The stars?" Now she knew he was looking upward too. "Yes! We've put them all into neat little packages ... joined them together ... named them so that we can pretend we know something about them. We really don't know anything, do we?"

They fell silent. She didn't want the walk to ever end. The night seemed thick and velvet, dense with emotions and feelings.

The exit gates of the park loomed and she longed to turn back. The lighted street seemed to issue a command to face reality. She could almost count the number of steps to her front door and wished they could be on a backward-moving ramp that kept them ever just approaching but never finally reaching.

He released her hand at the gate. "Thank you!"

"For what?"

"For being a lovely girl." He turned and, with a quickening step, moved away. She stood watching him, but there was no backward glance.

He didn't turn up at the cast party. He phoned to let Moira know he had a conflicting engagement.

For months afterwards she couldn't bear to go to church. She found all kinds of excuses to stay away. She didn't want to see Stephen and Joan together. Her parents were obviously disturbed about her change of habits but didn't say a word. Frequently, she overheard her mother talking to her friend Pat on the phone about Elizabeth's "phases," as she called them. They would put this change of habit down to another of her "phases."

It was September before she went to church again. She dressed carefully, wearing a deliberately sophisticated suit. Inspecting her face in the mirror, she felt irrevocably changed from child into adult. She was sure everyone would notice the difference the months had wrought.

Stephen and Joan were already seated in the usual pew. She tried not to look at the familiar back of his head. Everything about him so well-known, so lovingly recorded in her memory. Hardly anything about the service registered. She only noticed his solicitous hand on Joan's elbow when they rose to sing one of the hymns.

This was something new. A tiny ache of self-pity made her tighten her grip on the hymn book. This was what she'd promised herself would not happen.

It was customary for everyone to file out in orderly fashion. From the front row to the back. Elizabeth longed to flee first but stood frozen. When it was Stephen and Joan's turn to come down the aisle, Joan stepped out and Elizabeth at once saw the bulge of her stomach. She was pregnant. Very pregnant, perhaps six or seven months gone. When Stephen passed them, she knew he had looked at her, but she pretended interest in something up front. She couldn't bear to look him in the eye.

It was only the prod of her mother's hand in the small of her back that made her move out of the pew. Stephen and Joan stood talking to people outside the church. Her mother hung back, looking towards Stephen. "Joan's pregnant. That's nice," she said. "We should say something."

"Please, let's go. I don't feel too well."

Her mother looked at her with concern. Elizabeth knew that Stephen was looking towards her again, but she couldn't meet his eyes. Joan was pregnant, and *she* was the one with morning sickness.

The following spring, she was in the bus one day when she saw him wheeling the baby in the stroller down the road. He looked proud and happy. She felt a burning sensation in her chest and remembered suddenly how his fingers had brushed her breast when he touched the fertility goddess around her neck. When Moira had disturbed them, he'd let the pendant drop. The sharp little pain it had caused as it hit between her breasts was with her again. The resonance surfaced and the ache deepened.

She looked down quickly to the book she carried with her, *Notes From The Underground*. She read the same page twice. None of it registered. When she looked up again, he was gone from her sight.

The Paisley Mug

JOANNA

After the last moving van had gone, Joanna remembered she'd left her coffee mug behind at number 34. For want of an ashtray, the coffee cup held not only the dregs of her coffee, but at least three cigarette butts. It was her favourite mug, too. No doubt the moving men had wrapped it up and taken it off in the van. Years before, when they'd first moved to Winnipeg and she was unpacking boxes, there, carefully wrapped in newspaper, had been an ashtray, ten lipstick-imprinted butts sitting staring at her, ash and all.

Alice would get to Toronto and find the paisley cup. She would unpack it carefully and be reminded that not only did Joanna smoke too much, but that she drank far too much coffee. She was glad a little piece of her would go with Alice, for it might be the last memento of her Alice would ever see.

Joanna lay down on the bed, the familiar feeling of nausea creeping through her body, seeping upward from her gut into her throat. "Chemothoroughly," she always joked to Alice, for therapy it surely wasn't, and it made her thoroughly miserable. Why did she have so little faith that it was doing anything for her? All the little marching men with swords that Alice always insisted she summon up in her mind, were off with Alice, gone in the moving van. In their place were a gang of layabout civilian militia with no organization and little faith in their ability to conquer.

The chemotherapy was a last-ditch attempt. She thought of it as a bombardment of napalm that would knock off her freedom fighters for sure, but might leave the territory of her body so stripped and empty that what remained wouldn't be worth saving. Why in God's name she thought of it all in military terms she had no idea. Her support group, like Alice, talked like a bunch of commandos. They met once a week to discuss army strategy. They also talked about the psychology of cancer rather than the disease itself. Encouraged by the group leader to think of her illness as a disease of the mind, rather than a real illness, she sometimes thought it was all too much to bear. Bad enough to have a growth gnawing away at one's innards, but double the burden to have the responsibility for it too.

When she'd first resisted the therapy, the kids all came to her one by one and talked about doing something to save herself. "What about Dad?" each one asked, as though she were responsible for him as well as herself. Seven children, seven individuals who scrapped and yelled their way through childhood, at times making her wonder if they all detested one another, and suddenly they were a common voice over the medical treatment.

For a year she had felt low, tired, and drained. It was assumed that raising seven children was a naturally depleting effort, and it was right and proper that with them all gone except Jamie, she should now collapse with exhaustion.

Sitting by the open window, she lit a cigarette. With the mid-April sun warm and insistent now over the prairie, the last of winter's chill was being edged out, melting away like the bank of snow on the lawn. Large patches of the previous summer's seared yellow grass were reappearing. Water dripped steadily from the eaves, a somewhat melancholy sound, as it punctured little holes in the snow banks that fringed the lawn.

She would think of the chemotherapy as the sun. New images were needed now that the band of soldiers were gone. Her body was the ground underneath the snow: seared somewhat, but perfectly capable of re-nourishing itself, capable of greening and renewing.

The cigarette butt would have to be buried at the bottom of the garbage. Des hated her to smoke. She didn't like disappointing him. Never had liked disappointing him. He could smell it off her breath, she knew that, but he said nothing. She was considered too tender these days for reproach, and yet she longed for someone to scold her. How she would miss Alice.

Through Alice she had lived vicariously. Alice was divorced and had a son and daughter, Martin and Suzie, who lived with her. It was a perfectly amicable divorce, one that had given her enough money for the house and enough shared-custodial freedom so that she could finish her doctorate at the University of Manitoba. Alice was fifteen years younger than Joanna. What had drawn them together was their shared sense of humour. They laughed at the same jokes, saw the irony in things. Perhaps the only trait they didn't share was optimism, the old "half-full, half-empty bottle" thing. She tended to be negative, Alice always positive.

When Alice had moved to the street, it was early April, the same time of year as now. Only it had been a terrible month with snowstorms one moment and raging hot weather the next. The entire population of Manitoba seemed to be suffering from flu. Desmond was inundated with sickly patients and always came home exhausted. He arrived late that first night when Alice was over for dinner. They were both standing in the kitchen. Joanna saw them look at one another, eyes holding for an overly long second. Then Desmond spoke. "So this is our new neighbour? Welcome!" It was as though she disassociated for a moment. They looked like the perfect couple — Alice just an inch or two shorter — a perfect physical match.

Desmond wasn't large for a man, average height, a perfect size forty in suits. Whereas she had, at least after the last three children, jumped two sizes in clothing. When she saw their reflections in shop windows as they walked in unison, they seemed ill-matched, herself taller and slightly wider, as though his image had simply bled outward.

He would joke about her love-handles in bed. Telling her warmly that he liked his women with flesh on their bodies, but he'd never been one for hurting anyone. Now, when she was finally back to her pre-wedding weight, he admired her figure.

Because Alice had no husband, Joanna lent her Des, sending him over to help her start her car, fix her plumbing, have a look at her lawnmower, help her with the pool filter, trim the large tree that hung over their garden. Des went happily, and Joanna would watch them from the kitchen window, always marvelling at the look of them together. She felt no jealousy, just a little sad.

Everyone from their house spilled over into Alice's in the summer time. Jamie, her youngest, was the same age as Martin, and they played together. Alice had given the entire family rights to her pool, and on the hottest of summer days, the air was alive with shouting and yelling as everyone from both families invaded the water.

Sometimes, standing at the window and watching, she imagined that she was alone and that they were Alice's family, not hers at all. At times she almost longed for that. It was odd how Alice seemed to have so few problems with her children and appeared so in tune with Joanna's brood.

Alex, Joanna's oldest, her poet, her difficult one, spent long hours at Alice's house. He baby-sat for her without a protest. A some-time student at university, he always jumped at the opportunity to do Alice a favour. She noticed he hung around even after Alice came home and she felt a twinge of jealousy, but then again, wasn't that typical, children often preferred to confide in people outside their own family. Alice told her not to worry about him, that he would eventually find his way.

Betsy, Joanna's second youngest, was dyslexic. Here again, it was Alice who had diagnosed the problem, not the school, not the counsellor, not herself. She had felt totally inadequate when Alice had worked it out, showering Joanna with articles detailing every aspect of the learning problem. Somehow, with seven children constantly making demands, she'd not had much time for reading up on the latest in learning disabilities, or even for trooping Betsy off for assessment.

When she was young she had imagined what it would be like having kids. The idea of big happy families thrilled her. Swiss Family Robinson style they would all look after one another. It hadn't quite worked out that way. With Desmond's huge medical practice, she had felt the weight of most of the decision making. At times it had been overwhelming.

Joanna walked upstairs. She had to pause on the landing, out of breath. A fit of coughing racked her body. The bedroom was warm from the afternoon sun. She went onto the verandah and stood staring down at the yard. She looked over at Alice's now-empty patio. The lone chaise that she'd brought out a week ago when it had suddenly turned warm, was gone. The pool, empty of water and full of debris and dirty incrustations of ice, seemed forlorn.

On summer nights, the pool turned a shimmering aqua when the sun finally set and the underwater light came on. *That evening she opened her eyes and saw Desmond standing by the dresser, stripped to the buff, putting on his swimming trunks. She'd been in bed asleep when he had finally come home; she'd heard him moving around the room, opening drawers. Frequently, if he'd been working hard, he took a late-night dip, doing numerous laps of Alice's pool, lashing out at the water as though angry with the surface.*

He didn't come near the bed to kiss her or even see if she were awake. She closed her eyes again and feigned sleep. He'd been gone for more than half an hour when the men came to fog the street. They made their usual racket. She got up and stood at the window watching them. The first time she'd ever seen them in their white zootsuits, they'd looked like men from Mars. Aliens come to poison the planet. The horrible smell of DDT started to permeate the room. They always kept their windows and the balcony door open so that they got a through-draft on hot nights. She felt herself choking, so strong was the insecticide. She closed the windows and went to the verandah to close the door. Stepping out for a moment she saw Desmond's body like a dark long fish slide through the water of Alice's pool, with none of the usual thrashing. He was doing some kind of deep breast stroke that took him under the water, gliding for long lengths before he surfaced for breath. Standing in the shadow, dressed in a housecoat was Alice. She had her arms folded, watching him. Not making a sound, Joanna stood very still. She lost track of how long she stood. The smell of DDT was now seeping around to the back of the house.

At least Desmond wouldn't be attacked by mosquitoes when he came out of the pool. She saw him rise suddenly and heave himself out. He had brought no towel and shook himself like a dog; the water spiralled off his body, droplets spinning and catching the light. Alice disappeared inside, coming back with a towel. Laughter drifted up, a bonding sound in the heaviness of the night. Alice moved first into the house and then he followed. Joanna felt her body burning with all kinds of sensations. Her bare feet tingled against the wood of the verandah as though the wood were smouldering. As in a trance, she moved towards the bed. Her body felt aflame from head to toe. There were no options available to her. Desmond going into the house with Alice and whatever ensued was inevitable. She lay in bed in a dream state, feverish and alert at the same time, like a young bride awaiting that first experience. Her fingers felt the warm wetness between her legs and she imagined Desmond and Alice coming together. With them in her imagination, her body stretched and arched in ecstasy, experiencing it all herself.

She didn't hear him come home; she fell into a deep sleep and in the morning awoke with a feeling of calm and well-being. Desmond was his usual gruff self. Never a morning person, he moved silent and self-absorbed around the bedroom. She watched his every move, disappointed to see no change in him when she herself felt suddenly enlarged and all-knowing.

The sun had moved behind a cloud and it was instantly chilly on the balcony. Joanna coughed again, doubling up with the effort. She slid down onto the rocker in the corner and pulled the shawl that was draped over the back of the chair around her shoulders. God, bring back my army! she silently prayed, but there was no real conviction that it was about to happen.

ALICE

Amid the chaos of cardboard boxes and half-unpacked china, Alice came across Joanna's paisley mug. She sat startled, holding it in her hand. There was a faint crescent stain in the shape of Joanna's mouth around the rim of the mug. Her lips had pressed here. Poor sick Joanna.

She'd felt like a rat deserting a sinking ship leaving her at this particular time, but the job offer had come and she simply couldn't refuse. It was hard enough getting anything in the university system, and even the offer of a one-year post was better than nothing. At the same time, watching Joanna's decline had been almost unbearable. Impossible to describe the relief when the offer had come through. Then all the feelings of guilt. Worst of all had been breaking the news to Joanna.

"Desmond will miss you." Joanna looked away, staring out the window. She rapped the window sharply at a dog who was squatting in the yard doing his business.

"Damned dog! I've told the Korwins to keep him tied up."

"What about you?"

"Me?" Joanna looked up and smiled a wistful smile. "I thought you would be helpful afterwards," she said briefly, and Alice wanted to shake her awake. It had struck her over and over how unaware Joanna was of the family's and Desmond's devotion to her. She was like a big dumb animal at times, surprised at displays of affection from anyone,

59

even her own children. It was as though she didn't feel deserving of any kind of love.

"I wish you'd stop talking that way."

"What way?"

"As though it's all inevitable." This was the first time Joanna had said such a thing. The dialogue had all been in Alice's head. Joanna turned her large dark eyes on Alice; the yellowish tinge underneath was like a recovering bad bruise.

"I want to talk about things. Arrange things ... just like when I'm going on a trip. I have to plan, only it's as though nobody else wants to talk about it. I want to be cremated." She ran a fingernail along the top of the wooden table. "I can't bear the thought of going into a coffin. I mean, what if I'm not really dead and wake up buried ten feet under? I would die."

To laugh right then seemed impossible, but it was spontaneous for both of them and brought tears to their eyes: tears which quickly changed to ones that burnt.

"Look after them for me!" she said, wiping her face with her hand. "I mean Desmond and the children."

Alice pulled a tissue from the box on the table and blew her nose noisily. A little of what Joanna was saying began to seep in. Had it indeed been Joanna's idea that Desmond come over all the time to help her with things? All those years ago had she known even then she wasn't well? She talked about planning things. Was this part of the planning? Alice felt struck dumb at the thought. It would be unbearable to do what Joanna asked.

It had never once occurred to Alice that Joanne thought she might be interested in Desmond. She knew the thought had never occurred to him either. They were friends, nothing more. Desmond was one of those myopic individuals who missed signals all the time. If a woman had been attracted to him, she would have had to send a telegram, write a letter; eye contact would never pass the message on to Desmond. The first time they'd met, the thought had crossed her mind that he was an attractive individual, but he was a man so tied to his routine that he'd shut out his emotions. Even the way he attacked her pool was a clue to his personality. She wasn't surprised that Alex, beautiful Alex, had problems with his father.

Sensitive, tender Alex, with his immature poetry, all passion and incorrect syntax. He brought it to her time and time again, and it was as though he'd opened up his heart and offered it to her on a platter. All critical faculty left her at those times.

Setting the mug down, she ran a hand down her throat, tracking a rivulet of perspiration. Her body felt awash. Already she'd phoned the landlord twice to let him know the air-conditioning wasn't working. The children had obviously been able to fall asleep, but she hadn't. Unpacking seemed like the most sensible thing to do under the circumstances. It was like one of those early August nights in Manitoba, when everything became utterly still, suspended in a thick heat.

There had been no air-conditioning in the house in Winnipeg and perhaps that had been the cause of her madness. There was something about those nights that aroused the senses. Not only the heat prickled the body, but mosquitoes buzzed in a frenzy over the pool, gone mad for the promise of cool blood.

Alex came over often just like Desmond. She used to watch him from the window, vowing she wouldn't go down. Several times she'd been in the pool when he came. His body wasn't as well proportioned as his father's, his shoulders not as broad, his legs not as muscled. Where Desmond was a well-oiled machine who swam classic strokes and seldom faltered on his dives, Alex was gangly and uncertain. Then that was the story of his life. Nothing Alex did quite fitted into the groove. It was his intense vulnerability that was so appealing. It was the reason, too, that she felt an unwillingness to criticize his poetry. His poetry seemed so much a part of him that to tamper with it in any way would remove its charm. And charming it was, spontaneous and deeply felt. It was odd how he had affected her right from the beginning. He made her feel unbalanced and slightly out of control, full of raging sexual desires and incestuous passion. Never in her entire life had she felt emotions like these. With other people she felt in charge, could offer advise: to Joanna she'd given the little men with swords; to Mark and Suzie she mouthed

61

clever motherly adages to help them deal with their daily problems. With Alex she was struck dumb. It was as though she waited for him to tell her something about herself.

Listening to Joanna's gentle cavils about his shortcomings, which mostly had to do with his uncertainty about where he was going in life, she was wordless. To say anything to Joanna about Alex would expose her feelings, so instead she listened, wanting all the time to scream out that Alex was perfect. That nothing would ever change him for the better. In her heart, she knew he was like an open wound waiting for infection, and she had proved to be the infection. Leaving him was the worst thing she had ever had to do, but somehow she knew that a little hard crust would form over the wound and Alex would survive.

He taught the children to play chess when he came to baby-sit. He brought encyclopedias. He taught them about robber crabs and comets, about lapwings and plovers, and long after he'd gone, the information would filter out, sometimes over cornflakes and toast in the morning, sometimes at night over dinner. A one-man font of information, he made the world interesting for all of them.

Pages of paper were strewn over the coffee table one night when she came home from University. One of her photo albums was open, and he hastily folded up a sheet of paper on which he'd been writing and shoved it into the pocket of his jeans. She saw the album page open at a photograph of herself laughing up at the camera.

"The kids brought it out." He closed it almost instantly. She knew it wasn't the truth. She even wondered if he delved in the drawers in her bedroom when she was gone. She'd noticed things were arranged differently since he'd been baby-sitting.

She poured lemonade in the kitchen, and he hovered behind her, talking non-stop. Pauses and silence had never entered their relationship. He was eager to know what she thought of the possibility of his pursuing an academic life. She surprised herself with her own vehemence. She might be headed in that direction, but it was not for Alex. Turned lecturer all of a sudden, she tried to articulate what it was that intellectuals did to literature. "They are vivisectionists, pathologists, working on live bodies. They cut the beating heart out of literature. They must do that to exist, and if you tell them that you read somewhere that the author intended it to be a certain way, they say, 'Nonsense, what does the author know?' They miss the irony in that. They denigrate the explicit, they hate the simple because it says it all, it takes away their reason for being. They only operate in fog, negotiate through bad weather conditions ... not content to let metaphor and symbolism alone, they probe it until it's tattered from mishandling" ... She realized that she was describing herself in detail. Outlining what her life was to become. She also knew that long before it was all over, she would loathe her job.

Alex was full of enthusiasm. She couldn't bear to think of him thirty years later turned into a facsimile of the man who had supervised her doctorate; his passion long suppressed, his creative energy soured and turned to political in-house wrangles over authority and tenure. He had even confided in her his discontent with the life he'd chosen. Alice talked to Alex long and perhaps extravagantly about the academic life, and he looked at her perplexed, perhaps wondering why she was about to choose it for herself. They moved to other topics, and then, finally, he reached into his jeans pocket, and taking out the paper he'd hidden earlier on, he smoothed it out and set it in front of her. It was a long passionate poem about his Oedipus complex and she felt her cheeks flush under his gaze.

"It's about you," he said when she eventually set it aside and looked at him.

"No, Alex!" She shook her head. "No!"

"I only ever feel right ... feel complete when I'm here with you." He didn't have to go on. He was explaining her own feelings totally, and she had to force herself to stay calm, to keep her hand steady on the table.

"You like me too. I know you do."

How painfully accurate that was. Everything inside was liquefying even as he spoke. The warmth was like a spreading fire that she had to control at all costs.

She nodded simply. "I do like you. Far too much, but it isn't possible."

Had her intense emotions somehow set off vibrations through the house? Suddenly Suzie was standing at the door. Her hair all tousled, she looked at them sleepily. "I had a bad dream. I thought something ran over the covers ... a rat. Was it a rat?" she asked innocently, as though Alice could confirm that it was. She looked from one to the other, and for a moment Alice had the bizarre idea that she'd been eavesdropping.

"Of course not, darling. Just a dream."

"Can I have something to drink too?" She was a child again, all innocent and thirsty from her bad dream. Relief flooded through Alice's body. Temperatures cooled, none of it had been said. Next time she needed a sitter she would choose someone else. Alex would be disappointed, even hurt, but surely he would understand.

She didn't go back for Joanna's funeral. It was impossible to get a baby-sitter. That was what she told Desmond on the telephone. That was what she told herself. She took the paisley mug to the campus and used it every day for coffee. It stained easily and she only ever ran it off under the tap, so that often there would be the crescent shape of a mouth on the rim. As she put her own mouth over it sometimes she whispered, "I'm so sorry, Joanna," uncertain of how many things to apologize for.

She started letters to Alex but never sent them. Often young men came into her lectures who looked like Alex: vulnerability thick on them, messy hair, undernourished bodies and pleading eyes. She avoided them, avoided those eyes, dismissed them quickly. Some days she handled the paisley mug roughly, almost hoping it would break. Other times she treated it tenderly, regretting that the paisley pattern on the mug was fading, every day losing just a hint of its colour.

Tangerines and Brussels Sprouts

The kitchen steamed with condensation from the clothes boiler. Huge turkeys, like bodies in a steam bath, reclined on all the countertops. The birds reminded Cassie of Bertie Strathdee.

Bertie lived three doors down, and when the weather peaked to a chilly sixty in spring, Bertie was the first man on the street to shed his shirt, displaying his mammoth white-breasted torso to the world. His arms squeezed so tightly into their hairy sockets that they hung limp, giving the impression they were threaded wrongly and inoperable. The turkey legs hung just so now. Impossible to imagine the skin on these birds ever turning tight and dark from the oven. Just as it was impossible to imagine Bertie with the slightest tan.

Christmas Eve these large, waxy, inanimate offerings would start arriving early in the morning, and by noon the kitchen looked like a mortuary for turkeys. Shortly thereafter the van from Gallagher's, the butchers, would come and pick up all the birds except one. Then preparations for Christmas would be in full swing. Cassie's mother painstakingly reducing the stale bread to crumbs in the large, cracked, yellow bowl, the only one large enough for the vast amount of stuffing that would fill the bird.

Her father came home from work and the kitchen filled with the sourish odour of whisky. Her mother sipped on her gin while she chopped onions, and her father sharpened the chopping knife with the energy of a master butcher. Flailing at the parsley, he reduced it to tiny pieces on the chopping board.

"I saw your father coming out of Milligan's pub the other night," Moira Ferguson told Cassie smugly in front of Florence McAuley and half a dozen other girls during milk break at school.

What bliss it would be to belong to a teetotal family like Florence McAuley's, the form captain. Christmas for Florence was filled with lots of church-going and ceremonial stuff, like singing carols around the doors in Sandy Row and distributing her mother's knitted scarves to the poor.

Forehead glistening with sweat, her mother lifted the lid off the boiler. Mutely, she stirred the sheets that ballooned up into tiny blisters from the boiling water. At a time when she should have been full of joy, her mother's face was etched with lines of ill-temper and weariness.

"What do we get for them?" Cassie stared at the birds through a fog of steam.

"Get for what?"

"The turkeys."

"Gallagher sells them for half price to the poor," her mother said.

Cassie couldn't tell whether there was irony in her mother's voice or if she was stating a fact, but she had no opportunity to question, for her mother thumped the lid of the boiler back on and drew an arm across her forehead to wipe away the moisture from the steam. "Peel the onions and stop asking eejit questions!"

A stupid question always rated an indirect form of mild punishment. Peeling onions was a job Cassie detested, but since she was already being punished, she risked another question. This time directed to her father.

"Daddy, do you go into Milligan's on the way home from work?"

The question stopped both parents in their tracks. A familiar "I told you so" look appeared on her mother's face.

"Maybe he was dropping off temperance pamphlets?" Moira had supplied archly once she'd dropped her bomb. Cassie had no idea what "temperance" meant, but anything that came out of Moira's mouth was never simple or well-intentioned. She had felt her face burn red hot. Florence's sympathetic hand on Cassie's elbow had been no help. Florence's Baptist charity was ready and willing to drape itself around Cassie's shoulders. It would have been double suffering to appear to form an alliance with Florence. She had no desire to be one of her charity cases.

That Moira classified herself as Cassie's friend was always bewildering, just as Cassie's own belief in the conjunction was peculiar. Their odd, tottery relationship was one minute sweet, the next moment bitter. When Cassie had come to school on the second-hand bicycle her parents gave her for her birthday, and put it in the slot beside Moira's shiny new one, nothing had disguised its oldness. The plastic basket, the new lights, even the new red handlebar grips served only as contrast to the rusting spokes and worn-out tires. Moira stared at it with scorn. "Is that all your father can afford?"

Later, perhaps as an apology, she had invited Cassie over to her house: a big, stucco, grey box, set well back on a huge manicured lawn and all but robbed of light from its backdrop, the looming shadow of Cavehill. Cold inside, it was furnished with ugly, boney sofas and high-backed chairs, almost characterless. Cassie thought of her own warm cluttered house and felt less angry with Moira.

Moira's father owned land and cattle, which gave him immediate dominion over Cassie's dad, a customs officer and mere civil servant. "Civil servant" was a term Cassie had come to loathe because it was always pronounced by Moira with a sneer, as though she knew something about civil servants that Cassie didn't.

The magic was gone from Cassie's Christmas this year and it was all Moira's fault. The birds in the kitchen were a reminder of what she'd been trying to forget. On the last day of school before the Christmas holidays, Cassie had been in the locker room putting away her coat. The final bell for assembly was just ringing when she closed her locker and heard Moira's voice.

"The farmers need him to turn a blind eye to the smuggling. Daddy says he doesn't take too much persuasion."

Cassie knew right away she was talking about her father. She felt the blood draining out of her legs, and if she hadn't held on to the locker door, she would have fainted dead away. The voice drifted off and Cassie knew they were gone. She should go to class, but her legs wouldn't move. Her heart fluttered feebly in her chest. Closing her eyes she leant back against the locker and slid down until she was sitting on the oak floor. What had Moira said after all? If he did turn a blind eye to what went on across the border that divided the north from the south of Ireland, it wasn't for profit, but because he felt the unfairness of the system. Cassie had heard him go on about it many times. The British Government allowed a subsidy on cattle from the north, and of course many a southern farmer smuggled a cow or two over the border to get the subsidy. Cassie knew for certain money never changed hands, but there was the odd bottle of whisky at Christmas time, not to mention all the turkeys. All the joy she'd been feeling at the approach of the Christmas holiday was suddenly wiped out.

Christmas Eve in Belfast was always magic. The tree in front of City Hall was an enormous spruce, sprung overnight like a huge, spiney, green church steeple, dwarfing Queen Victoria's statue, causing the resident pigeons to waddle far from it in disbelief.

It twinkled with a thousand lights that looked as though they had dropped from the milky way. Carollers sang all through the day and into the evening. Cassie imagined heaven would look like that. Not that she dwelt for long on what the afterlife might be like, but whenever she did, the City Hall on Christmas Eve was what came to mind.

The stuffing had to be finished, the sheets all washed, and the house dusted before they got dressed up and went downtown to stand in line in front of City Hall to see the Crèche. After that, it was always tea at Thompson's Restaurant: a mixed grill, toast, and then Thompson's Christmas cake to finish off the meal; all of it drunk with rust-coloured tea.

The line-up to see the Crèche was twice as long as usual this year, and when it finally moved and Cassie was there at the Crèche, it looked messy and amateurishly made. For the first time she felt nothing, no great heaving in her breast, no tear in her eye. She moved past it quickly; her mother pulled her arm as though to say, don't move so fast now that we've waited so long, but Cassie felt no inclination to linger.

They were renovating Thompson's and the family had to sit among scaffolding and bits of fallen plaster. The service was slow and disorganized, and her mother was irritable because she was tired. She was always tired at Christmas, but this time more than ever. She had dark circles under her eyes. Cassie hoped she wouldn't have another gin when the waiter came around. One gin made her cheerful, two depressed. Cassie had no idea what a third might do.

Cassie watched her mother loop her pearl necklace around her reddened fingers. Her nails were short and uneven. Never in a million years would she have taken time to file them or try to make her hands look pretty. She was ashamed of her hands. Often when she talked, she would fold her arms and bury her hands under her armpits. She was already speaking louder than usual and complaining about the poor service.

Cassie focused on the dusty scaffolding and imagined it coming crashing down on their plates; a little bit of violence to distract her mother from her growing irritation. Her father, across the table, wasn't hearing. He had that blank look on his face that came whenever her mother complained of things. Cassie knew he wished that the meal was over and they were on their way to Auntie

Ellen's for the usual Christmas Eve party. He suddenly looked across the table and smiled conspiratorially at Cassie.

She and her sister were always taken home and then her mother and father went off to the party. They would come home in the wee hours of the morning and her father would perform his Santa Claus act, putting the presents at the bottom of the bed — insurance against being woken too early on Christmas morning — something to keep them quiet while her parents made up for lost sleep. Florence's parents would be at home with her on Christmas Eve. Cassie was sure of that.

Christmas morning Cassie woke late, her throat sore, her eyes running. She lay looking at the wrapped gifts on the bed but made no move towards them. She could hear the rest of the household come awake and yet she felt no urge to move. There was no curiosity to know what was in the parcels.

She closed her eyes again and tried to swallow. She lay until the door opened and her father put his head around.

"You're not up yet?"

"No!"

"Well, Santa made it last night, didn't he?"

"He did. He was noisy," Cassie said grumpily.

"Isn't he getting a bit of age on him? What do you expect?" He came over and looked down at Cassie.

"Are you all right?"

"I don't know."

"And what about all that?" He pointed at the gifts. "Are you too sick to have a look?" He sat down on the edge of the bed and felt her forehead.

"You can't get sick on Christmas Day."

He handed Cassie the smallest parcel from the foot of the bed and read the label out loud. "Love from Auntie Ellen and

70

Uncle Frank." He pushed it at her. "Go on, open it!"

"It's perfume," Cassie said, holding it in her hand.

"Don't you want to know how it smells?"

"It's 'Magi.' It's always 'Magi.'"

"Here, try this one!" He handed her the largest parcel, putting it on her lap.

"What is it?"

"Open it and find out."

He was more excited than Cassie and impatient that her fingers were unhurried on the wrapping paper. Cassie knew the minute she saw the box that it was the ice skates that she had wanted so badly and had been told they couldn't afford. When she and Moira went to the King's Hall to skate, Moira always had her own skates and Cassie had to rent a pair. Moira's boots were white, and Cassie's rental boots were scuffed black-leather uglies with gaudy yellow laces. They never fitted properly.

These were magnificent, exactly like Moira's, supple white leather with shining blades and exactly the right size. Also in the box was a pair of emerald green stockings to wear with the boots. Cassie felt no joy, only a worse tightening in her throat.

"Where did *we* get them?" she asked, looking up at her father. The smile faded off his face.

"*We* stole them from Robinson & Cleavers, what did we think?" His eyes were reproachful. She knew he didn't understand what was wrong with her and for an instant she felt ashamed.

"They're great! Thank you."

She could see his disappointment. "I'm glad you like them."

"I do." She tried for more enthusiasm, but with his dear, scruffy, early-morning face, the stubble thick on his chin, he suddenly looked like one of the gangsters from a film she'd gone to see the week before. She felt she was seeing him for the first time. She smelled, too, the sour after-breath of a night of heavy drinking and felt the old anger again. He pulled his dressing gown tighter around his body and got up slowly, moving to the door.

"Do you want to stay in bed?" he asked, turning to look at her.

"No. I'll get up."

"Your mother could do with some help then."

Cassie flung the blankets back resentfully. It was always Mother he thought of first. Marjorie and she could be dying and her mother would always need help. Cassie loathed their mutual support system that left her out. She sometimes thought she was only incidental, only put on earth for their convenience.

Feeling even more sorry for herself, she opened the other presents. Everything seemed better than other years, only adding to her misery. There was a huge fat sketching pad and an assortment of sketching pencils and charcoals, something she'd always wanted; an Arthur Ransome book that she hadn't yet read and a pair of fur-lined mittens. She wanted to burrow back under the blankets and forget, wake up sometime in the new year and be someone else.

She eyed the box of Peppermint Creams that had probably been smuggled up from the South of Ireland. She had a passion for peppermint creams; just looking at the box made the saliva buds moisten in her mouth. But this time she wouldn't touch them. It would be a form of protest, a demonstration of strength. Even her very favourite, the tangerine in the toe of the stocking, would go uneaten. It fitted almost sensually into the palm of her hand. She could nick the skin ever so slightly and luxuriate in the delicious scent of the fruit, but she couldn't bear to waste that pleasure in her present frame of mind. She put it back in the stocking.

Her sister, Marjorie, poked her head around the door. "Are you dead? The Queen's about to come on any minute."

This morning Cassie didn't want to hear the Queen's voice with its high nasal tones reminding the world of "those less fortunate." She was less fortunate. Her throat felt even more sore and she could feel a sort of thickness in her chest.

"I've had to do everything: peel the spuds and do the brussels sprouts. I suppose you're lying there deliberately — trying to get out of it all?"

Why did they have to have brussels sprouts on Christmas Day? Still, it wasn't as bad as having a goose. Moira had goose on

Christmas Day. Cassie pitied her, but Moira seemed to think it gave her some kind of moral superiority. Florence's parents invited orphans for Christmas dinner. Cassie pitied her too. How could you avoid their envy over the things they could never afford? Another friend, Nancy, had her dinner at some aunt's house. The aunt was a terrible cook. Cassie knew she had a lot to be thankful for, but why brussels sprouts, those noxious wee cabbages she so detested? Still, it was small penance for not having to have goose and orphans for dinner.

"Are you all right?" Marjorie came closer and peered at her.

"No, I feel awful."

Marjorie bent down and examined her face more closely.

"You don't look too great." She sat down on the bed and rustled around in the paper that surrounded Cassie.

"What did you get?"

"Skates."

"So did I."

Cassie blinked at her. "How did they afford it?"

"The dogs."

"The what?"

"Father won 150 quid on the dogs."

"How do you know?"

"I heard them talking."

Her father had never talked openly about betting on horse and dog races, but there were frequent baffling phone calls that had always puzzled Cassie in earlier years.

"One straight on Fairy Godmother and five each way on Arabian Nights."

"Run away and play!" her father always urged before he made those phone calls and she never could resist the temptation to listen outside the door.

"A tenner on Rumplestiltskin, straight. Two on Dancer's Mate." It sounded like something she should have been allowed in on, a terrific game, but when she asked, he always said, "It's not for children." Cassie was amazed. It sounded exactly right for children.

It was funny how much less sick Cassie felt suddenly. It was marginally better to have a gambler for a father than someone who took bribes. She threw back the bed clothes with new-found vigour.

"So you're getting up?" Marjorie stood up. "You're a right wee skitter!" she complained bitterly. Cassie smiled and handed her the box of peppermint creams. "Have one!"

Marjorie looked at the box. "It's not even open yet."

"I told you, I wasn't feeling well."

"You can't be."

When Cassie came down, her mother and father were already stationed by the radio. They were drinking coffee in the best china cups with the yellow roses, but it was coffee that smelt suspiciously like whisky.

"You've recovered?" Her mother looked up.

"I'm fine ... throat's a bit sore, that's all."

The Queen's voice came on, high and strained. She sounded as though she'd come from another planet and was speaking to people she suspected might not understand her language.

Her father had shaved especially for the speech and was almost sitting at attention. The fire burned brightly in the grate, none of the usual banking of coals to save energy. It was a special day and it required a special fire. The entire room seemed alight with the glow from it and from the lights winking on the Christmas tree. Cassie thought suddenly of Moira and the great, empty, gray house.

"... and for those less fortunate than ourselves we pray at this special time of year ..."

"Here, do you want a sip of Irish Coffee?" Her father handed Cassie his mug.

"Harry!" her mother admonished.

"She wasn't born yesterday this one. It'll do her no harm."

"... and for all those both at home and away who must be without loved ones, we offer a word of comfort ..."

Cassie loved the sting of the whisky on her tongue. It reminded her of all the times when she'd been sick in bed with a bad cough and her father had come bringing hot milk laced with whisky and dotted with butter. Sitting on the edge of the bed he'd patted her back. "There, butterface, this will take the bad cough away," and it always did.

"... and for all those in hospitals and for those of us who have recently lost dear ones ..."

Then "God Save the Queen," and they all stood up solemnly to attention right there in the living room, the fat sticky fig, only ever a Christmas treat, momentarily stuffed into the recess of Cassie's cheek while she observed the moment with a still jaw and quiet mouth. There was maybe even a tear at the corner of her eye, oiled and unctuous as she suddenly was, full of good cheer and loyalty to family and Crown.

"Is there any reason why we have to have brussels sprouts every Christmas?" she asked when they sat down again.

"Your mother likes them." "Your father likes them." They spoke in unison and then looked at one another with raised eyebrows.

Streets, Avenues, and Roads

When I was growing up, I always felt a bit ashamed of living on Derravogie Avenue. The very idea of being associated with an "avenue" gave me the shivers. In Belfast, in those days at least, if you lived on a Dominion Street or Tully Street or any other number of streets, you were immediately identified as lower class. On a Derryamore Park or a Malone Park, you were upper class. To be on a plain old avenue, like Derravogie, you were worst of all, middle-class.

I had no aspirations to be at either end of the scale. My longings were more for the "roads." Antrim Road or Lisburn Road would have done. Living on a road meant you were harder to classify. In fact, you didn't really belong in any identifiable social milieu. Soldiers, sailors, candlestick makers were known to live on roads — adventurers, self-made interesting types — scorned by some, admired by the more imaginative among the population.

The one thing I knew about avenues was that the adults kept themselves to themselves. On streets, you could hang out around the front door and chat to everyone who passed by. On parks, you socialized with your own class. On avenues, you were on the borderline, so, according to Mother, the safe thing to do was to keep to yourself. It was a concept I found hard to handle. I talked to everyone on the avenue and everyone talked to me.

Most of the people were average, ordinary, pleasant people, a little stodgy, a little dull, but there were exceptions. The family in No. 32 Derravogie interested me. Out of No. 32 tumbled an incredible number of people.

"Breed like rabbits ..." Mother scoffed when I mentioned the McCartneys' name. "... and they live on fish and chips, I'll bet."

"We should buy more fish and chips then." Father winked at me. "They all look good on it. Especially the mother."

"She has her hair done, twice a week. Who couldn't look good. He sells vacuum cleaners and she has her hair set twice a week."

"Maybe it's lucrative. Besides, if I had eight children, I'd probably have my hair done twice a week too," Father rallied to Mrs. McCartney's defense.

"You'd think she got the kids from under a cabbage patch, with that smirk on her face."

Father started to laugh and had trouble stopping. "How do you expect her to look? Guilty?"

There was much frowning then and nodding towards me. Certain things were not for the ears of children, especially since my best friend on the street was the youngest McCartney child, Eileen.

Mother didn't really mind my roaming. I'd been in and out of most of the houses on the avenue and I was a natural blabbermouth. I was able to relate to Mother exactly how everyone lived, and usually did.

The other house of interest on the avenue was No. 60. The mother of the Bamford girls who lived there, was dead or had run away. Nobody on the street seemed to know for sure. There were two Bamford girls, Vivienne and Veronica. Their father was only a vague figure, a natty-looking commercial traveller with a round, jovial face. He was given to wearing bow ties and yellow jerseys, and saying "What ho!" in a phony English accent. He came and went irregularly, and had, according to Vivienne, lots of girlfriends, all of whom she detested. I was fascinated by the unusualness of their lives and of the way Vivienne controlled Veronica as though she were her natural mother.

Vivienne stayed home to keep house. She was a homemaker beyond compare. Both girls sewed their own clothes, made the curtains and upholstered their furniture. Vivienne seemed to exist on a frugal budget, but she could transform potatoes, carrots and ground beef into a meal fit for a king.

We haunted the Bamfords, Eileen and I, bringing with us our dolls. We loved going there. Vivienne had a big barrel of left-over material which we were allowed to plunder, and with a little help from Vivienne we fashioned clothes for our dolls. We vied for who had the best-dressed doll. We wanted to be good at something, but nothing we did could compete with Vivienne's accomplishments. And she was dazzling to boot. A softer version of the Red Queen from Snow White with jet-black hair, milk-white skin and vivid red lips. Eileen and I hero-worshipped Vivienne. We were less sure about Veronica, the sister who was our age. Veronica, compared to Vivienne, was soft, pink, and blonde. So different that we surmised she came from a different mother.

Veronica wore lipstick to school and had conspicuous breasts that puffed out her pleated school uniform, making it short at the front, showing off her spectacular legs. Veronica was interested in boys while Eileen and I were still terrified of the male sex. All the McCartney boys whistled at her when she walked by. They would have whistled at Vivienne too, but she would have clipped their ears as soon as look at them.

Mother plied me with questions when I came home from either house. Mother approved of the Bamfords. She thought Vivienne noble for having taken over the function of looking after a younger sister and a wayward father. She had seen Mr. Bamford turning up at the house with an assortment of showy blondes and her heart bled for the innocence of the girls.

Vivienne lapped up the neighbourhood warmth. She let Mrs. Allen, her next door neighbour, in on the secret of how to upholster a chesterfield, and Mrs. Allen was never done talking about how wonderful she was.

When I was fifteen, Vivienne showed me how to lay out a pattern, read it, and cut out a dress for myself. She then taught me the finer points of putting it all together. Mother was enchanted. From her I also learned how to lather my hair in salad dressing, stick a plastic cap on my head, and apply the hair dryer. Twenty minutes later my hair would be shining. She coached me on how to be reticent with men, too. Not that there were any boys in my life to practice on.

"Never let them see you like them, sweetie. Fatal!"

I never discussed things like this with Mother. She was convinced Vivienne was turning me into a homemaker. She couldn't envisage a better fate.

A few weeks before my sixteenth birthday I heard a rumour that Mr. Bamford wasn't coming home any more. Word was out in the neighbourhood that Vivienne had set herself up as a home consultant and offered interior-decorating advice. It explained the sudden increase of traffic on the street.

Veronica stopped going to school and through the grapevine it was circulated that she was doing a secretarial course at the Belfast Technical School. I never saw her come and go with books, but then I knew nothing about the workings of secretarial school. All I did know was that I envied her. I hated school with a vengeance. I had no clues as to what I wanted to do with my future, but I was certain that whatever direction I took, school would not be a help.

Sometimes I popped in after school to say hello to Vivienne. The door wasn't open as it had been in the past, and often nobody came when I rang. Still, Vivienne was as friendly as ever when she was home and always invited me in to chat and gossip. Despite Mr. Bamford's absence things were luxurious in the house. Potatoes and ground meat were no longer dished up in imaginative ways. Instead, smoked salmon and steak graced the larder. In the dining room there was an impressive array of alcohol all set out on a new buffet.

"Have you ever thought about giving your hair a colour rinse?" Vivienne asked me one day, fluffing out my hair with her competent hands. I giggled at the suggestion. I knew my mother would have fits if I mentioned such a thing.

"You're very pretty, but your hair is mousey." She ran her hand through it again and I allowed the invasion. "A little light perm, too. I could do it for you."

I was thrilled.

"You don't have to tell your mum. Just surprise her."

"Right! Why not."

I noticed Vivienne had taken to carrying a diary. She leafed through it and I saw over her shoulder that there were markings on just about every day.

"Wednesday night. Come over and we'll fix you up."

Eileen came with me Wednesday night, hopeful that Vivienne might extend the service to her. Vivienne was not terribly interested in Eileen and treated her as though she were a child. Eileen had been pretty when I first met her, but now she was overweight and spotty-faced. Mother never tired of saying it was because of the McCartney diet. She would look to me for confirmation, but my lips were sealed about the fish and chips.

Vivienne was true to her promise. She wrapped me in plastic sheeting and then concocted something in a bowl that looked like motor oil. With competent fingers she plied it into the roots of my hair. Eileen sat beside me, head in her hands.

"I can't do anything with yours," Vivienne said, looking at Eileen. "Besides, the red is nice."

"You think so?" Eileen pulled at her curls with vicious fingers. "I hate this."

"Most people would give their eye-teeth to have curls like

81

that." Vivienne was nothing if not tactful.

"They can have them!" Eileen swore at her reflection in the mirror.

"You'll lose the puppy fat soon," Vivienne assured Eileen.

Eileen let out a long wounded sigh. She had hoped nobody would notice. I was beginning to get nervous. My hair was turning a strange colour, all reddish.

"You're going to be a redhead like me," Eileen said, grinning now.

"I think we'd better rinse it out." Vivienne poked and prodded and rubbed one of the strands, peering at the colour.

Mother and Father stared at me dubiously when I got home. Because they approved of Vivienne, they were willing to be lenient. Anything Vivienne suggested or did seemed all right to them. I liked what I saw in the mirror, the strange new reddish tint made my face look more interesting.

Weeks later, as I was walking home from school I saw Vivienne ahead of me on the Malone Road. I ran to catch up with her.

"Hello you!" She smiled at me.

"How's business?" I asked brightly.

"Business?" She frowned.

"Yes. Your consulting business."

"Consulting?"

"Right. Mrs. Allen says you advise on interior design." She laughed.

"Well, don't you?"

"No! But mum's the word."

I couldn't tell from her expression whether she wanted me to pry any further.

"I give massages."

"Oh!"

"We both do." She stared at me. "You're shocked?"

I didn't know what she meant or why I should be shocked.

"Father ran off with some floozy and we had to eat. It's money for jam."

"Is it?"

"You could do it too, if you wanted." We walked on silently. I was trying to think why she had told Mrs. Allen she was a consultant.

"How much do you get?"

"Twenty quid an hour. Sometimes it's only for fifteen minutes."

I was overwhelmed. I also didn't know what she meant. Perhaps fifteen minutes of massage was all they could stand. In films I'd seen huge women masseurs and had heard people groaning as they were worked on. Mind you, I couldn't see Vivienne having that much muscle, and I wondered that her customers didn't feel short-changed.

"I don't know anything about it."

"It's easy. I could show you."

I was thrilled by the prospect. I saw myself rolling in wealth, ditching school and eventually dressing like Vivienne. I would introduce Mother and Father to the wonders of smoked salmon which, incidentally, I'd only ever tasted in Vivienne's house.

"Come over Friday night. I'll give you a massage. Show you how it's done."

"Can I bring Eileen?"

"Better not, she's a bit naive."

I was puzzled by this, but at the same time flattered. Vivienne obviously thought I was grown-up. I was delighted by her confidence in me.

Friday night came and Vivienne took me up to the third floor in the house. It was pretty bare, except for a couple of chairs.

"You'd have to work up here, but we're planning on fixing it up. Making the atmosphere a bit warmer. She showed me some material she had draped over a chair. "This is for the windows. We're getting another massage table." She touched the shelf. "This is for the massage oils."

"I'd have to talk to Mummy and Daddy about it all."

She put a friendly arm around my shoulder. "Don't rush things. They probably won't agree. We'll try you out on a part-time basis, and when things are really rolling, you can tell them then."

She took me down to the second story and into the front bedroom. It was wonderfully decorated, but totally startling. Everything was black and gold. I'd never seen anything like it before. I'd imagined something white and clinical. The massage table was set up in the middle of the room. It was covered in black velvet. Her bed had been pushed over to one side.

"Right off with your clothes. I'll show you how it's done."

I stood, embarrassed, arms crossed.

"It's me, come on. Don't be shy. I've seen it all before. Keep your pants on."

I stripped self-consciously, but Vivienne didn't seem to be paying any attention.

"Hop on the table, face down!"

I did her bidding. I loved the feel of the velvet against my bare skin.

"I haven't got the heater on now, but you have to make sure the room's warm."

I turned my head sideways and watched her oiling her hands.

"We work on the spine first." I felt her hands competent and pleasurable on my back.

"How did you learn all this?"

"Reading. I got every book I could. You should do the same thing. Drop a few phrases here and there, but believe me, they don't care after a while."

"Don't you have to have a licence or anything?"

"No. Besides, who's to know?"

There was no doubt she was good at it. I began to feel really sleepy after a while until she gave a light smack to my bottom and said, "Right, that's it! They turn over on their backs then and you'll know how to continue."

I was baffled by this. Was this to be the extent of my training?

"I have some of the books you can take home with you. Don't let your mum and dad see them yet."

"When can I start?"

"Read up for a while, then we'll see."

I was a quick study when I was motivated, and the image of all that money made me even learn the name of all the major muscles and tendons in the body. I found it quite thrilling in a way to be learning something none of my friends knew anything about.

Eileen was quite miffed that I was spending less and less time with her and more in my room studying, but my parents were impressed.

"Glad to see you're finally doing some work," my father said, smiling at me, when I made a move to leave the living room.

"If Eileen calls, what shall I say?" Mother asked.

"Tell her I'm studying."

"Maybe it's a hint she should take. She'll be qualified for nothing that girl, except maybe streetwalking."

Normally, I would have jumped to Eileen's defense, but Eileen was getting on my nerves of late. She was always developing a passion for some boy who, as far as she was concerned, was utterly unattainable. All she wanted to do when we met was go for a walk and talk non-stop about her current "pash." The walk usually took us past the home of the object of her desire. On the odd occasion he emerged from the house and ignored us as completely as though we were a couple of worms. She would imagine he'd glanced her way. If he did, I was sure it was merely to avoid stepping on us.

I'd had Vivienne's books for about a week when I came home from school one day to find Mother flushed and excited-looking, and Father home from work early. They both stared at me with a look of half-dread. On the kitchen table were the books Vivienne had lent me.

"Where did these come from?"

"From Vivienne."

"What were you reading them for?"

85

I shrugged and took off my coat, flinging it down on a chair.

"Do I have to tell you everything?" I felt defiant and angry, but also disturbed because of something intangible in the air. I started to move out of the kitchen, Father blocked my path.

"Sit down!"

I looked from one to the other. It was always the pattern that when one was severe, the other showed some weakness. The expression on both their faces was the same. It frightened me. I felt my legs go weak.

"What's wrong? All I was doing was reading."

"What did you do last Friday night when you went over to Vivienne's?"

"Nothing, she gave me the books then."

"You did nothing?"

"No, of course not." I felt my face flushing.

"Well, my girl, your friend Vivienne and her sister were picked up today for keeping a bawdy house."

I'd only the vaguest of notions what a bawdy house was. To my mind it was consistent with images of something sloppy and sleazy and people drinking mugs of ale."

"You said she was a great housekeeper," I accused Mother.

"Dear God!" Mother looked at Father and for a moment I felt their resolve weaken.

"Servicing men!" Mother said sharply, and I knew it had burst out of her against her better judgement.

I knew about bulls servicing heifers and I could only assume this is what she meant. The enormity of what she was saying hit me full force. I remembered Vivienne's phrase about the clients turning over and then I would know what to do. I felt suddenly queasy. There was only one muscle I would have had to be learning about and, strangely enough, in most of the anatomy books that one had been ignored.

It was about then I must have fainted, for the next thing I remembered I was sitting on the couch in the drawing room and Mother and Father were hovering anxiously over me. Mother had made tea and poured me a cup. It was strong and sweet, and I supped it gratefully.

"What did you do over there?"

"She gave me a massage to show me how ..."

I got no further. Mother let out a yelp. "You mean she interfered with you?" Mother held a fearful hand half over her mouth.

"She kneaded all up and down my spine. It was nice."

Mother and Father exchanged a look. "What else did she do?"

"Nothing! I got dressed."

"Holy God! You had your clothes off."

"No, just some. She said I would know what to do when the clients turned over. I thought she meant the same as on their back."

"You mean she wanted you to work ... there?" Mother's voice was faint.

"She said maybe I could, if I wanted."

"And you agreed?"

"It was twenty quid an hour, or sometimes only fifteen minutes, she said. Where else could I earn that kind of money?"

Mother sat down. "Nobody ever listens to me. You all think I'm unfriendly not wanting to get to know people on this avenue. Now you see the kind of people who live here."

"Oh, for goodness sake. You're over-reacting," Father said calmly. "You're the one thought Vivienne was great at everything. Looks like she was."

"How can you?" Mother turned on him. "She corrupts your daughter and you're treating it like a joke."

"Nothing happened."

"Something would've, if the police hadn't come."

"It won't now."

Mother turned to me. "I don't understand how you could be so naive?"

"You're always protecting her. What do you expect?" Father sat down opposite me.

"What about Eileen. Was she in on all this?" Mother asked.

87

"No."

"That girl has a lot more sense than you."

Just at that moment the door bell rang. Father got up from his chair and a few minutes later he came back in, followed by a flushed and excited Eileen.

"Did you hear the news?"

I nodded. There was a dead silence then, and Eileen looked back and forward between Mother and Father.

"My Maam's been giving me the third degree too."

"At least you didn't dye your hair," Mother said, putting a friendly hand on Eileen's arm. "You're a sensible wee girl."

Eileen looked smug but didn't mention anything about Vivienne's lack of interest in her.

Weeks later, a For Sale sign went up at number 60. Eileen and I had resumed our walks. We never went by the house without casting regretful glances up at the windows — half expecting to see Vivienne, a wing of shiny black hair falling over her face. Years later, I heard rumours that she had married a wealthy man and gone to live in London.

One good thing came out of the whole adventure, though. Plain, boring old Derravogie Avenue had acquired a status all its own. "That's the place where the Bamford girls ran their brothel, isn't it?" people would ask. "It is," I always anwered proudly, "... and didn't I know them. Och I! Butter wouldn't have melted in their mouths."

Three Good Days

Charlene, sucking on a coke bottle, watched her grandmother pounding the dough patiently, totally intent on the job. Flour covered her apron and there were traces on her face too, even the lashes on her left eye were covered in flour.

"Pizza!" her gran said, looking up at Charlene.

"Great!"

Nobody could make pizza like Gran: heaps of cheese, tons of pepperoni, and anything else she found left over in the fridge, but all of it tasting great underneath the mountain of cheese.

The phone rang and they both looked toward it, but neither of them moved.

"You get it," her gran ordered.

Charlene lifted the phone off the hook on the wall.

"Yeh?"

Someone at the other end asked for Bertha Shymko. Charlene was about to say they had the wrong number, then she realized it was her gran they wanted.

"Hold on!" She held out the phone to her grandmother.

"Me? What do they want me for?"

Charlene shook her head. She was as baffled as her grandmother.

"If it's one of them advertisers, tell them I'm not interested."

Charlene stood dumbly looking at the phone.

"Well, ask them!"

Charlene held the receiver away from her ear as though it might bite her.

"Go on, goose! Ask them."

"Whadya want?" Charlene asked tentatively.

She listened to the response. She shook her head at her grandmother and held out the phone again.

Bertha frowned and wiped her hands on her apron. Pieces of dough still clung to her fingers as she took the phone from Charlene. Charlene ambled over to the counter where her gran had been working, picked up a lump of the dough between her fingers and rolled it into a tiny log.

There were a lot of "Yeahs?" and "No kiddings" coming from her grandmother. Then she began to laugh, and Charlene gawked at her for she seemed almost to go out of control. Finally she stopped and seemed to be listening for an awfully long time.

She waved an arm at Charlene. "Pencil! Get a pencil, quick." Charlene scrambled in the jam jar on the counter and produced a stub of pencil.

"Paper!" She took the pencil from Charlene and pointed towards a pile of newspapers on the floor. Charlene lifted one of the newspapers and handed it to her grandmother. With the phone tucked in the crook of her neck and the newspaper jammed against the wall, Bertha wrote a number in the margin of the paper.

Charlene leant back against the counter and watched. Her gran hung up the phone eventually, then the laughing started again and she laughed so hard that Charlene could see all the gaps in her mouth where teeth should have been an' she could see the one gold tooth her gran was so proud of right at the back of her mouth.

"What is it, Gran?"

"That old bastard's dead ... he left me forty thousand dollars."

"What old bastard?"

"Yer lovin' gramps," her grandmother said.

"I din' know I had one." Charlene lifted a piece of pepperoni off the plate on the counter and took a bite.

"Oh, you had one okay. I left him thirty-five years ago and he goes and dies and leaves me forty thousand dollars. He's been living with some poor ninny, common-law like, and never bothered makin' no will. So it goes to me. She's fightin' it though, an' I have to go to Vancouver if I want the money."

"An' are you goin' to go?"

"Darn' tootin' I'm goin'. Forty thousand dollars," she repeated. "Where'd the no-good get that from? Musta robbed a bank or somethin'."

That night her gran didn't go into the basement when Charlene's dad came home from work the way she usually did. Charlene knew her grandmother didn't like her dad and the feeling was mutual. He hated the idea they were "carryin'" her, as he called it. She gave them her old-age pension in return for her room in the basement.

Charlene always felt guilty sleeping in her own bed at night and thinking of her gran in the basement. Her gran always said she didn't mind, but Charlene knew she did. The basement smelled damp all the time, and when it rained the four small basement windows leaked water, and sometimes, if the rain was real heavy, the floor flooded. Her gran slept on a terrible old mattress that they'd thrown off their bed and had been stored for years in the shed at the back of the house.

It was good to see her father's face when her gran told him about the money.

"Forty thousand! Jesus! I thought you said he was a bum?"

Her gran nodded. "Once a bum, always a bum. No forty

thousand dollars changes that."

"Holy Jesus!" He disappeared into the kitchen cupboard, getting out a bottle of whisky and three glasses, and poured a whole tumblerful into each. Her gran looked at the whisky and then at her son-in-law and shook her head. She went towards the basement steps.

"Heh, where you goin'?" her dad yelled after her gran.

"Where I always go."

"Now come on, there's no need for that."

Her gran turned and gave her son-in-law a long look. Gran wasn't good at mean stuff, so you weren't real sure what was goin' on in her head.

When she'd gone to the basement, Charlene's mum rounded on him. "Stupid bugger! It's her money. What the fuck are you celebratin' for?"

"Her money? She's been livin' off us for months, hasn't she?"

Her grandmother had lived on her own until she got sick, and then Charlene's mum had brought her to live with them. Charlene knew her gran hadn't wanted to move, but she'd been too sick to argue.

"Livin' off us? You mean we've been livin' off her cheque."

"Whose side are you on anyway?"

"It's her money. If she wants to give us a bit, that's nice. If she doesn't, we aren't going to say nothin'."

Charlene couldn't imagine her mother keeping her mouth shut if her grandmother did decide to give them nothing. Her mother could be a real hypocrite.

"Oh, we aren't?" her father shot back.

"No, we're not!" Her mother slammed the table with her hand. "She can move out to-morrow now an' you can't do a damned thing."

Her father ignored that and drank his tumbler of whisky and her grandmother's too, then he began to do a lot of whistling. It was nice to see him in a good mood for a change.

After they'd eaten the pizza, he started talking about getting rid of "the little shit box" of a car. Charlene's mum said nothing.

The next couple of weeks her grandmother was on the telephone a lot with some lawyer, and then one day when her mother came home from work her grandmother announced to her that she was goin' to Vancouver for some court case over the money.

"I'll come with you," her mother said, all sweetness and light in her voice.

"Why would you?" her gran said quietly. "I can go on my own, thanks."

"Don't be a fool. You can hardly walk the length of the block without gettin' out of breath."

It was true of course. Her grandmother had been worse than ever since she'd been sick.

"I'm goin' on my own," her gran said firmly, and then she began to rock in the creaky old rocking chair she sat in when Charlene's dad wasn't around. The rocking seemed to shut out all the unpleasant things Charlene's mum was ranting and raving on about ... like how her mother didn't give a damn about all the sacrifices she'd had to make to keep her there. At that, her gran opened her eyes and shot her mum a funny look.

Charlene's Auntie Shirley and Auntie Gloria were brought in to argue with gran, but she was firm and said she was goin' on her own. Then Charlene's dad started yelling and shouting and it was awful. Her grandmother took herself off and it was like she pretended they were all fighting about something that had nothing to do with her.

Charlene's aunts and her mother and father finished up all the booze then and began to talk about the things they was goin' to buy with her gran's money. Her mum seemed to have forgotten what she'd said to her dad about it being her gran's money.

The next day, when Charlene got home from school, her gran was soaking her feet in a big basin in the kitchen. She said she'd been to town to buy herself a new coat for goin' to Vancouver.

Charlene inspected the coat. It wasn't no new coat,

Charlene decided 'cause there was a button missing, but still it was better than the old brown thing she owned — the only coat Charlene had ever seen on her gran's back.

"How'd you like to go to Vancouver with me, Charlie?" she asked Charlene out of the blue.

Charlene couldn't believe she was hearing right. She'd only ever been to Niagara Falls, and that was so long ago she barely remembered it.

"What about school?"

"It'd do no harm to miss a few days. You're smart as a whip, you'd catch up."

"Could I really go?" Charlene felt she was gonna bust with excitement.

"Sure."

Charlene suddenly remembered the whole ruckus over who was going to go with her grandmother. They'd be mad as hell. Sure to say no.

"I'll fix your mum an' dad, if that's what you're thinkin'?"

"Could you?"

"You bet."

Her father's face turned purple when her grandmother mentioned it to him. He started bellowing at her, but her grandmother just turned on her heel and disappeared down the basement steps.

"That was jus' shit stupid," her mother said, shaking her head.

"Shit stupid, was it?"

"Yeh! You got it. Dumb!"

"Please, can't I go?" Charlene pleaded, aware suddenly that her voice had come out in a whine. She thought for a minute her father was goin' to hit her and she covered her face, but instead he smiled.

"Yeh, maybe you're right," he said to her mother. "Maybe Charlene should go. She can keep an eye on the old bat, make sure she doesn't do something damned stupid with the money."

"She's only a kid," her mother said. "Besides, we shouldn't count our chickens. They might give the money to the common-law."

"They won't give it to her. She had no child. I already checked it out. Your mum brought up three kids on her own with no help from that old bastard. The judge'll be sympathetic to that." Her father patted Charlene on the shoulder. "Good to have the kid along. The judge'll see what a good kid she turned out to be."

Charlene felt like yelling for joy. *She was going. She was going.* She rushed off down into the basement to tell her grandmother.

"Sure," her gran said with no change of expression." Di'n' I tell you you was goin'?"

Later, at the table, they talked about cars. Her father had already been looking at cars. He'd seen just what he wanted.

"Split three ways, you might be looking at a motor scooter," her mother broke in finally.

"Those sisters of yours? You kiddin'. I di'n' see them makin' no rush to take her in when she got sick. No sir, sucker here," he jabbed his chest, "... lets her come here. She knows that, she ain't stupid, that's for sure."

Charlene was dreaming of something else altogether. She saw her gran and her in Vancouver. Saw them getting the money and staying there, just the two of them. Never coming back. She knew that you weren't supposed to hate your parents, but right then she did. She couldn't think of one good thing about them. All she could see was her gran sitting in the damp basement while her mum and dad were splitting up the money.

She'd heard her gran goin' on at times about when she'd been a kid on a poor farm in Gimli, Manitoba. *"We had nuthin', but we was happy as clams."* She usually said it when she heard Charl's mum goin' on about wanting a new fridge or a microwave oven or something else that they couldn't afford. She was glad to hear her gran saying things like that. Glad to know that there had been one part of her life that had been good.

Charlene often told herself that if there really was a God he couldn't possibly make the whole of a person's life rotten. If he was any good at all he would give everybody a little bit of a good time. She knew that life had been very hard on her grandmother. She'd brought up three daughters on her own, scrubbing floors day and night to keep them all alive. Now, at least, she would have the money. That was something. And way back when, if what her gran said was right, she had once been happy.

Charlene's Dad drove them to the airport. As they drove, he talked the whole time about the car falling apart. Charlene knew he was thinking of the new car. He was actually trying to be nice to her gran for a change, but he never said a word to Charlene. Never said, "Have a nice time!" Nothing.

She wasn't scared of being in the plane. She knew somehow it would never crash. God wouldn't allow a thing like that. Especially since her gran was about to get a bit of good in her life. Charlene sat contentedly sucking on the candy the hostess had given her and felt her tummy fill up with butterflies at the excitement of the whole thing. Gran took her hand and squeezed it.

"We're off to China," her gran said cheerfully. "I wanted to go to China all my life," she said with her eyes half-closed.

"You could now." Charlene looked sideways at her gran.

"Could what?"

"Go to China. With your money you could go to China."

"No, I couldn't do that." Her gran shook her head. "Better to imagine it."

Charlene couldn't work that one out, but she didn't say anything. Besides, she was staring out the window in awe as everything flew past the window. The earth was disappearing beneath them like they was in a rocket. Gran let go of Charlene's hand and crossed her hands in her lap. Charlene could see her knuckles all tight. When she looked up into her gran's face, there was sweat on her forehead. She looked uncomfortable in her new coat with it buttoned all the way up the front.

"Gran, you can take your coat off," Charlene said. "I seen someone put their coat up there." She pointed to the storage bins above them.

"Nope! Got it to travel in, an' that's what I'm doin'," her gran said solemnly.

"It'll get hot, Gran."

"I'm fine."

Charlene relaxed beside her grandmother but took her own coat off. She held it in her lap, not wanting to disturb her grandmother. A man from across the way looked at her and stood up holding out his hand for her coat. He put it away in one of the storage bins for her.

"Keep your eye on it!" her grandmother said. "Someone'll go off with it, for sure."

Ladies came up and down the aisles with drinks an' things and nobody seemed to be paying for them, so Charlene took a Coke. Then came the food. Great food in little trays. Then more drinks and one of the hostesses gave Charlene some extra bags of peanuts. Then before she knew it, the captain was talking about landing, and Charlene felt sorry. It felt as though they'd just taken off.

Her gran was all pink in the face by the time the plane landed. She'd kept her coat buttoned up the whole time, and there was a great big stain on the front of it where she'd spilled some food. Charlene said nothing because her gran never noticed things like that anyway.

They had to wait for ages for their suitcase, and Gran complained saying her legs felt like overstuffed sausages, and sure enough, when Charlene looked down at her gran's feet, they were all blowed up and sort of bulging over her shoes as though someone had pumped them up like balloons.

"I guess my legs went on a trip too," her gran said with a grin. "Got filled up with air."

They were staying at the Holiday Inn and Charlene had never seen anything like it before. The room had a bathroom and two huge double beds, and there was a television set on the dresser and a bathroom with thick towels and soap in little packages.

Her gran was too tired to do anything but sit when they arrived, but Charlene was perfectly happy. There was a Coke machine in the hallway, and she still had some of the packages of peanuts from the aeroplane, so they both sat and watched television.

Next day, the lawyer came to talk to her gran, so Charlene decided to do some exploring on her own.

"Mind you don't get lost," her grandmother warned. "Keep the hotel in sight!"

Charlene rode up and down in the elevators for a while, puzzled that she could find no thirteenth floor. Then she started going up and down by the stairs and there was still no thirteenth floor. It was a total mystery.

She went outside. It smelt different from Toronto, but she couldn't exactly say why. She liked the smell. People walked real slow on the streets. Looking into their faces, Charlene would have said they looked happier than the people at home.

She found a shop near the hotel that had lots of Indian things in the window and went inside. She found a key chain with a pair of Indian moccasins on it, all yellow suede and white fur. It was only five dollars. Her gran had given her ten dollars to spend, so she bought the chain for her.

She knew her gran didn't really have any keys except the one for the door of their house, but she could at least put that one on the chain. The girl behind the counter wrapped the present in white tissue paper and gave her the box. Charlene felt happier than she'd ever felt in her life. She would have bought a lovely Indian doll for herself as well, but it was expensive.

When she got back to the hotel, her gran was pacing up and down the lobby, looking worried.

"Where were you?"

"Shopping." She held out her package. "I bought you a present."

"Silly girl, spending your money on me. It was for you, not for me."

"If it's my money, I can do what I like with it, can't I?"

Her grandmother smiled. "You can."

Her grandmother put the present away in her handbag, and Charlene felt hurt that she hadn't wanted to open it right then and there.

"We have to go to court for two oclock. The lawyer's comin' to get us," her grandmother said.

"I can come too?"

"Sure. That's what I brought you for."

Charlene couldn't imagine what it would be like to be in a courtroom. She'd seen plenty of courtrooms on television, but she wondered if this one would be different.

"Her name's Rose Litsky," Gran whispered to Charlene when they were in the lawyer's car. They both sat in the back seat while he drove, and it was like he was a taxi driver. Charlene wondered how he felt about them sitting at the back, but he didn't look as though it bothered him one bit.

"Who?" Charlene whispered back.

"The woman the old bugger lived with," her grandmother said.

It was lovely sitting in the big car and being driven around. Vancouver was nice, mountains all about and masses of flowers everywhere, not like in Toronto with its puny flower beds and the few measly geraniums people liked to plant. Here there were big bushes all covered in tons and tons of purple and pink flowers the size of a person's head. Charlene had never imagined it would be like it was, and she was thrilled. Everything seemed white and blue: the sky blue, the sea blue, and then the buildings and houses like a lot of smiling white teeth all around the harbour.

She had never sat in a car just riding and riding around up and down big wide streets. Maybe they weren't any wider than at home, but there were fewer cars, that was for sure.

It would have been nicer if the lawyer hadn't talked so much, but he kept reminding her gran of all the things she shouldn't say and her gran just kept nodding and looking out the window as though she wasn't really listening.

She could see the lawyer's face in the mirror and he looked a bit mad. Her gran had that effect on people. She always had a sort of peaceful look on her face, a bit punchy, so you never knew for sure if she heard when you talked to her.

Charlene saw the lawyer's neck was red an' he kept jabbin' his finger back at them, trying to make sure he had Gran's attention. His voice seemed to get louder and louder. It would have been nicer just to have had a quiet ride, like in the taxi coming from the airport.

When they got to the court they were too early and had to wait. The lawyer didn't want them leaving the courthouse, so they had to sit on hard benches outside the courtroom and watch all the people coming and going.

"What was he like, Gran?" Charlene asked her grandmother, thinking of the grampa she'd never seen.

"No good!" she said, staring straight ahead.

"He was all right at first, but when the kids started comin', that's when it changed ... never home ... out drinkin' his head off ... beatin' up on me ... disappearin' for days." She smiled a sad smile. "Then he'd come home an' call me a bitch and begin slappin' me around." She seemed lost for a minute. Charlene took her hand and squeezed her grandmother's fingers.

"An' you left him?"

"No, not then. I just kep' bailin' him out of pokey ... Oh, yeh, I left once and he came an' found me. Swore on his mother's grave he wouldn't drink no more. He got a job in a lumber camp and he found a place for us to stay. So I decided I'd give him one more chance. Things was just the same ... him workin', drinkin' an' fightin'." Her voice tailed off here and Charlene thought for a minute she'd decided not to tell her whatever it was she'd started to

100

tell. Charlene squeezed her hand again.

"One day they found the cook at the camp with his throat slit. He swore black and blue he didn't do it. The RCMP came an' arrested him ... but they finally let him go ... couldn't find no weapon on him ... never did find no weapon and nobody could say he did or didn't do it."

"An' you ... What did you think?"

Her grandmother shrugged. "He had a mean temper an' all ... but I couldn't believe he'd kill a man."

"Then what?"

Her gran laughed and looked at Charlene. "You don't give up, do you?"

"Then what?" Charlene repeated. She knew she would have to keep after her gran or she'd drift off on another train of thought.

"We moved to Parry Sound an' he got a job with a construction company and he was all right a for a while ... cut back on the booze, stopped yellin' and hittin', but then by the time yer Auntie Gloria came along he was sick of kids ... he started beatin' up on me again. It was my fault we had three kids he said ... He started drinkin'... lost his job ... we damned near starved. Then one night he got drunk and came home, punched me on the mouth an' started screamin' at me ... said I was a stupid bat ... didn't know nothin' from nothin' ... never had ... an' he started braggin' about killin' the cook."

"Wow! He killed him?"

"He got out his knapsack and showed me some knife he said he killed him with."

"An' had he?"

"Probably not. Jus' tryin' to scare me. I don't know. I knew I'd had enough, that was all I knew. When he was out the next day, I packed up the kids and hitched a ride to Toronto."

There was a smile on Gran's face now at the memory.

"Did you have any money?"

She laughed. "I had two dollars in my pocket. A guy in a semi-trailer picked us up. He thought I was off my rocker. He dropped us off part an' parcel at the Sally Ann on Jarvis Street."

"And?"

"They took us in. Helped me look for a job. Gloria was only two. I went out cleanin' houses an' offices, workin' morning, noon and night. The four of us lived in a one-room dump off Queen Street with cold water an' roaches the size of yer thumb."

"An' him? What happened to him?" Charlene asked eagerly.

"That was the last I saw of him or wanted to see."

"That's somethin', Gran. Doin' all that on your own."

Her grandmother put an arm around Charlene. "You do what you have to do an' no lookin' back. I never looked back."

Charlene studied her gran's poor old worn face and felt a great swelling of love for her. She looked at the thinning hair on her gran's head and the way hair sprouted in little fountains out of her chin, like the hair had decided to grow on the inside instead of the outside and then just came burstin' out in odd little patches here and there.

Charlene felt her own chin and wondered if that would happen to her too when she was her gran's age. Although she couldn't really think she would ever get to be her gran's age. Charlene had decided long ago that she would like to die at fifty. Fifty seemed the right age to die.

It seemed they had to sit and sit on the hard bench forever before they were finally called. She could see her gran was tired and her feet had begun to swell again. That always happened when her gran didn't get to put her feet up. Charlene held onto her arm as they walked into the courtroom.

The Rose woman was sitting on the other side of the aisle from them. She could see her gran take a good hard look at her and the woman did the same to Gran. Neither of them cracked a smile.

The woman looked pathetic, like a balloon that had started to loose its air. She wore a faded pink knit dress that came to her knees. She had awful yellow hair with black roots. Her gramps had sure picked no beauty queen, but then no beauty queen would have wanted him by the sounds of things.

The judge called the woman up to the stand first and she told her story. She'd lived with him for twenty-five years. She told it all in a kind of whine an' you could see right away the judge didn't like her voice. He kept leanin' his head to one side on his hand, maybe to cut out the noise of her voice.

"Could you tell the court what your present income is?" the lawyer asked her.

"Nuthin!" she replied. "I get the Old Age next year."

"What a wimp," her gran said under her breath.

Her gran's lawyer took over questioning her and she started to cry. Everyone waited politely for her to stop.

"Is it true, Miss Litsky, that you hadn't lived with the deceased for the past year?"

There was another pause and some more crying, and then she admitted she hadn't.

They called Gran to the witness stand next and it took her the longest time to get there. Charlene knew her legs were hurtin' bad from the long wait. She held her gran's arm. Charlene went back to her seat and listened. She was proud of her gran. She told her story well and you could see the judge liked the look of her.

"Did you ever try to get any support money?" he asked her at one point.

"Are you kiddin' ... I'd rather stay lost."

Everyone in the room laughed.

"Thank you, Mrs. Shymko!" the judge said. "Mr. Edwards, would you like to cross-examine the witness?"

"Thank you, Your Honour!"

The lawyer stood up and went over to Gran.

"Mrs. Shymko, during the years together with the deceased did he ever fail to provide for you?"

"All the time ... he was in and out of the pen. I had to scrub floors. Sometimes he was in a drunk for a week."

"Thank you!" he cut her off quickly. "Now, is it true that you left him and there was no forwarding address?"

"Forwarding address ... an' what would he have forwarded

103

'cept himself?"

Everyone laughed again and even the judge smiled.

"Thank you, Mrs. Shymko, that will be all."

Charlene went up and helped her gran back to her seat. She was puffing and panting and Charlene knew she wasn't feeling so hot. Charlene wished it was all over and she could take her back to the hotel room, but it wasn't to be. The lawyer called the Rose woman back on the stand.

"Miss Litsky," he began, and Charlene wanted to laugh 'cause she sure didn't look like no Miss, "... during your time with Mr. Shymko, was he given to fits of violence?"

"He punched me out a few times ... sure."

"A few times ... once a year? Once a month? Or once a week?"

"He didn't mean it, though ... he was always sorry."

"Please answer the question!" the lawyer snapped. You could see he was sort of mad at her now.

"Once or twice a week." She began to sob, and it only took a few tears to bring half the mascara down her cheeks, so that she looked like a real dog's dinner.

"She's so dumb!" Gran whispered, and I thought that was somethin' for her to say because apart from saying things about Gramps, she never did say nothin' bad about people as a rule.

"If that is all, Mr. Edwards, we will take a break. I will give my judgement after lunch.

"Yes, Your Honour."

When the judge came back after lunch, he took his glasses off and rubbed the indentation on the bridge of his nose. Then he squinted towards Rose Litsky's lawyer.

"While my sympathies are with your client, Mr. Edwards, for having endured twenty-five years with the deceased, I'm afraid I find the case, through strict interpretation of the law, quite straightforward." He looked at my gran and gave a smile of encouragement and I knew she'd won.

"I must rule for the defendant, Mrs. Shymko. Although she had the good sense to withdraw from the relationship with Mr.

Shymko, she must have endured equal, if not more, hardship during the past thirty-six years, having had to rear the children of this unfortunate union on her own and without any financial assistance from the deceased. I therefore uphold the will."

Charlene saw the Rose woman crumple, and you could see her whining away again an' you couldn't help feeling sorry for her. She wasn't as tough as gran. Gran hardly looked pleased at all, just tired, but she shook hands with the lawyer, and for once he was smiling. Charlene guessed he knew he'd get paid for sure. She didn't like him, and when he dashed off leaving them both at the courthouse, she liked him even less.

They managed to get a taxi back to the hotel, an' her gran kinda collapsed on the bed and fell asleep almost right away. Charlene turned on the telly real low and waited for her gran to wake up.

Later, when she woke up, her legs had gone back to their normal size and she seemed quite cheerful, but Charlene was surprised her gran wasn't happier with her good luck.

"What do you want to do tonight, Charl, to celebrate?"

"I don't care," Charlene said. "If you're tired, I can go an' get us somethin' to eat and we can watch the tube."

Gran swung her legs over the side of the bed. "No way," she said fiercely. "I di'n' come all this way to lie in no hotel-room bed. What would you like to eat?"

Charlene shrugged. "Anything."

Gran got up slowly and went over to the table where the telephone book lay, and she started leafing through the yellow pages for restaurants. She went through it slowly, pronouncing names as she read through: "The Lobster Trap, The Shrimp Kitchen, Maggie's Hut, The Seafood Den." She grunted and looked up at Charlene. "I don' know."

"Stab a finger at it, Gran. It don't matter none."

She looked down again. "The Steak Pit," she read out, and giggled. "Sounds like The Snake Pit." Then they were both laughing and couldn't stop, and tears were running down their faces. That's what Charlene liked about being with Gran. Gran could always see the funny side of things.

"All right, girlie. Get your good dress on. We're goin' to dine in style."

Her gran changed her blouse, but it was like exchanging one stain for another. Her gran was no good at keeping food from dropping on her when she ate, no matter how hard she tried. An' even though her blouses were clean, the stains somehow never came off proper. Charlene's mum was always on at her about it, but she always said that as long as they were clean it made no matter. An' neither it did, when you thought about it good.

Charlene hoped the restaurant wasn't too grand because she didn't exactly look like no fashion plate.

They needn't have worried, for it was like the restaurants at home, with a full course meal for $9.95, and they didn't give you no kind of "once over" when you walked in. Charlene could see they was happy just to have customers.

Charlene had the "surf and turf." The name made her want to laugh. It was like you should expect a wave on a patch of grass, but it was real good. Her gran had a steak an' kidney pie because it was soft to eat and didn' need a whole pile of teeth to get it down. There was cherry cheesecake for dessert and Charlene felt like a stuffed pig by the time she'd finished.

"It's great you got the money, Gran," Charlene said as she laid down her napkin.

"Is it?" Her gran pushed her cheesecake away only half finished.

"Well, isn't it?"

"If you could have anything you wanted, what would you want?" she asked Charlene suddenly from across the table.

"To stay here forever an' ever," Charlene said with a grin.

"Besides that?"

Charlene shrugged. "I don' know. Maybe a bike."

Her gran wiped her mouth on her napkin. "A bike, you'd like that?"

"I suppose."

"Then you're goin' to have a new bike."

Charlene looked down at her empty plate. "I don't really want it that much," she said, quickly thinking about all the wants of her mother and father.

"Sure you do! You get a bike, no matter what."

"Isn't it too bad we couldn't just stay on here?" Charlene said with longing.

"Yes, but we can't."

Charlene knew she would have liked it too, by the look on her face, but she knew it was no use going on about it, for it wasn't about to happen.

They walked back real slow to the hotel and Charlene thought it was a shame about her gran's legs, for it was a beautiful night and she could have walked on an' on. She loved the reflection of the lights on the water. Also seeing the people strolling, sometimes arm in arm. She tried to overhear their conversations. She felt real grown-up, but she knew that eleven wasn't grown-up enough to walk around by herself at night.

They had one more day, an' Charlene hoped they would be able to see a bit more, but just being away the two of them was good enough, and so what if they didn't see any more of Vancouver. So what?

They had a big breakfast next morning an' Charlene was allowed to order anything she wanted on the menu. She had waffles and then pancakes and couldn't really finish them, but her gran said it didn't matter.

When they went past the front desk, the man behind the counter called Gran over and gave her an envelope. Gran took it and turned it over a few times and then finally opened it. It was a cheque for the money she'd been left. Her gran had to sit down when she saw it, and then they both sat and stared at it and it was hard to believe that right in her hand was all that money.

"What are you goin' to do with it, Gran?"

Gran put it away silently and didn't answer. She didn't look so happy any more, and Charlene imagined she was probably hearing in her head the voices from back home. The aunts and her mother all arguing about how it was goin' to be spent.

"We're goin' to get our coats and then we have some things to do," her gran said firmly.

The first thing they did was stop at a bank, and Charlene had to sit on a chair and wait and wait for her gran to finish her business. When her gran was finished, she handed Charlene a letter from the lawyer. "What's the address on that?" She pointed a finger at the body of the letter and Charlene knew she'd forgotten her glasses back at the hotel.

"It says somewhere this Rose woman's address," her gran said.

Charlene looked down at the letter, and there it was. She wondered what her Gran wanted it for.

"Now be a good girl. We'll stand on the corner and you call a cab when you see one."

Charlene liked doing that. She felt very grown up, just putting her arm up and making a car stop. She also liked travelling by cab. When the taxi pulled over and they were safe inside, her gran said, "Give him the address!" Charlene read out the address to the cabbie, and he cocked an ear to hear what she was saying.

"Why are we going there, Gran?"

"You'll see."

It was a poor street she lived on, with a lot of crumbling houses and porches with people hanging around on the steps or by the front door.

Even with Charlene's help, her gran was slow getting out of the cab. They walked up to the front door of number thirty-seven and knocked. The door wasn't properly closed and when she rapped, it opened slightly and you could see the floor with dirty, peeling linoleum and the wall with torn wallpaper.

The Rose woman came to the door and, if anything, she looked even worse than she had in court. She wore an old bathrobe in a dirty grey colour, and without her lipstick and rouge, her face was the colour of the robe. She looked at Gran with a real mean look on her face.

"What do you want?" she asked suspiciously.

Gran fumbled around in her bag and brought out some paper and handed it to her. The woman looked down at it, and her eyes grew wide in amazement.

"Thirty thousand? ..." she said, her voice tailing off. "Is this some kind of joke?"

Gran shook her head. "No joke." Charlene tugged on her gran's arm. She couldn't believe what she was seeing. She thought perhaps all the water from her gran's legs had gone to her head.

"What are you doing, Gran?"

Her grandmother shook Charlene's hand from her arm.

"You're serious?" The woman's voice was full of disbelief.

Her gran nodded. "I managed this long without his money." With that she turned on her heel and started down the steps. Charlene rushed after her. She knew it was no use to argue once her gran's mind was made up, but she could only imagine what would happen when they got home. Her father would probably slap her around for letting her gran give half the money away. She felt a kind of sick feeling in her stomach.

Charlene looked back a the Rose woman, an' her mouth was still open like a fish's.

"Heh, thanks!" the woman called out, but her gran didn't turn around.

Charlene felt like running back and grabbing the cheque out of her hand. Instead, she followed her grandmother to the cab.

"Whadya want to go an' do that for?" Charlene said when they were on their way again.

"You'll have your bike, never fear."

"I don' want no bike. I don' want anything," Charlene said miserably. "Mum and Dad'll yell like hell."

"So, what'll be different? You think I want to go back with that cheque and have them all divvying it up and fightin' and squabblin' over who's getting what?" She smiled suddenly and laughed, "... But best of all, can you see that ole bugger on his

109

deathbed thinking he'd screwed up that poor dumb bitch. Now who has the last laugh?" She turned to Charlene. "Cheer up! I feel real good."

"But what about you, Gran? Dad'll be so mad he'll kick you out."

"No, he won't, Charl. I'm not goin' back there anyway. I'm getting my own place again. I have enough with what's left and with my pension. So he can rant and rave all he likes." She patted Charlene's hand. "An' you're comin' with me till he gets used to the idea of there bein' no money. Then, if you want, you can go back." She set her mouth in a firm line. "But let him lay one finger on you an' I'll have him up in front of the courts." She smiled at Charlene. "I reckon I can handle courts now. I'll get a court order to have you quick as a wink. You'll see."

Charlene had never seen her gran so happy-looking. She was glad all of a sudden about what her gran had done.

They had a lovely day. They sat down at the water's edge, ate potato chips and drank Coke and fed the crumbs from the chips to the seagulls, and then when the light was beginning to go, her gran looked up at the sky. Charlene thought at first she was talkin' to God but then realized it was the ole' bugger she was talkin' to, wherever he was.

"Yes sir, I got along fine before you ever came along, an' I've managed fine since." Charlene didn't like the idea of her gran talking to the dead. She took her hand and squeezed the fingers.

"Gran, you didn't open your present yet."

Her gran kept staring up at the sky, and then finally looked down at her handbag.

"You always keep the best things for the last, you know," she said, opening her bag and taking out the present.

She took the lid off the box and held up the key chain.

"Nicest present anyone ever gave me, Charl."

Charlene knew she meant it because she could see there was a tear at the corner of her eye, but she brushed it away real quick and gave a sort of cough.

Later in bed that night, when Charlene was lyin' with that whole big double bed to herself and she could hear her gran in the other bed begin to snore a bit the way she always did, she thought that those three days probably were the good bit that God was going to allow her. Despite what her gran said she couldn't imagine her mum and dad letting her live with her gran. She sighed deeply and snuggled down into the blankets. She was only damned glad that God had let her have these three good days with Gran.

Mr. Hussein

afez Hussein checked himself in the hotel mirror and approved of what he saw: an average Middle Eastern business man, of average income and of average expectation, who was finally about to find out what it was like to travel without his usual princely entourage. Hafez was travelling incognito.

It had been no mean feat to convince his loyal staff, not to mention his wives, that he had to try this venture. They had warned him of the danger, but that had only firmed his resolve. Just once he had to find out what it was like without all the advantages of birth.

Perhaps his shirt was a trifle too ordinary. The check a bit too large for good taste. The cravat perhaps not quite right, but he felt it gave him a certain debonair look of a world traveller.

He was now well rested after the incredible debacle at the airport. He had been assured he needed no special passport to visit South America but he had been detained for an endless time at the

Miami Airport, strip searched, and put under the ghastly third-degree. He had of course been warned that this might be the case, but had almost looked forward to the challenge of dealing with it like a gentleman. Eventually, the Kuwait Embassy had been contacted to handle it all. That was a disappointment, but there had been a certain sense of triumph at the round of apologies which had followed. He only hoped he wouldn't have to resort to such a thing again.

He checked his itinerary. Today there was a trip to Chiloe, a small island south of where he was staying at Puerto Varas, Chile. He checked the battery of his video camera. The camera, he decided, was exactly right for a tourist; perhaps he should not have had Selim buy him the best, but what matter, it was easy to operate and made him just another tourist.

Still, he felt some trepidation. He wasn't used to dealing with things himself. He had been studying Spanish for six months, however, and loved to hear the Spanish phrases sliding off his tongue.

He stood outside the hotel and breathed in the air. As the morning mist cleared, the volcano across Lake Llanquihue was beginning to appear. His guide had promised that the visibility would be good today. He was glad of that. Naturally he had seen volcanos before, but their splendour had been spoiled by the cacophony produced by his loyal subjects determined to destroy his pleasure with their unbearably mundane clucking.

He drank in the grandeur of the Osorno Volcano. He knew all the statistics by heart: 2,660 metres high; snow-capped all year round. He made it his duty to memorize details like this and loved the look on people's faces when he relayed the facts. He knew they admired his erudition. Too bad he wasn't as quick as he used to be, but with a little more work the details were eventually fixed in his mind, firm and correct.

A woman he had noticed in the hotel the night before came and stood on the hotel steps beside him. She was pleasant-looking. Somewhat taller than himself, but he liked that. There was nothing as wonderful as impressing a tall woman. He particularly liked the colour of her hair, just a hint of chestnut. It could even be out of a bottle, but it was not garish. Nothing about her was showy. She wore sensible, flat shoes, but wasn't old-maidish. Her dark green track suit was just the right colour for the tint of her hair. She smiled at him, a pleasant smile, and he returned the greeting with a slight click of his heels and a bow.

"*Buenos dias,*" he said immediately, knowing perfectly well the Spanish wasn't necessary, but enjoying the rolling sound on his tongue.

"*Buenos dias!*" she returned in less perfect tones.

"Ah, you are English?"

She nodded.

"And are you going to Chileo?" he asked with a smile.

"I am."

"Ah! That too is my destination."

At that precise moment a grey-haired woman joined her on the steps, and she turned her attention away from him. He was disappointed. The night before he had noticed her in the lounge having a drink on her own. He had contemplated approaching her, but something had warned him that she was not the type to enjoy this kind of overt behaviour.

He strolled onto the promenade in front of the hotel and imagined the two women enjoying this view of himself.

"What a peculiar we besum," Morag Finlay observed to her companion. "Struts like a peacock who does nae know he's got nae feathers."

Jill Eldred laughed. "There's something awfully strange about him."

"You hae talked to him?" Morag enquired.

"'*Buenos dias,*' that's it, but he has eyes like grey bullets. He doesn't seem to have dark pupils in his eyes like other people."

On the bus the two women observed Hafez Hussein hanging back from the crowd, and then when everyone had filed on the bus, he came last, giving a slight bow as he passed them. "Ladies!"

Mr. Hussein could hear the older woman's voice over all the other voices on the bus. He also could tell that the two women weren't well acquainted, for the grey-haired woman was talking endlessly about her job which seemed to have something to do with a United Nations Agency. He couldn't place her accent, but he guessed she too was from the British Isles. The other woman deserved to be rescued, and he would do the rescuing.

A finger to her lips, Jill leant across the aisle to her newly made friend, "Arms dealer," she offered speculatively.

"Goha," Morag replied.

"Goha? What is a Goha?" Jill asked.

"He's very popular in Arabian mythology. A sort of little man living out his fantasies. He's quite revered in the Middle East. A kind of Arabian Walter Mitty."

Jill felt a tiny rush of shame for having so blithely stereotyped the man. It was wrong of her to think of every Arab she saw as a potential assassin or drug dealer, but she had Hollywood to thank for that weakness.

Mr. Hussein was happily unaware of the speculations going on two seats ahead of him. He thought it highly likely he might be being discussed, but in his mind the conversation was totally different.

"What a distinguished man. Lonely, perhaps? A man of depth and feeling." They were possibly even arranging to rescue him from his loneliness, but it would no doubt have to be a subtle exercise. Women were ever the same. He considered himself an expert on the subject, having four wives. Still, his were taught obedience, and it was a commodity he had long tired of.

His brothers and cousins would have been shocked if they'd understood the depth of his discontent with life. In his weekly *diwaniyahs* they naturally talked about all nature of things, but seldom of things personal. At times he had longed to question the other princes about their private lives, but politics and business were the usual themes. Often some foreigners would be present. To talk of private matters would have been unthinkable.

He had written out a job description for himself so as to get all the details correct. Selling oil was naturally what he was doing travelling the world. This minor jaunt to the countryside was a distraction from the rigours of contracts and delivery.

It was a nuisance that the bus was full. It was also a nuisance that he was such a gentleman, for he let all the women leave the bus before he did. And precisely because so few of the other men were gentlemen, he was usually last to dismount and the women were well ahead of him at each stop.

They stopped to view a fort where the occupying Spaniards had finally lost the day to the indigenous Indians who were fighting to regain their land. He did not need to listen to Juan, the tour guide. He had read extensively on the subject. He was irritated because there were many facts that Juan had left out of his speech.

He hurried to catch up with the women. Suddenly there was a commotion. Everyone was huddled around something on the road down to the fort. He pushed his way through the crowd. The auburn-haired woman had missed one of the steps and fallen down. She was in some distress and was rocking back and forward in obvious pain.

"What is the problem?" he asked the man beside him.

"She fell on her knee. Perhaps it's even broken," the man answered in Spanish.

"Clear a space!" Hussein said loudly, "... and get a doctor!" Nobody paid him any attention.

A veritable Goliath of a man bent low over the woman. Hussein had noticed him on the bus. His pink shirt kept slipping out from his pants, displaying a mammoth belly.

"She needs a doctor," Hussein repeated importantly. Juan, the tour guide, shrugged and raised his shoulders helplessly.

Mr. Hussein was used to being obeyed and wondered for just an instant if perhaps his Spanish weren't as correct as he had assumed.

"A doctor!" he re-iterated, this time more forcefully.

"That man is a doctor." The grey-haired woman was

suddenly at his elbow. "I really think she'd rather there not be any fuss."

"Naturally not," Mr. Hussein said apologetically, "... but this could be serious."

"Nothing seems to be broken," the fat man said, ignoring Mr. Hussein. "*Heilo*," he added, ordering ice. Juan immediately hustled off in the direction of the restaurant at the top of the hill to get the prescribed ice.

Mr. Hussein felt irritated that this huge, sloppy man could get such immediate attention.

"She should try to stand," Mr. Hussein persisted.

"Not at the moment," the man said. "Cold compress first to take down the swelling and then we will get her to her feet."

"He's an orthopaedic surgeon," the woman's friend said to Mr. Hussein.

"How convenient." Mr. Hussein's voice had a slight edge. One could of course be anything one wanted in this world. He, best of all, knew about that. Somewhat affronted he moved off. The rest of the crowd were now walking down the hill also. There was no one else Mr. Hussein felt like talking to, so he focused his interest on his video camera. Holding it up, he directed it on the landscape. He felt a prickling of sweat on his forehead and was suddenly warm and clammy all over. He felt much less sure of himself.

Later, much later, the auburn-haired woman appeared at the upper wall of the fort. She was leaning heavily on the arm of her companion. Mr. Hussein didn't move immediately when he saw them. He deliberately hung back until most of the others had gone forward to ask her how she was feeling.

Taking his time, he allowed his camera to pan the horizon. He was no expert on how to handle the camera, he wasn't even terribly interested in its focus. It was merely a device. Viewing the landscape through the lens made everything more real to him.

He walked casually up the hill and arrived just in time to see both women disappearing into the yellow hotel that overlooked the bay. The injured woman had obviously recovered enough to manage the walk. No doubt they were going for tea. He would give them a moment or two and then put in an appearance. It would of course look merely like a coincidence.

                        *

"That funny little man," Jill said to Morag. "Ordering everyone around, demanding a doctor."

"There was a certain authority in his voice," Morag said. "I suspect he's a sheik in mufti. Someone used to people listening. Did you notice the long nail on his little fingers? The sign in his culture of someone who wouldn't dream of dirtying his hands with menial jobs." Morag looked at Jill with mock seriousness. "He jus' might be on the luk out fer another woman fer his harem. A think he fancies you."

"Surely, they don't still have harems? Isn't that the Turks?" Jill sat down stiffly, her swollen leg extended.

"The Arabs too," Morag assured her. "I think I'm cramping yer style. I shuld get on the bus an' write ma diary. Let you sit with Goha."

"Speak of the devil," Jill said quietly.

"Ladies, what a coincidence." Mr. Hussein made a small bow. "And are you fully recovered?" He addressed himself to Jill.

"Almost. Thank you for asking."

"May I join you? Or am I being too forward?"

"Certainly." Morag smiled.

"My name is Hafez Hussein. I am from Kuwait." Mr. Hussein offered Morag his hand, showing respect for the older woman. Morag shook his hand.

"Morag Finlay."

Mr. Hussein turned to Jill. "Jill Eldred."

"Both from the United Kingdom?" Mr. Hussein asked with a raised eyebrow of enquiry.

"From Scotland," Morag said, "... but of no fixed address

as a rule."

"How interesting."

Jill added nothing but studied the menu the waitress had brought. She was aware that Mr. Hussein was staring at her.

"My friend is from London," Morag said. Jill looked up briefly into the mortar-shell grey eyes of Mr. Hussein.

The waitress came to the table. "*Buenas tardes*," she said, smiling, fixing her attention on Mr. Hussein.

"*Te, por favor*," Mr. Hussein said without consulting the two women.

Morag swiftly interrupted his order, "*Quisiera cafe con leche.*"

"Excuse me." Mr. Hussein turned to Morag. "I assumed that like all British women you would be drinking tea."

"Wrong assumption," Morag said crisply.

"I do apologize."

"There's no need." Morag smiled.

"You speak Spanish well," Mr. Hussein said ingratiatingly to Morag.

"Being able to order coffee hardly constitutes fluency in any language," she replied tartly.

"Ah, but I was eavesdropping earlier when Miss Eldred fell down, and I heard more than basic phrases."

Morag smiled politely. "I've worked in South America for many years now, one picks up a thing or two here an' there."

There was a pause for a moment or two while all three drank in the view from the terrace of the hotel. Mr. Hussein broke the silence by delivering a treatise on the history of the area, covering territory Juan had only touched upon. He fingered his cravat to make sure it was still in place. He was aware of the eyes of the two women watching him as he spoke.

Mr. Hussein enjoyed the sound of his own voice. He knew it had a lyrical quality, he had been told so on many occasions. He outlined how the Spanish had pillaged and raped their way through South America.

"I've done much travelling and working in South America,

Mr. Hussein," Morag interrupted. "I a'ways consider it ma solemn duty to thuroughly know the countries where a work."

He felt a twinge of pain in his chest. No woman in his circle would have dared such an insult. He tried to force a relaxed smile, but he feared that it was almost impossible under the circumstances.

He hated robust females like this one. She might have grey hair and be ten or fifteen years older than the other woman, but she had the kind of pink-and-white complexion and gleam in her eye that assured her a long and annoyingly healthy life. No fear that she would have fallen.

He had noticed the bag full of medicinal equipment she carried around with her. He'd seen her dispense several things to people on the bus who had various medical problems. He had heard her proclaim how she always carried a dispensary but seldom needed it for herself. He didn't doubt it.

Jill Eldred broke into the conversation. They were suddenly talking about Turkey, but how they'd got onto the topic he had no idea. It was beyond belief. They were extolling the virtues of the Turks. He felt horror growing in his chest. That race of unspeakable despots was actually being elevated and praised.

"Ladies, I cannot believe what I am hearing. The Turks are a barbaric race, without a single redeeming feature."

"How far back are we going?" Morag asked equably.

"Do you have any concept of what they did to the Greeks?"

"There's barely a race that doesn't have skeletons in its closet." Morag smiled. "The Arabs haven't a'ways been wee angels, now have they?"

Mr. Hussein felt his lips tighten. This woman was impossible, but at the same time she seemed to have very little fear of anything. He felt compelled to find her totally wrong on some subject.

They forged on in their conversation, covering thousands of miles as tourists often do, comparing countries, talking about hotels. While Mr. Hussein had stayed at the Dorchester in London, Morag Finlay had been a guest of Lucas Morgan, a renowned British philosopher whose opinions were sought on every subject on the face of the earth.

While Mr. Hussein had been in the diplomatic suite of the Waldorf Astoria in New York, Morag Finlay had been staying with a relative of the Kennedy family on Long Island. While he had travelled to Niagara Falls in a three-hundred-dollars-an-hour white limousine, used the previous day by Elizabeth Taylor, Morag Finlay had been given an escorted tour by the premier of the province.

Jill Eldred occasionally entered into the conversation to add something, but mostly it had become a competition between Morag and Mr. Hussein.

"The Japanese are a fascinating race." Mr. Hussein felt it was now time to talk about something of which he had intimate knowledge. Here he was on solid ground. He had spent many days in Tokyo as a guest of the royal family. He safely could drop names and quote statistics to prove that of all the nations the Japanese were the most progressive in almost all respects.

"They might be, but they cut the redwoods down here in Chile," Jill Eldred said quietly.

"For every tree they cut down, they plant three," Mr. Hussein countered with complete assurance.

"Aye, three pines for every redwood. Hardly a fair exchange," Morag said dryly.

"To slightly distort Gertrude Stein's words, a tree is a tree, is a tree," Mr. Hussein recited. They no doubt would be impressed by his literary knowledge.

"Aye, but it's not," Morag ground on. "The pine is not indigenous to this country. It creates acidic soil and totally wrecks the eco system."

Mr. Hussein felt a kind of desperation building. He was glad when the the other woman, Jill, began to talk about Poland, but he wondered how the subject had jumped to Eastern Europe. He felt himself go completely limp. He even contemplated having no further input to the conversation, but that was unthinkable and would be evidence of defeat.

He delivered a little speech about Poland and both women

were suddenly silenced. Mr. Hussein felt some kind of calm returning. Neither woman said a single word. They might not even have been listening, but again that was unthinkable. Both faces in front of him were intent on the horizon and he, too, turned his attention to the sinking sun as though the event was something he'd never witnessed before.

Later, he picked up the tab, leaving a generous tip. He walked slightly ahead of the two women out of the restaurant. His shoulders were finally squared again and he felt some confidence returning.

❧❦❧

On the return trip Mr. Hussein sat well back on the bus, beside a solitary Australian man.

"Gadday!" the Australian greeted him.

"Good-day to you too!" Mr. Hussein replied. "What a fascinating island Chileo is. We are very lucky to see Chileo in the sunshine. They say it rains more than 220 days a year here."

"Ye don't say?" The Aussie turned to Mr. Hussein and gave him all his attention.

Mr. Hussein thought with fondness of the *diwaniyahs* he would be missing while he was travelling. He understood now why his group resisted the inclusion of women. Today was a perfect example of how the equilibrium could be disturbed.

Morag looked around to see where Mr. Hussein was sitting.

"We were very hard on him," she said, turning to Jill.

"Poor Goha," Jill sighed, putting her head back against the headrest.

"No, not Goha," Morag said thoughtfully.

"You've changed your mind?" Jill asked.

"There's a story about Goha. Mr. Hussein is certainly no Goha. Actually, there are many stories about him, but one in particular excludes our Mr. Hussein from that category.

"Goha and his faithful donkey travel to a mosque. He gets up to talk to the people there and asks, '*Do you know what I'm going to talk about?*' They say no, and so Goha says, '*Then there's no point telling you something you don't know.*'

"He comes back the next day and asks the same question. The people say yes and Goha replies, '*Then there's no use telling you something you already know.*' On the third day when he returns, some people say yes and others say no.

"Goha says. '*Those who know tell those who don't know.*'"

Morag shook her head. "No, our Mr. Hussein is certainly no Goha."

Fly Me to the Moon

Cher, Bette Midler, Madonna, Liza Minelli, all sashay and swing in front of us. Moving the way no real Hollywood movie queens would ever do.

"Let me congratulate you." A Nancy Reagan look-alike, with a skull-like head and the body of a gnome, takes my hand in hers and caresses it. "You look wonderful. Exactly like a woman. The others are overdone. Why is it transvestites have to go so overboard?"

Peter had insisted on the ball gown. I'd been less certain, nervous about being over-dressed. Still, having the fun of dressing up, I'd rationalized, might compensate for the dreaded boredom of the evening. "You're the president's wife, people expect you to dress the part," he'd insisted. The men, I now note scanning the room, dapper as penguins, are mostly accompanied by women in discreet knee-length afternoon dresses, even blouses and skirts. No wonder I'd been mistaken for one of Les Girls. Around me everyone giggles into their drinks about the transvestites from La Cage Aux Folles.

"Charles Evans's idea to spice things up," Peter announces to every new arrival. "Idiotic!" he mutters. "Everybody feels uncomfortable."

I don't. I feel right at home.

"You look great, hon!" Liza Minelli, with lashes a foot long, lips like a couple of shiny red fishhooks and black stubble already sprouting through the acrylic layer of make-up, tweaks my arm with her black-satin fingers. "Love the dress! It's so retro. Like the one Kate Hepburn wore in 'Woman of the Year' ... Just what they're wearing now. Don't ever donate it to 'Second Time Around.' When you're finished, send it my way."

If I had to choose to be anyone, it would be Katherine Hepburn. Inside, I know Kate is waiting to come out, hiding in the wings, longing for the current lead actress to get sick or throw away the part. Peter is taller than Spencer Tracey, not quite as stocky, but he'll do.

One by one, Les Girls make their way over, fingering the copper satin of my skirt, lusting after the yards of stole, admiring the choker around my neck. We are all girls together. I admire their dresses, their hairdos, their jewellery. Want to tell them to swing their hips less, move their arms in smaller motions, but maybe that's part of it all? Perhaps they want to be recognized as fakes? It might be too painful to be taken for what you are not.

At dinner, later, Les Girls sit at their own table; their laughter rings out loud and clear over the dull thrum of other crowd noises. Everyone at our table is suffering from some kind of stasis. It feels like hours between courses. I know the flower arrangement at the centre of the table intimately. I've studied the platform, where the band members are playing unobtrusive dinner music. Conversation has run out.

"Do you have children?" I ask the girl beside me. Silence had gone on too long.

"No, two cats. We have two pussy cats ... They're so cute ... They wait for us in the hall at night ... they know just when we are coming home ..." On and on the dialogue goes ... feeding the cats

... playing with the cats ... the psychology of cats ... the different nature of cats ... the cuteness of cats ... Was it ten minutes later or ten hours later? "... Am I boring you?"

Yes, you're boring me to death. Yes, I'm dying. Can't you see the colour draining out of my face. Starting at my brain, I am numb. I have been numb for so long I barely remember any more who I am. But my dress sets me apart from the crowd – apart and yet so with it.

"I suffer from the environment," the woman on my other side intones through a stuffy nose.

Is that not what I'm suffering from too? Hasn't she stolen my line?

"I have to stay in the house for days before coming to an occasion like this. I'm so allergic to everything, that I just have to rest up."

"You saved yourself for this?" The line slips out before I can stop it — out of my memory. *It was the waiting room at O'Hare Airport in Chicago. A little blonde woman with big hair and a sequined denim jacket is telling me the story of her life. "My mother always said, 'Save yourself for marriage! Men don't respect girls who give themselves. Wait. Save yourself!' So I did. On our wedding night Murray comes to bed. Slam! Bang! It's all over. This is what I saved myself for? That's all I could think. This is what I saved myself for?"*

The woman with environment problems is still sitting in stunned silence. Perhaps I've said something even more outrageous. I can't remember. All I know is I have to leave. I get up and move to the table with Les Girls. Peter's eyes are boring holes in my back. Bending over Liza Minelli, I ask her to give us a song.

"Really?" He smiles up at me. "How about 'New York, New York?'"

"Good! I can do it with you? I know the words. It's something I've always wanted to do."

"Whadya think, girls?" He puts the question to the table.

"Absolutely!"

He gets up. Never mind that he's a head too tall and that the waist is too large for Liza Minelli — the black sequined mini-dress is just right, the cut of the wig perfect. I'd always suspected Liza Minelli was a man in drag anyway.

We go to the microphone together. The M.C. stands looking a little stunned. I take the mike. "A little diversion — Liza Minelli and I are going to sing 'New York, New York.'" It's impossible to see anyone's face in the crowd, the light is too bright.

When it's over, the crowd is ecstatic. Bows and more bows. Suddenly Spencer Tracey is there to collect me from the stage. I tell him to buzz off. I'm not finished. We exchange slick banter, *or is it angry words?* He accepts his rebuff with good-natured humour. "Kate, honey, you were brilliant!" *Is that what he says? or, "Elizabeth, you're making a damned fool of yourself?"*

He throws a mink stole around my shoulders, picks up a bottle of Dom Perignon from one of the tables, and we leave the ballroom. *Or is it my purse he collects?* We move through the crowd pressing around us, and out to the lobby.

Alone in the washroom, I stare dazed at my image in the mirror. No mink stole. Just a vacant look on my face. Going into one of the cubicles, I lift the layers of satin and plonk down on the toilet. I could easily sit here for the rest of the evening. A door slams.

"Jesus! Talk about uptight! These people make Jehovah's Witness look like Hell's Angels."

"Do you think we should be in here?"

"You wanna risk goin' to the men's be my guest. They'd have us up for soliciting. They're so fuckin' uptight, these people." One of the cubicle doors closes, and after a moment a sound like a garden hose plays down the toilet.

"Phew! What a relief. This girdle's so damned tight I thought I'd never be able to use it again," a voice calls out to the others.

I wait for a minute and come out of the washroom.

"Well, waddya know," Madonna says grinning, "If it isn't Kate Hepburn."

"If you're going to use the women's washroom, you've got to

learn to pee slower," I advise, watching Bette Midler etch an outline around his already crimson mouth.

"Urine interruptus!" he says with a grin. "Women pee slower, do they?"

"Much."

"I'm sorry about what I said."

"What you said?"

"About the crowd."

"Don't be. They *are* uptight. How long do you have to stick around?"

"Ye mean here?"

"Right?"

"Another half hour, then we're on our ever lovin' way."

"Can I come too?"

They exchange looks. "Where to, hon?"

"Well, wherever you go."

"We're not fuckin' vampires, sweetie, we actually sleep at night."

"Kate here wants to see how we live. What about it, Bette? How's about your place?" Cher says.

"You can come back to my place for a drink, sweetie, but don't expect no Four Seasons."

"I'd love that."

I stay in the toilet, hiding from the various people who no doubt have been sent to find me. My skirts hitched up, I perch on the toilet until the girls come back. We leave the hotel, piling into a rusted white van: a paddy wagon with purple shag carpeting on the long benches. The floor is littered with car jacks, spare parts, and empty coke bottles. Madonna turns her ankle on a bottle. "For Chrissake! Why don't you tidy up this shitbox?" Cher pulls her skirt from whatever it's attached itself to on the floor.

"Like asking me to tidy up the truck that picks up the garbage, hon! Waste of time," Bette carols and revs up his engine.

Bette lives in little Portugal, in a semi-detached house with weeping brick and a sagging verandah. It's surrounded by red-brick houses with elaborate metal-work fences, postage-stamp sized lawns with ornamental fauns and bird baths. His living room is painted maroon and his couch, a modular thing, is black velvet. A huge white cat reclines, vampish as its owner, on the back of the sofa. Moulting hairs from the cat strafe the velvet upholstery. The lights are low so that it's almost impossible to see the rest of the room. The cat expands under my hand, arching its back.

"She's a slut," Bette says, throwing a feather boa from her shoulders onto a chair.

"Like mother, like daughter," Cher sings out.

"Her name's Regina ... from 'The Little Foxes' ... she was such a bitch."

The cat settles on my lap, but not before walking back and forth across the satin, her paws caressing the material.

"She knows quality when she feels it," Bette says.

Bette moves through the room and a light goes on, displaying hat boxes, material piled high on the floor, a veritable fabric store, only not as tidy. Two sewing machines sit along the side wall. At the back of the room, a rack holds a kaleidoscope of rainbow-coloured dresses.

"You make your clothes?" I ask.

"He's a fuckin' genius." Cher throws her lengthy form down onto a cushion on the floor. "Talk about Scarlett O'Hara making a dress from the drapes. He could make a bikini for Princess Di out of a tampax."

"You're too generous, sweet one," Bette called from the kitchen.

"Seriously, he's dangerously talented. Liza here won the title this year and all because of him."

"Title?"

"Queen of the Night!"

"Do you just make clothes for your friends?" I ask as he comes back with a bottle of wine and glasses on a tray.

"No, hon, I like to get paid. I make clothes for little old ladies in Forest Hill. I do Bar Mitzvahs, weddings, funerals, you name it. I'm seriously into transformations. I make humps disappear, backsides shrink, and give people breasts where they have none." He pauses and pours some wine into a glass. "Incidentally, hon, you don't make the best of yourself."

"I don't?"

"If you're going to go décolletage, then do something about your bra."

"Like what?"

"You wanna push them together and up. Take your bra, cut it right up the middle with a pair of scissors, overlap the two pieces, sew it up again and voilà, Dolly Parton."

"Maybe she's not the Dolly Parton type," Cher suggests from his cross-legged position on the floor. His dress is completely hitched up, displaying muscular thighs.

Before I even take the wine, I have the extraordinary feeling I'm drunk already. Hours go by, or perhaps minutes. More wine keeps coming and I'm having trouble focusing on the room. I've forgotten my anxiety about Peter.

I want to ask them why they do what they do, but it seems inappropriate. I can't see any of them as men. I feel as though I've found my fraternity. People who live in disguise. Liza Minelli who is sprawled close to me on the sofa is beginning to metamorphose in front of me like Dorian Gray; the five-o'clock shadow is turning into a beard. With the beard comes a change of character.

"This wine pukes," he says, staring down into the dregs of the glass.

"Yes," Bette offers dryly, "I notice you hate the stuff."

"Nothing harder?"

"No!" Bette says curtly. "What about all your promises?"

"Fuck that! You've only got one life. Right?" There's a small, meaningful silence, and minutes later I see tears glistening at the corner of Bette's eyes.

Liberated by the wine, insulting banter flies around easily now.

I finally ask, "Why do you do it?" Somehow I know they

won't be offended.

"Because we're freaks, why else." Bette raises her glass. "Here's to freaks everywhere! Try growing up in a small town, a girl in a boy's body. Everything in you says you're a girl, and yet because of one little difference, you're thrown in with the jocks."

"You poor deprived baby," Liza says cynically. "Dramatize your story and sell it on video along with 'Cinderella.'"

"Shut up, Gord!" Cher says.

It was the first time I'd heard any of their real names. "Well, I mean, give me a break." Liza straightens up on the sofa beside me. "At least there were no perverts in the family rolling him over on his stomach."

"Personally, I like nice clean stories like Bette's. Especially for present company." Cher says.

"Funny most of my life has been spent thinking how much easier things are for men, and here you are wanting to be women," I contribute.

"Now it's time for your life story, Kate!" Bette sits down beside Liza on the sofa and puts an arm around his shoulders. "Aren't you scared you'll get the shit beaten out of you when you go home?"

"No! I feel guilty, sorry, if Peter's upset by my leaving, but I'm not scared."

"So, what's the story? Why are you here?"

"I'm a reporter," I improvise.

"Neat." Bette pats my knee. "Who for?"

"The New York Chronicle," I say with bravado. I can see doubt in their faces.

"So what's this husband like ... the one who dragged you off the stage?" Marilyn asks, looking up at me from the floor.

"Did he?"

"You mean you don't remember?"

"I remember Spencer Tracey coming with a magnum of champagne ..."

"Wow! I like it." Bette lets out a joyful little whistle.

"Isn't that what it's supposed to be like?"

"Sure!" Liza stretches beside me and for the first time I see the purplish patches like sores on his arms. The same marks are beginning to appear on his face through the make-up. Aware of my scrutiny, he shifts away from me uncomfortably. He stands up suddenly and breaks into a rendition of "Fly me to the Moon." He drops his hands when it's over and there's dead silence in the room.

"I should get home and cut out all this shit." He swipes at his eyes with an arm and his mascara is all over his cheek.

Someone phones for a taxi ... I remember only vaguely a lot of kisses on my cheek and then it's suddenly morning and I wake up on the sofa with Regina licking my face. Someone has flung a blanket over me. I'm sneezing, mega-sneezes, and my mouth feels dry as a gorse bush. I can't control the spasms and Regina backs off, offended by the involuntary spray.

I sit up gingerly. A pulse, insistent, like a small ugly drill is boring a hole in the side of my head. Collapsing back on the sofa, I turn my head and see Bette wrapped in a white satin kimono covered in huge bright red poppies, with a pin cushion strapped around his wrist, pinning and tucking a dress on a tailor's dummy. His wig is gone and there's a quarter of an inch of stubble all over his head. He looks incongruous. His lips, still rouged from the night before, are indecently garish amid the five-o'clock shadow of his beard.

He removes a pin from between his lips. "Good morning, Kate!"

"Good morning?" I watch him speechless for a while. He stands back and squints at his creation. Either he's drunk less than I have or he's used to late nights, overindulging, and working the next day.

"Where did you learn to sew?"

"From my mother. She was the hair dresser in our town. I used to hang around her shop all the time. What I really wanted to do was women's hair. She was a good sewer, too. She taught me all the tricks. The whole town used to feel sorry for her. Four good children and then one freak ... 'Don't worry, hon, he'll grow out of it ...' I used to think they meant I would shed the penis. I remember being fascinated by the whole caterpillar thing. I imagined that there would come a stage when I could just creep out of my skin and be what I really wanted to be ..."

"I know what you mean."

"Still a freak. That's what those people think."

"You're not a freak."

He comes over and perches on the arm of the sofa, "Thanks, luv, for the endorsement, but didn't you see their faces last night? Anyway, who gives a shit. I'm only ever really happy when I'm dressing up. I love to sit in front of the mirror and see my face change in front of me. Once I've finished, the thrill's over. Isn't that what life's about? One big show after another. It helps me to forget things I need to forget."

"Like Liza?"

He nods. "Like Liza," he says sadly.

"How long will it be?"

"Today, tomorrow, next week, maybe a year. Who knows." He plucks a pin morosely from his wrist and stabs it absentmindedly back into the pin cushion. "We were lovers for four years."

"I'm sorry."

He brightens up suddenly, a false brightness, his eyes squinting slightly as he looks down at my bare feet. "Cinderella's lost her slipper, has she?"

"I've no idea how I'm going to get home without shocking the neighbours, not to mention the entire town."

He giggles, and we sit in companionable silence for a minute or two. "If Audrey Hepburn could do it in *Breakfast at Tiffany's*, so can you."

There's a loud knocking at the door. "That will be Maria." He gets up without any explanation of who Maria might be. A minute later he's back. Spencer Tracey is standing behind him.

"How on earth did you find me?"

"Somebody saw you leave. Charles Evans talked to La Cage, got some of the girls' numbers, and then I began phoning. I've been up just about all the night."

Suddenly I don't want to leave. I want to prowl the room, curious as the cat. Stretch along the back of the sofa and observe the women Bette transforms come for their fittings — see the miracles he performs. When tired of the sofa, I'll lie indolent on the window ledge and soak up the sun.

"Are you coming?" Spencer's voice is sharp.

"Have you got my stole?"

He throws a wrap around my shoulders, the mink, or does he pull my arm slightly as though thoroughly disgusted with me?

"Can't I offer you coffee?" Bette asks.

"No, thanks!" Spencer is churlish, at his worst. I kiss Bette's cheek. "Thanks for a lovely time."

"You're welcome, hon ... Any time."

Spencer bundles me into the car, and we're off. I'm vaguely aware of what he's saying, but I concentrate fiercely on the early-morning bustle of people coming and going. Though the day's only beginning, already-tired-looking people with lunch buckets and heavy bags wait for buses. Scattered words enter only peripherally into my consciousness, "... fool of yourself! Idiot!" Pejorative, ugly words spew out, but then again they might be from the radio. The radio is on. I'm sure the radio is on.

I smile at a man who is peering in from the street at my half-naked shoulders. He gives a little nod of approval. No doubt he remembers *Breakfast at Tiffany's*. I close my eyes and lean back.

When All the World is Old

"Always walk tall, m'dear!" she would say, drawing me toward my reflection in the full-length mirror on the wall of her shop. I stood shyly viewing the hunch of my shoulders, feeling her hands on my shoulder blades as she forced them back, smelling the whiff of lemon from her hands when she nudged my chin in the air. Mother would have been cynical about the lemon smell, say it was from the slice she always had to have in her gin and tonic. I preferred to think it was from a favourite perfume.

She haunts me now that I'm reaching the age she was when she died, and only wonder how it was that I knew so little about her. It was her walk I remember best: a proud walk, a tall walk.

I recall her shop in incomplete flashes: the wide window that had once been large enough to display a grand piano, the dark shelving, and shining but uneven oak floors with great knotted whorls of wood. The small, cluttered office behind the shop was where the chaos began. A dark hallway then led to the awful kitchen and pantry. The walls of the kitchen were plaster and always peeling from the damp. The floor was grey slate. The cold from it penetrated upward through feet and legs, so that the very bones ached. Even the big black stove that filled the end of the kitchen couldn't take the chill out of that floor. The enclosed back yard had a high brick wall that blocked out the light from the two tiny rooms.

Before I was born, the shop had been Uncle George's piano shop. It had been a Belfast landmark, renowned for pianos of all sizes and makes. Then came the Depression, then the War, and pianos were suddenly a luxury no one could afford. The business had been in Uncle George's family for years. He viewed the bankruptcy as a personal failure. Mother agreed with the assessment.

"It's the times. Just the times," Father offered more charitably.

"To think she could have married anyone she wanted," Mother complained. *"He was never a businessman."*

"For God's sake ..." Father's anger was unusual and explosive. *"Hasn't she long ago made her bed? What's the use of dredging up old stuff?"*

Uncle George still owned the premises, so Auntie Peg took over and transformed the shop overnight, stocking the shelves with baby-goods and lingerie. An odd mix that seemed to appeal to people. Their two sons were off on their own by this time, which meant Auntie Peg had more time to devote to buying and selling.

Uncle George seemed to do very little any more. My memories of him are vivid. I remember him taking me on his knee to read from *The Water-Babies*: "When all the world is young, lad, And all the trees are green ..."

It surprised me that he could read in the dim light, but the pages of the book were heavily thumbed. He had parts memorized: "Once upon a time there was a little chimney-sweep, and his name was Tom." Always the first line to remind me how the story began. I needed no reminders. I remember the story vividly, and the strange light in his eye when he told of Tom shedding his clothes

138

and lying in the water: "I will be a fish; I will swim in the water. I must be clean, I must be clean," with heavy emphasis on the last "clean." He downed more whisky from his glass. "Only to clear the throat mind," he claimed. The pungent smell made me pull away from him.

Those days Auntie Peg drank very little, but she said nothing to him about his drinking. There wasn't a lot of dinner dialogue; I seemed to be the focus for both of them, as though they'd forgotten how to communicate except through a third party.

"Uncle George died in the night," was all Father told us when I woke one morning and found Father had been sleeping on the sofa in the drawing room and Auntie Peg upstairs in bed beside Mother. Only years later were we told it was suicide. I thought then of his favourite verse: "Creep home, and take your place there, The spent and maimed among; God grant you find one face there, You loved when all was young."

Even when Auntie Peg got up two days later and finally came down to get herself ready for the funeral, she was still crying, her face unrecognizable from grief.

She was never the same afterwards. That single event started the downward spiral. Soon after that, her youngest son, David, did something that plunged Mother and Father in gloom and brought the entire family together for long discussions.

Her two sons were years older than me, for Peg was the oldest in Mother's family. David seemed more like an older man than my cousin. He had Auntie Peg's outgoing personality and was handsome as a film star, but I was terrified of him without ever knowing why. "He could charm the birds out of a bush, that one," my mother said frequently, but it was said disparagingly, not with admiration. "Little liar, and does it smooth as silk."

"What does he lie about?" I enquired.

"Ask him how he's done in his exams and he says, 'a cinch, Auntie Anne.' Ask Peg and you find he's failed."

"Maybe he thinks he's done well," I rationalized.

"He knows right well," Mother said cynically.

"Sure last week I saw this cloud of smoke coming up the street. David behind it. When he saw me coming he threw the cigarette in the hedge."

"You were having a smoke, David?" I asked him.

"Smoke?" He looked as though butter wouldn't melt in his mouth. "You know I don't smoke, Auntie Anne."

"Bare-faced liar. I saw him as plain as I see the nose on your face an' he had the gall to deny it. There's a right streak of larceny in that one, take it from me."

Mother had been right, but if we thought we were going to find out what David had done, we were mistaken. Murder? Theft? Rape? We wrote the script so well for him that a year later, when I saw him coming towards me on the street, I wanted to run away.

I could see he was hurt by the expression on my face, but by this time Auntie Peg had started to smell of gin all the time and Mother was never done blaming it on David. The caring, loving Auntie Peg I'd always known became a crumpled, distracted woman, who let her stock of merchandise dwindle to an alarming degree.

I used to go there regularly after school. Finnegan, the cat, lay indolent and warm inside the shop window, smart enough to sprawl near a baby's christening robe or alongside a shawl, but never on top of any of the merchandise.

I sat on the stool behind the counter and watched the shop for Auntie Peg while she sat in the office behind the big roll-top desk and worked away on invoices, nipping gin from small bottles she kept tucked away in the myriad of drawers.

Perched on the stool, I could hear the opening and closing of drawers and saw her unsteady on her feet when she heard the ping of the shop-bell and came out to greet a customer. They mostly came to talk to her and not to buy now, and sometimes they even went into the back where I could hear the rill of their laughter drifting out.

I was happy enough. I'd learned how to make toys for babies with simple rings of cardboard and bits of coloured wool. I would make endless numbers of these. Although I saw them decorating the shop window for a whole year and was certain she never sold one, she gave me sixpence for each one I made.

I went less and less to the shop as I grew older. I had my own friends and after-school activities. Perhaps we were all careless about monitoring Auntie Peg's decline; our own lives were busy enough.

One summer, in what seemed like an act of loneliness, she invited Mother and Father and me to go with her to visit Brian, the good son as people now christened him. He lived in Wales where he'd married a Welsh girl and sold life insurance.

Stray pictures of the trip come back now in vivid recall: the strange channel crossing, where the boat pitched and rolled; Auntie Peg staggering and falling over herself in the gloomy, tight little cabin I shared with her: a weird smile on her face as if she had a secret she wasn't about to give away to anyone; the train trip out of dark old Liverpool with its blackened buildings and fading grandeur, past rows of red-brick houses that looked just like Belfast houses; and then on through fields of green to the mysterious, dark Welsh hills, with sheep like white stones, dotting the landscape.

Cardiff itself fades totally in memory, except for the remembrance of eating prawns from a paper poke: a cupful of prawns for fi'pence, bought down by the dock from one of the fishmongers; the very taste was like drinking the sea.

A few days into the visit and I knew I was there for a purpose: to keep a watchful eye on Auntie Peg and also to mind Brian's and Myfanwy's child, a wee girl of ten months who needed constant jiggling and entertainment. I was expected to take her for walks day after day.

Truculently I pushed the pram up the street with a deep shored-up resentment at being used as a baby-sitter, banging the pram up and down grey pavements, past grey houses and grey walls, almost toppling the child out onto the road.

One night they all went out to the picture show and left Auntie Peg behind with the baby and me. A while after they were gone she stumbled and fell on the stairs. Crumpled and astonished-looking, she lay half on and half off the bottom step. She smiled briefly at me as I bent over her, and then promptly passed out.

The baby howled in its crib in the upstairs bedroom. Terrified, I prodded Auntie Peg. She lay heavy as a bag of wet sand, the laughter gone. Snivelling, I pulled her by the legs, but there was no sign of life. Gathering cushions from the chesterfield in panic, I propped one under her head and the other under her feet. I climbed over her, went up to the bedroom and lifted the baby. She sensed my terror and screamed even louder. Taking her downstairs and over the dreadful hump on the bottom step, I dropped her like a hot potato into the pram and went to heat milk on the stove in the kitchen. With shaking hands I filled a bottle with milk, slopping it all over the counter and floor. I didn't want to go back and see Auntie's body on the stairs. I momentarily hated her. Rubbish, all rubbish about walking tall, when everything inside amounted to no more than that crumpled heap.

It seemed as though years had gone by when the others finally came home, and not once had Auntie Peg stirred. The baby was with me on the sofa now and finally quiet. I had cried myself out and sat drained and resentful.

"She's had a bad turn," was the only comment my mother made. I detested her for her untruthfulness. It was typical. Drunkenness could only be discussed in terms of the past or future. In the present, in all its sordidness it was often renamed. It was like the big "C." For years when Mother talked about somebody having the big "C," I had no idea what she meant. I had images of some huge letter imprinted on the person's chest.

When I think of Peg, I have trouble imagining her as she had once been. As Mother told it, she was the one in the family who had everything going for her. Personality, stamina and, if not exactly raving beautiful looks, at least a kind of patrician, strong face. I could only see this from old photos, for in my memory she had grey hair, teeth that were a bit stained from nicotine, and cheeks that sagged into little pouches at the sides of her mouth. The nose was still regal and strong. Only tiny, red, broken surface veins on either side of the nostrils spoiled that feature. The only thing about her that hadn't changed, I imagined, was that walk. She carried herself as though she was keeping her chin just atop some water level. Then there was her laugh: a kind of joyous shout that pulled everyone in, if not to the joke, to her enjoyment.

When Auntie Peg sold the shop and moved to our street, I supposed it was because she wanted to be nearer to Mother, nearer to us. It didn't help matters at home.

"If she thinks we're going to be in each other's pockets, she has another think coming," Mother said uncharitably.

Father came to her defence. "Maybe she's lonely."

"She was never lonely a day in her life," my mother said. "Doesn't every Tom, Dick and Harry on the street get invited in for a drink?" The familiar crease on Mother's forehead deepened as she dished out dinner. "She's the laughing stock of the street."

Auntie Peg knew all the tradesmen on a first-name basis, and Mother felt that this somehow demeaned the whole family.

She looked up at my father and shook her head. "I know, I know. You don't have to say it. She has reasons for it all. God knows I feel sorry for her, but I have my reasons to stay away from it."

When I walked past Auntie Peg's house, I always looked for her at the window. Often she would be there, stroking Finnegan who always sat on the window-ledge. Then one day she wasn't there. I didn't think about it much until the end of the week, when I realized that there'd been no sign of her for days. There was no need for me to hold my chin high and pretend I was keeping the water from lapping over it, for she wasn't there to see.

It bothered me, too, that the cat wasn't on the window-ledge. I walked past the house and then, turning back, went up the path and knocked tentatively on the door. I thought of ringing the upstairs boarder's doorbell, but I doubted he would be home yet.

When there was no response, I tried the door handle. Auntie Peg hardly ever locked the door. Unlike my mother she had no fears about burglars. I even remember my mother joking about it.

143

"God help the poor burglar. He'd have to have a drink with her."

I was almost sorry when the door opened.

I called out, "Auntie Peg!" and again there was no response. No lights were on anywhere. Often in the winter she kept the hall light on, for it was dim inside even at the best of times.

The living room for some unaccountable reason smelt of sardines. Papers were strewn everywhere. Open books had been tossed down as though she'd been searching for something between the pages. A range of empty glasses occupied every table top and ashtrays with scrunched-up cigarette butts were filled to overflowing. Some of the cigarettes were only half smoked.

I moved down the hall and stopped outside her closed bedroom door. I think I already knew what I was going to find before I opened the door. The smell stung my nostrils the minute the door opened. If it hadn't been for an open window, the stench would have permeated the whole house. Several empty bottles stood on the bedside table. Her body lay half out of the bed. Her face was a dreadful grey-white; her mouth and chin were smeared with her own vomit.

To turn and run would have been natural, but I was mesmerized. Finnegan sat on the floor so still that he might have been a china cat. His gaze didn't leave her face. The other thing that registered was that the bottom part of her body still had a skirt on; on top she had a nightie, but I could still see the broad straps of a vest and her bra showing, as though she'd made some efforts to dress for bed and then forgotten what she had started to do.

I might have stood forever if I hadn't heard a door bang somewhere up above and then footsteps. I knew for certain there was no need to hurry anyway, she was dead. I wanted to cry, but everything seemed stuck in my throat. Then, before I could move, my body spewed up its own bile, bitter and convulsive, but it made no difference in the horror of that room.

"Why did you go in?" my mother asked later. "You'd no business going in."

I know now that my mother was possibly even more scared than I had been; that was what had kept her away. When she looked at my aunt, she didn't see drunkenness and death as a result of a hard life, she saw drunkenness and death from bad genes. Only much later did it begin to make any kind of sense. I realized that Mother thought she was saving herself and us from the Finlay curse: booze. We were seldom allowed to forget about our grandfather and his battles with the bottle.

This might explain why Peg had died alone, but certainly never excused it. It might also explain why Mother seldom talked about her death and never showed any sign of regret for what might have been if we had seen more of her. Maybe, when I was at school during the day, Mother did go to see her, but I doubted it.

I've even thought that perhaps Mother wanted one of us to find her. Perhaps she thought that kind of lesson would never be forgotten. In that she was right.

We inherited Finnegan. He sat on the window-ledge day in, day out, his head moving back and forth as though searching the street for her. When any of us paid him any attention, he drew himself away and looked at us with what could be described as undisguised scorn.

When we couldn't find him some days, more often than not he would be up the road at Number 76, lying on the dormat as though waiting for Auntie Peg to come home. I know old habits die hard, for I could barely stop myself from staring at the window every time I passed and half expected to see her friendly face stare back at me and then the hand come up to wave, half beckoning, half greeting.

The Enchantress

"This is not bloody Calcutta!" Wozek slammed his briefcase down so that it shuddered briefly against the wall and then slid flatly to the floor. Elma ignored the comment. She'd grown used to the depth and viciousness of his spleen when it came to the Bhatnagars next door. For Wozek it was bad enough to have East Indians in Devonshire Park, but to have them as neighbours was a worse insult.

"Bloody trailing around in that thing she wears." His eyes narrowed, and he looked squinty and fleetingly mean. Wozek's appearance, so leonine, almost elegant, could at times like this be transformed into ugliness.

The shouts from the children swimming in the Bhatnagars' pool came fractured but joyful through their open window. "Thinks she can buy her way into the neighbourhood." He slammed the window shut, closing out the sounds of the neighbourhood children's pleasure.

Next door, Rada had noted Wozek returning from work.

Quietly she had rounded up the children shouting and splashing in the pool and told them it was time for home. The children dog-paddled disconsolately, trying to prolong their minutes of joy. She smiled as she bent down and hauled out the smallest, wearing his life jacket.

"Home Michael! Tomorrow," she promised.

When they'd all gone, Rada surveyed a piece of turquoise blue chewing gum floating in the pool. She scooped the gum from the water with the net she kept for retrieving foreign objects from the water. A great happiness filled her. In four months' time she would have her own child. It would be some years before it was frolicking in the pool, but when that happened, she wouldn't put a limit on swimming time.

She lay down on the lawn chair. The faint odour of the *murgh masala* she was simmering on the stove filled the air. It took her back, back to New Delhi. Only the dust, the ochre colours, and the noises of New Delhi were lacking. Often she missed it all bitterly.

Up at her window, Elma looked down on the unaccustomed sight of Mrs. Bhatnagar at repose, the ends of her saffron-coloured sari trailing on the ground: she was a Rousseau painting come to life, only she had escaped the one-dimensional flatness of his canvas, the earth's moisture having turned her into an exotic glistening beauty. Elma had never exchanged more than ten words with her, but often fantasized about being her friend. At times Elma imagined that one day there would come a knock on the door and Mrs B. would be there with an offer for Elma to go and swim in the pool. It was of course unthinkable.

One day, going through a suitcase filled with old clothes, Elma found her ancient swimsuit. It was turquoise with a great black flower across the belly. It looked nothing at all like any of the skimpy suits people wore today. Nevertheless she stripped and put it on. There wasn't an ounce of fat on her body. If there had been she probably would have looked better. The skin on her thighs offended her, like the skin of a week-old chicken left out to dry in

148

the heat: puckered and useless-looking.

Elma heard the sound of the Bhatnagars' door closing. She hurried to the window, ducking behind the curtain. Mrs. B. passed beneath her, a shimmer of gold in the daylight. She looked purposeful. Circling the pool, she left by the gate, closing it firmly behind her. Elma went quickly through the front bedroom and watched her progress down the street; her slim figure seemed to cut like a laser beam through the drabness of the avenue. It was almost a surprise that the pavement showed no trace of her passage.

Elma looked at her watch, then quickly took it off and laid it on the dresser of the spare bedroom.

The water in the Bhatnagars' pool was warmish, although not warm enough to stop the little shiver that accompanied her chest-high venture into the pool. It was quickly displaced by pure pleasure. Her body, so dehydrated, would absorb some joy, surely plumpen in the pool.

She was as natural in the water as a dolphin, always had been. It was one of the things she'd put behind her when she'd married Wozek. He hated holidays, hated the sea, hated swimming pools. Closing her eyes as she swam, she felt as though she were possessed. She was pushing her way through years of oblivion, of time unnoticed because of a lack of events. She was going back to a past when things were important. When finally her body felt totally exhausted, she reached the end of the pool and opened her eyes. All she could see was the saffron-coloured sari, then her eyes rose from thigh to waist, to chest, and finally to the look of pure amazement on the face of Mrs. B.

Elma's legs went weak. Her head submerged, the chlorine stinging her eyes, blurring her vision, then she came up again, hoping she wasn't seeing what she was seeing.

"Hello!"

Wearily Elma climbed the steps of the pool. She was shivering now and almost at the point of collapse. Mrs B. handed her the towel.

"I'm terribly sorry."

"Don't be."

"I don't know what came over me. It's unpardonable."

"Not at all." Mrs. B. smiled warmly. "It is a temptation, isn't it?"

"I should have asked. I should have at least asked." Elma felt tears come to her eyes and rubbed them fiercely with the towel. She couldn't bear the woman's warmth. She felt a great welling of self-pity, and stuffing the towel in front of her face, she fled. Tears poured hotly from her eyes, blinding her retreat, so that she stumbled on the steps from the cement patio to the garden and almost fell.

Two days later, shortly after Wozek left for work, the doorbell rang. Mrs. B. stood on the doorstep, a smile on her face. She held out her hand. She was holding a key.

Elma stood stunned.

"It's the key to the gate. I usually lock it when I go out — in case the children decide to come in when I'm not around. Please feel free." Before Elma could think of anything to say, she was gone again.

Elma took up Mrs. B.'s offer of using the pool but didn't use the key; instead, she went when the children were there and got to know most of them by name.

It was a sad moment for Elma when she saw the pool being drained for the winter. She packed away her swimsuit and felt a wave of depression. There would be no more excuses to see Rada almost every day. She would miss her small excursions dreadfully.

Elma racked her brains to think of some way of repaying Rada for all her kindnesses. When there was a snowfall, and it came after Viraht had gone to work, Elma nipped over with her shovel and cleared the snow for Rada. Inevitably she was invited in for tea.

By December, Rada's slight figure had turned into a plump fig. One evening in mid-December, Rada called from the hospital to let Elma know she had a little girl. When Wozek wanted to know who had called, Elma merely said, "Wrong number."

The first time Elma saw Rada's baby, Asha, she fell in love

with her. Peering down at the child, she thought the tiny, brown, bruised face was hard to praise, it looked like a little pecan, or walnut, fresh from the shell. Elma found it difficult to find the right adjective to describe her looks, but she was exquisite in her own way.

"Isn't she lovely ... so ugly." Rada smiled fondly at the child. It was an unusual response from a new mother, but totally accurate. "Mother always says babies should be ugly at birth ... then they grow into beauties." Rada touched her lips to the baby's forehead.

Elma found all sorts of excuses for bringing presents to the baby. She took up knitting again, and when Rada and she had tea together she either held the baby or knitted.

"You're wonderful with her," Rada said one day as she poured some tea into Elma's cup. "Viraht and I were talking. I'll be going back to work in another month and desperately need someone to look after Asha. Would you be interested?" What Rada didn't tell Elma was that Viraht hadn't been enthusiastic about the idea of having Elma as a baby-sitter.

"*Very narrow people! Will that be good for the child?*"

"*She isn't narrow, she's rather lovely and good-hearted.*"

"*I want the child to have a big heart,*" Viraht said, looking at the child fondly.

"*Elma will be looking after her, not Wozek. She'll help her with that.*"

"*If he'll let her.*"

"*Yes, there's that to consider.*"

"We would pay you very well."

"That isn't necessary," Elma said, smiling.

"Oh, but it is. We would never accept you doing it otherwise."

"I'll have to talk it over with Wozek."

"Naturally."

She waited several days before she broached the subject. Wozek looked at her in amazement. She found herself relating everything about the summer and the swimming.

"You lowered yourself ... those foreigners?"

"I married *you*, Wozek ... *you* were a foreigner."

She knew it rankled him to think of her working for the Bhatnagars, when he thought it should be the other way around.

"They are going to pay me very well." She saw him pause at that.

"How much?"

She cleared away the dinner dishes and left him to ponder the dilemma. Wozek loved money. For the first time in their married life she was about to contribute. He would have a hard time turning it down.

"How can you look after the house here and the child at the same time?" Of course he meant how could she look after him.

"I can bring her over in her basket during the day, do the housework while she sleeps, and then take her back."

"I don't want to see the brat ... that's all."

"You won't." Elma trembled, trying to hold back her joy.

She found her days taking on new meaning with the addition of Asha to her life. The child was only a couple of months old and none of the beauty that Rada had been talking about had yet appeared. Her huge, dark, liquid eyes overcame her entire face. Elma thought of her as a little tadpole and felt helpless with love for her. Asha fixed her with a gaze so intense that Elma felt a slight shiver, as though that tiny infant had sized her up right away. She was sure this child knew instinctively that Elma would always be a captive to her charm.

She brought Asha over in a bassinet when it was time to clean her own house and do other chores, and she always lay quietly, fixated by the delicate motions of the brightly coloured mobile Elma had hung on the bassinet.

One afternoon Elma was vacuuming and didn't hear the front door and Wozek coming home. Working in the dining-room, she glanced into the kitchen at the bassinet which was set up on the table. Wozek was leaning over it, looking in. She couldn't see his face, for his back was to her, but suddenly he put his hand out and she saw the baby's arm rise and grasp his finger. His profile was turned slightly towards Elma, and wonder of wonders, he was smiling down at the child.

"Hallo! I didn't know you were home."

"So I see." He nodded towards the table.

"She's a very good baby, hardly ever cries. She won't disturb you." Elma moved to the bassinet and lifted the child out. "You're a lovely girl, aren't you?"

Wozek shook his head. He snatched a look at the child, however, now that she was out of the crib.

"What's her name?"

"Asha."

"What kind of a name is that?"

"Quite a lovely one."

He didn't say another word but left the room. Elma felt a little ray of hope. At least he had asked a question about her.

Rada bought a Jolly Jumper contraption for Asha and Elma set it up in the kitchen. When Asha was a few months older, Elma tried the harness on Asha and she danced around, squealing with delight. With her little legs stretched to the utmost and like an elastic she bounced and leapt with complete abandon.

Each day Wozek came home a little earlier and although he didn't go near Asha, Elma knew he was watching. One day, as he was making himself his customary tea, Elma took Asha from the jumper to change her diaper.

"Could you hold her for a minute?" She held the child out.

"I don't know how."

"Just hold her." She thrust Asha into his arms and went to get the changing pad and the diaper. When she came back, the baby had a clump of his white hair in her hand, and his head was bent allowing her to pull it. The child giggled with delight. Wozek was grinning.

"She likes you."

"Nonsense!"

Asha put a hand on Wozek's mouth, and for an instant

Elma could have sworn Wozek had kissed the child's fingers. It didn't surprise her. One would have to be wooden not to be affected by the little girl.

"Can you help me put her back in the jumper?"

Wozek frowned but nevertheless helped Elma hook the baby in. He stood and watched as she bounced and laughed, and a smile came to his face. The baby looked up at him happily, as though she were willing to accept him as her family. He turned away.

The routine was now established. If Wozek came home early and Asha wasn't there, he was visibly disappointed. Still, he had barely any greeting for her parents when he met them on the street.

One early-spring evening Wozek was on the front lawn trying to start the lawnmower. Elma, watching from the window, saw his face becoming quite red from his exertions. Viraht's car drove into the driveway. Wozek never raised his head. Getting out of the car, Viraht watched Wozek for a moment or two and then walked over to him; he touched Wozek on the arm. Miracle of miracles, Wozek relaxed his grim look.

A few minutes later Viraht wheeled his own lawnmower out and set it beside Wozek who bent and pulled the starter. It roared to life. With a friendly wave Viraht left. Wozek raised an arm in a half salute of thanks. He immediately looked around as though to make sure nobody had seen the exchange. He moved his own unresponsive machine to the pathway, went back to Viraht's mower and began the task of cutting the grass.

Elma let the curtain drop and bent down to Asha who was bouncing around on her jumper. "You're a wicked little enchantress, that's what you are."

The child giggled as if she were a co-conspirator. Elma kissed her velvety cheek. "It's a start, isn't it? You're a clever girl."

Come Free the Spirit

"Come free the spirit," the blue pamphlet invited in bold print. "Explore the body's mysteries, dance yourself free! No steps to learn, no right, no wrong, only freedom. Contact Hathor (926-3015)."

Was Hathor a man or a woman? The name resonated in Adeline's head. Surely not a proper name. Perhaps symbolic of something?

Her trusty book of mythology put it in perspective. "Hathor, Egyptian deity whom the Greeks identified with Aphrodite. Hathor, protectress of women. She was proclaimed mistress of merriment and sovereign of the dance, mistress of music and sovereign of song, of leaping and jumping and weaving of garlands."

Was that what they would be doing then? Leaping and jumping and maybe even weaving garlands? No matter. It was something to do on Thursday nights, something to enter in the empty diary. Infinitely preferable to the other classes the church bulletin board advertised: "Wen'Do — Women Learn to Protect Yourselves from a Brutal World."

"The Art of Creating an Authentic Life," one poster read. What on earth was an authentic life? Was that not what she possessed now?

"Lesbos, Love and Literature," another read. That explained the girl at the mirror in the washroom whom she'd mistaken for a man; and the other one coming out of the john zipping up her pants as though she'd been tucking something away.

Adeline reinforced herself with a large Mars bar before going into the workshop. Damn! Mirrors and more mirrors. She could see the fat already unloading onto her hips. It would take all kinds of work to get rid of that.

Hathor was a big disappointment. She was tiny, thin as a steel wire, her black leotard showing every knob on her spine. Adeline saw herself as huge and clumsy by comparison. A wisp of dank, flimsy material was draped uneasily around Hathor's nonexistent hips. Her ghetto-blaster was gargantuan. How she had managed to lug it to the church was a mystery. If it had been an empty box, she could have climbed inside without any difficulty.

The others straggled in, everyone reticent, embarrassed. Ready, like Adeline, to turn tail and go home. The first arrival was a huge pumpkin of a woman wearing a leopard-spotted leotard and an orange sweatshirt. Another was a Chinese woman, with an iron grey monklike haircut and sinewy muscles who twisted herself into various configurations at the bar while she waited for Hathor to get herself together. The mirrors on the long walls were disconcerting. How would it be possible to dance yourself free with those reflections?

One lone man joined the group. Dressed in intern green cotton pants, his back turned to the wall of mirrors, he stood sheepish and uncertain. Stripping off his shirt, he displayed a yellowish undervest covering what seemed like a concave chest. His shoulders were thin as antlers. Not hard to pass judgement on such a specimen.

A young woman came in wheeling a baby carriage. Each new arrival went to view the baby carriage, only to see a head of cauliflower and sheaf of celery where a baby should have been. The girl gave no explanations. She looked almost fondly at the vegetables.

"Think of a colour." Hathor's voice was an odd lisp. "Pull the colour inside the length of your body. Feel the colour."

Adeline could only feel each knob on her spine in contact with the hardwood floor. The scarves Hathor had brought for them to lie on they had to imagine were mats or even padding. Adeline chose brown as her colour and imagined a big Cadbury chocolate bar.

"Now feel a sound emerging from the colour!" Hathor whispered. "Let it come. Help it out."

Somebody was snoring beside Adeline. Possibly the Chinese woman. What in God's name could the colour be that produced snores like that? A high tin-whistle sound came from the left. The room began to resonate with unsettling mewling, hums, and whistles, while Adeline's brown colour changed to purple, a deep and resentful purple. This colour was eating into her bones. It was not producing a sound but some kind of vitriolic acid.

It wasn't enough to assign a sound to the colour; they were now, in turns, to talk about their feelings. Adeline sat mute on the floor, legs crossed. A big sturdy woman with broad shoulders and narrow hips began to cry. Her colour had been pink, the colour of her conjugal bedroom. Her husband had just taken off with another woman. She must have produced the awful, unnerving mewling. More stories emerged. Hathor looked happy, more relaxed now as though everything made sense. None of it made sense to Adeline. When were they going to dance?

"Some of us found no sound for our colour." Hathor looked straight at Adeline. Adeline stirred the floor with a pointed toe and concentrated on concentric circles, wishing she were stirring a tub of melted chocolate and could disappear into the vat, her body sucked down and away from her present company.

She might have paid her money, but she didn't have to speak if she didn't want to.

"We are going to concentrate on different parts of our system," Hathor explained in less faltering tones, "... starting with the lymphatic fluids."

If she were to rise and leave now, it would be too embarrassing. Already she felt seven pairs of eyes focusing on her, the soundless one.

"Feel the flow. Let's free our feelings. Let's find 'oneness' with the warring parts of our body. Pull in the maleness, assimilate the femaleness into a whole ..."

"Bullshit!" Adeline felt like crying out, but looking at the others and seeing the intensity on their faces, she knew suddenly she was totally alone, walled up in her critical shell. She sensed bonding, sticky as syrup, all around her and felt more alone than ever.

The music finally started and they all rose to their feet. Adeline closed her eyes as Hathor had suggested and allowed the music to flow through her body. She'd come to find forgetfulness, not to dig, not to excavate. Music would free her.

Adeline concentrated on the joint of her knee which had been painful of late. She kneaded it with her fingers and let Hathor's voice slide by her. Now they were to start the dance. Adeline felt the purpleness melt out of her arms and legs. Corroding fluid was leaking like ink from a pen out of her body. If she opened her eyes, it would form inky ribbons all around her. She kept them tightly shut and swayed, mesmerized by the beat, allowing herself to move freely. It was lovely, and best of all, Hathor had stopped talking.

She opened her eyes and saw them all reflected in the wall-length mirror, gyrating and moving, everyone acting out, it seemed. The pink woman kept reaching up into the air and grasping at nothingness; the little Chinese lady was moving at double time and emitting grunts as though every movement needed sound to get it out. The lone, yellow man who had talked about never making connections was swaying like a limp flag in a breeze. The baby-carriage girl squatted as if she was trying to give birth and shunted awkwardly back and forth like a pregnant frog absorbed by some inner rhythm.

They all had their eyes closed. Hathor suddenly opened hers and looked straight at Adeline. Adeline saw resentment in the look. She had identified her "spoiler" and likely wished Adeline wouldn't come back to class. Adeline vowed she would have her wish.

The music finally stopped. They were all to sit on the floor again. This time they were to feel the blood flowing through their bodies and to try and detect where the stoppages were. Hathor seemed to find nothing funny about this. Adeline knew she was smirking and tried to control herself. Nobody else seemed to find anything funny about the command. More stories emerged.

"Jesus," Adeline thought with contempt. "This was supposed to be a simple dance class, not a psychiatric session." The room felt as though it were filled with sepsis. It was as if a smell accompanied the telling. This time she hunched over her knees and tried to pick a small scab that had formed on the point of her right knee. She focused on it and tried to shut out the voices, the camaraderie that sadness evoked. She felt out of sync with all of them and sensed Hathor's eyes boring holes in her body.

Like a writer who has no story to tell, she felt devoid of experience and therefore unable to express anything. Nothing in her life touched any of these stories, everything about her was too ordinary, too mean, too boring to relate. On with the dance! she silently urged.

They now had to choose a partner, and one was to dance while the other watched. Horrors! Boris, the lone male, chose her. He stared eagerly into her eyes which she immediately lowered.

"Watch and encourage each other." Hathor's thin voice scraped on and on. "Let your eyes appreciate what your partner is doing in the dance!" Why was it not possible for her to say things simply?

No mention of what to do if they looked ridiculous. Glances

towards Boris had already confirmed that he was no natural dancer. "You go first!" Boris smiled at her.

She accepted his urging, frightened she might laugh out loud if he were to start first. She closed her eyes as the music began. It wasn't fair, but it would be impossible for her to look at him. It was as though her body had suddenly lost its rhythm. She was just as conscious of his scrutiny when her eyes were closed as when they were open. She could feel judgement pouring out. Stupid, fat, idiotic, ungraceful, ugly, stilted, all the adjectives piled on top of one another in an ugly, crooked pile. The music was all wrong. It had an impossible beat. Had Hathor chosen this particular tape deliberately to show up the ridiculousness of their movements?

"Open your eyes!" Hathor commanded. "Some of you have them closed."

Adeline obeyed and met the smiling eyes of Boris. She concentrated on a tiny hole in his yellowish undervest and the idiotic twist of chest hair that protruded over the v of the neck. What a loser. All losers. What was she doing in a class of losers.

"Right!" Hathor stopped the tape. "Now switch!"

The music started. A far easier beat than the one she'd had to dance to. Was this deliberate too?

Boris' dancing was horrible, producing nothing but jagged and ugly lines. She tried not to look surprised as his arms shot out in spastic motions and his legs moved to a time of their own. Her antipathy spilled over. What a pathetic specimen. She felt like putting her foot out and tripping him up. Then she caught sight of herself in the mirror: the imperfections of her own body were surely magnified, the ugly bulges of fat revolted her, made her feel suddenly ill.

Boris looked at her with such pleading that she felt like an assassin. Something inside of her began to soften. He actually had rather nice eyes behind the goggle spectacles. A beautiful blue, with long lashes. She smiled back, trying to ignore the pitting of the skin of his cheeks and his weak chin. What was there after all that was beautiful about her? One look in the mirror had confirmed her own defects.

Amazingly, Boris was more fluid in his movements, as though that one tiny smile had freed something in him. Perhaps her face showed that she approved of the change, for suddenly he was looking almost graceful.

She forced herself not to look away. He turned, showing her his back which was just as unappetizing-looking as his front, but she found herself blocking out the sight of his body and concentrating on his movements. He seemed to invite her into the dance. She swayed slightly in response to his beckoning and began to think she'd only imagined his ungainliness.

Then, thankfully, it was over and they were in a circle again spewing out their feelings. Boris looked at Adeline and smiled, and she knew he was going to say nice things.

"Adeline moves like a ballerina. It was a pleasure to watch her. I think Adeline shouldn't ever talk, just dance." She had been given permission not to say a word. He smiled at her and his eyes were suddenly his entire face. The imperfect parts of his body didn't matter any more. He had seen that she wanted to dance, not to talk. A layer of ice melted from the block that was her inner core.

Then it was her turn. She could do it just as well as the others.

"At first I thought how stupid. I looked around the room and thought everybody looked self-conscious ... I felt awkward when I started to dance, then I suddenly didn't care any more, I felt better, more sure of myself. Then Boris danced and it was nice to watch." Hathor smiled at her for the first time. She had said all the right things. The circle in which they sat felt warmer. She wasn't sure how much of what she said was true, but she was part of the group, part of the camaraderie. Wasn't that the important thing?

Boris waited for her when she was leaving. She didn't want him to, but he hung around while she put on her coat and scarf. He pretended he was helping Hathor gather up her things, but he kept glancing over towards her.

She waited until he looked away and then she scuttled towards the door. He was behind her suddenly. He wore an extraordinary short tweed coat that ended around his knees.

"Can I walk you to the subway?" he asked.

She shook her head. "I live around the corner."

"Around the corner then."

She shrugged. The softness she had been feeling inside towards him dissipated in the chill night air. She didn't really want to be seen in the street with this scarecrow person. How did she know that anything he had said inside was true? Perhaps he had just zeroed in on her as a target and had used flattery as a tool to get to her.

"You are a lovely dancer," he said quickly.

"Yes, so you said."

"But you don't think you are?"

"I don't think about it."

"You should." He did a little double step to keep up with her. What was one single man doing in this dance class anyway? Any decent, self-respecting person would have turned tail and left when he found out he was the only one. There had to be something wrong with his personality.

"You don't trust yourself very much, do you?"

More psychoanalysis, she groaned inwardly. She had no intention of allowing this line of thought to go any further.

"You live around here?" she asked abruptly.

"No, across town actually."

She was glad of that. She wouldn't likely run into him again in that case. She certainly wasn't going back to the class.

"I'm just down here. You needn't bother coming any further." She stopped dead in her tracks and turned to him, putting out her hand. "Thanks for walking me this far."

"I can go to your door."

"Thanks anyway. I can look after myself." The rebuff was final. He looked bitterly disappointed. For an instant she regretted having cut him off this way. He nodded, and she knew

162

from the look on his face he felt he had seriously misjudged her. Behind his glasses his eyes looked terribly sad.

"See you next week then?" He left it hanging, half question. She nodded curtly. Not if I see you first, her cynic was saying.

She pushed open the door of the Mac's Milk store. She gathered up a collection of chocolate bars and a huge bag of marshmallows. She could reward herself now for having exercised. If she had let him walk her to the door, she would have had to come all the way back to the store.

Later, when she was kneeling at the toilet wiping off her mouth as the last trickle of her own vomit trailed from her mouth, she thought with some regret about the entire evening. What had it achieved? One false warm moment of communion that meant zilch in the overall scheme of things.

She would go back again tomorrow and look at the church bulletin board. Every day there were new classes posted. Every day out there somebody thought of something new. That at least she could rely on. Somewhere there would be some kind of class filled with people like her. She didn't have to go back to the dance class if she didn't want to. It was something she could think about later. Meanwhile there was the bag of marshmallows to be tackled.

Just a Wee Girl

Miss Greene's sweetie shop was housed in a white cottage at the bottom of the avenue where we lived. The back of the cottage had been built on, a semi-circular appendage that served as a dance studio for her partner, Miss Lindsay. Somewhere in between the sweetie shop and the studio, the couple shared living quarters.

It was a cottage that dealt in contradictions: a Hansel-and-Gretel house with one good old woman and one bad old woman. Sweeties dealt out with love, dancing classes delivered by a witch! Three nights a week — Tuesday night for beginners, Thursday night for intermediates, and Saturdays for the pros, all taught by Miss Lindsay.

I only knew Miss Greene from buying sweeties over the counter: fivepence for a bag of pomfret-cakes, sixpence for a bag of jujubes, sevenpence for sugared almonds. Miss Greene measured them out like pure gold. Aware that the army of kids who bought from her were spending their hard-earned pennies, she had to make as much of a procedure of it as possible. Sometimes there were line-ups, but she never altered her leisurely speed of delivery.

Black hair tight in a bun, she was shaped like a tea caddy but always had a cheery smile on her face. She was as different from her partner as could possibly be. Miss Lindsay was thin as a shoelace, Mediterranean-looking, and olive-skinned. To counter this, there were two hectic red spots on her cheeks and a vivid gypsy red flash of colour on her lips. There was nothing graceful or flowing about Miss Lindsay's everyday movements. On the dance floor she was minimally transformed. She knew all the steps, but she was stiff in her delivery and hard on the so-called "natural movers."

"And how's your daddy, dear?" Miss Lindsay always asked me. *Why didn't she ever ask after my mother?* There was always a weird twist to her lips when she asked, as though she knew something about him that nobody else did.

Tuesday nights, seven to nine, and you could always be sure Miss Lindsay arranged it so you never got to dance with the boy you liked best. If you happened to talk to him for two minutes, she was on top of you, whisking you off into a fox-trot. I was her favourite partner, and she seldom chose a boy, for then he would have had to lead and she wouldn't be able to teach.

Pressed to Miss Lindsay's bosom, I inhaled queer body-odour smells from her chest, but the whiff of something sweet from her mouth, like she'd been sucking on a perfume bottle. Up close, too, I could see the pencil marks, firm and arched, that served in place of eyebrows; observe the mouth, where her lipstick bled in vertical rivulets as though she'd been chewing on raw meat.

I hated dancing with her. Instead, I longed to be paired with David Kinley. Miss Lindsay was scrupulous about making sure no alliances were formed. She had no written list, but definitely in her head she knew who had danced with whom the week before. Not only was she the dancing instructor, she was the keeper of virtue.

David Kinley was big and a little rough looking, but he had

gentle eyes, and despite the size of his feet and hands and the general feeling that he would be better on a football field, he was a good dancer. Sometimes I saw him looking at me, but just as quickly he would look away.

On the last night of class before the winter, Miss Lindsay allowed us all to dress up. It was no treat for the boys, but for the girls, it was heaven. My sister had a beautiful long frock in pearl-coloured slipper-satin. I'd seen the actress Capucine wearing just such a dress in a movie about Franz Liszt. It had been hanging in the wardrobe for two years. Considered old by Jean's standards, it was the frock of my dreams. It was off the shoulder. Capucine's breasts had flowed over the confines of the bodice. I knew mine would be pressed no larger than poached eggs against the softness of the satin. But the ruching might easily hide this deficiency.

Jean said I could wear the dress for the class that night and even helped me get ready. Lipstick was out of the question, but she rouged my cheeks a little and put a dab of rouge on my mouth and said nobody would notice.

"You look lovely," she said, standing back to admire her handiwork. "Far too sophisticated for fourteen." She rooted through the dresser drawer and emerged with a pale pink rose. She stuck it behind my ear and pinned it there.

Jean turned me towards the mirror. "Here, have a decko! You're gorgeous."

It seemed like another person staring back at me in the mirror. Not one I knew anything about. Someone a little exotic and definitely too bold.

"You don't think it's too much?"

"Of course it is, but what do you care. Won't they all have stupid little frocks on and in you'll come. Can't you see the look on their faces?" Jean was given a bit to theatrics herself. Never in a million years would she want to disappear into the woodwork.

I sat down on the bed and wished all of a sudden that I'd opted for my Sunday dress, the one with the circular blue skirt and the neat, white, starched collar. How on earth would I get down the street with this thing trailing beneath my coat? I imagined the looks I would get from passers-by.

I solved the problem with a length of string, hitching the frock up above my knees. Ducking out of the house before my nerve failed me and before my mother and father could inspect me, I took off down the street, furtive and embarrassed. Mrs. Robinson next door was sure to be duking out from behind the curtains. If she caught a glimpse of the frock, I would get an earful. With the frock all bunched up under my coat, I felt like a shoplifter hiding stolen goods.

In the cloakroom, when I took off my coat, all the girls gathered around. They fingered the satin material and "oohed" and "aahed" over my bare shoulders. I fiddled around in the cloakroom, trying to stifle the urge to run home.

Somebody had given the dance floor an extra polish that day; it positively gleamed. Self-consciously I hunched my shoulders as I walked across the shining floor and wished myself a thousand miles away. The room had mirrors all around, and everywhere I turned I saw my own reflection. I could also see how out of place I was. The boys were marginally neater than usual, but their basic dress of blazer and flannels hadn't altered one bit.

They all stared, and one of them whistled. It wasn't David Kinley who whistled and I was glad of that. Miss Lindsay's eyes turned black as coal with condemnation.

"Maggie Porter, your father let you come out like that?"

My body burnt with mortification. Biting my lip, I looked down at the floor. *Again my father. Why did it have to be my father who was being questioned? What on earth was it that Miss Lindsay had against him?* Suddenly, I didn't care any more about the frock.

"Yes, he did," I said, bravely lying.

One of the boys hooted in support. Miss Lindsay's eyes blazed, and she went into their midst and brought out the culprit by the ear. She pointed at the other end of the dance floor and he went off sheepishly to sit by himself.

"You wait here!" she instructed me.

"She's away to get a sack to put you in," one of the boys called from across the room. The other boys laughed.

All the girls who had gathered around me in the cloakroom were suddenly silent. I looked at their faces and knew that their enthusiasm for the frock had been feigned in the first place, for there was a smug look of triumph on some faces, especially on the face of Wynne McPhee, who was usually the best-dressed girl in the class.

The idea about the sack wasn't that far off. She was back in an instant with an ugly brown shawl, which she quickly draped over my shoulders. There were titters from both sides as they watched the procedure. She had brought a huge pin with her, the kind people used on kilts, and was securing the shawl in place around my shoulders. I thought about poor Hester Prynne from *The Scarlet Letter*.

"There! Now you're decent."

I felt like crying. Total humiliation was swamping me. Should I run or should I stand? Miss Lindsay's mouth was set in a thin grim line. There was no doubt at all that I was destined to be her dancing partner for the night. She was bound and determined to protect me from my sins.

The wool of the shawl felt unbearable against my bare skin, and when I looked down later, an ugly red rash had appeared all over my chest. Once or twice I caught David Kinley's eye and thought I saw sympathy there. That was the only thing that kept me from total despondency.

There were to be refreshments at nine, and I was sent to the little kitchen to help bring out the sandwiches.

When the interminable evening was over, Miss Lindsay dismissed all the dancers, saying she hoped they would be back next year. Turning to me, she held on to my arm. I expected another lecture.

"Maybe you'd help me clear away the things, Maggie Porter?"

It was the only decent thing that had happened. I was only too glad not to be in the cloakroom with the other girls, glad not to see their faces. Wordlessly, I began carrying dishes into the kitchen, hustling so as not to have to talk.

Finally, when I was finished, Miss Lindsay thanked me gravely.

"Now, Maggie Porter, I hope you realize that what you did tonight was totally inappropriate. A wee girl like you turning up in this trumpery ..." Miss Lindsay waved a hand at the lovely satin frock. "You've time enough for all that sophisticated stuff. Doesn't your father even know you're just a wee girl?"

Anger burnt a flush into my cheeks. Here I was being called a "wee girl" when I felt like I was a thousand years old.

I was finally allowed to go to the cloakroom. Unpinning the ugly shawl, I let it drop to the floor. In the mirror I could see the red rash on my shoulders. Sitting down on one of the long benches, I started to cry. The emotions of the evening were finally let loose. I sat for a long time after I'd stopped crying. Then, getting my coat, I didn't even bother to hitch up the frock, just put the coat on top. The gate had barely closed behind me when I heard a voice. I turned and saw with dismay it was David Kinley. I never could cry without my face puffing up like choux pastry. I knew I must look a sight.

"Are you all right? Can I walk you home?"

I nodded.

We walked for a while silently. "She didn't like the boys looking at you," he said finally. "... Especially when she fancies you for herself."

I didn't understand what he meant. The memories of all those nights in Miss Lindsay's arms came back vividly. Surely, what he was suggesting couldn't be true? Why on earth would she want to dance with me? While I had been concentrating on the steps, had something else been going on? I didn't even want to think about it.

"I thought you looked lovely," he said, breaking into my miserable thoughts.

I should have been thrilled, jumping for joy. I felt only

numbness. He took my inert hand and held it in his own. I was too stunned to do anything about it. My face felt red and hot again.

"Didn't you hate havin' to dance with her every night?"

"I did," I said with force. "I did."

"I wanted to dance with you."

"I hated it," I repeated fervently, deliberately ignoring his admission. Maybe he thought I'd actually liked dancing with Miss Lindsay. It was important for him to know that wasn't true.

All I could think of now was getting home and getting the dress off. I never wanted to see it again. Never! Never in my life would I set foot in the shop again and certainly never take another dancing class. Something lovely had been completely destroyed, and the deliverer of the bad news was bounding along beside me like a big, rough dog, talking nonstop. I wanted to yell at him, tell him to shut up, but my vocal chords were frozen in my throat.

In the daytime I would have taken the short cut through the garages to get home, but at night, when it was dark, I had the strictest instructions to walk the long way around, where it was well lighted. When we got to the turn-off that would take us through the garages, David Kinley turned in there.

"I'm not supposed to go through here at night," I said as we continued walking in the forbidden direction.

"Am't I here to protect you?"

I wasn't certain of this at all. The garages at night were totally scary. There was one solitary lamp which cast eerie shadows on the dark wooden face of the garages. One would stumble on dead bodies here or run into some kind of evil.

"I hate this," I said vehemently, not sure whether I meant the garages, his holding my hand, or the riot of thoughts tumbling around in my poor mixed-up brain. He loosened his grip on my hand and put an arm around my waist pulling me closer. I was too scared to protest. There was a familiar odour coming from him. The same smell I sometimes noticed on the girls at school at the end of day. The whiff of erasers and pencil sharpeners and sweat. I wanted to push him off, but I felt limp and out of control.

As we turned the corner to where the lights were brighter, he stopped suddenly, and before I had a chance to think, he kissed me. The kiss didn't quite hit my mouth but skidded off onto my cheek. It was inoffensive enough and lasted for only a second. To make any protest would have been silly. It was odd how after dreaming about nothing else but David Kinley for weeks on end, I now only wanted him to be gone.

When we got to my front door, we stood for a minute under the lamppost. For decency's sake he'd removed his arm, but he'd taken my hand again. I was doing my best to behave normally but I felt as though I'd already left him and was closeted in my room.

Suddenly the front door opened and Father stuck his head out and called, "Maggie!"

"Yes?" I was mortified again. I was fourteen years of age, almost grown up, and was being called in as if I were a little child.

"Come in at once and don't loiter!"

"Parents are all the same," David said. He squeezed my hand. "I'll be seeing you."

I watched him go with relief. I knew I had handled things badly. Turning, I walked up the path. I'd forgotten all about the frock and it trailed the ground as I walked.

Father rounded on me when I got in the house. "What's that you're wearing?"

"Jean leant me it," I said dully. His anger seemed like nothing to me after all the emotions of the evening.

"A long frock?"

Mother came into the hall. She stood with arms crossed.

"Let's have a look at you!" she said. It was hard to tell from the tone of her voice if she was as angry as Father.

Reluctantly I unbuttoned my coat and took it off.

Mother smiled. "Well, don't you look a treat."

I looked from Mother to Father. There were suddenly things I wanted to ask them, but knew I never could.

"And who was that boy?" Father asked.

"Just a boy from the class, he lives on Deravolgie Avenue. This is on his way home."

"Miss Lindsay rang to say it was a disgrace we let you out half-dressed."

"Sure anyone can see she's just a wee girl," Mother said smiling. "Only a twisted mind would see anything wrong with this. Wasn't she just playing at being grown-up."

I swallowed hard. I almost preferred Father's anger, but at the same time I recognized Mother was only trying to help.

"Away on upstairs, and take that rig-out off you! It's past your bedtime," Father ordered.

"Give us a hug!" Mother said as I passed.

I let Mother put her arms around me, and with Mother's cheek against mine, the remembrance of the softness of David's mouth against my cheek came back — the smell of him too, and I smiled to myself.

"And I'm not just a wee girl," I said defiantly, breaking away from the embrace, and stared down defiantly towards my father.

"Of course you're not." Mother gave me a gentle push. "Off with you now to bed!"

Daphne

She was a girl who always sat at the front of the class under the teacher's eye. Whereas I was in the back row where, if I became bored, I could slyly read a book. She'd only been in school since September and I'd formed no real opinion of her.

I couldn't classify her as one of the other "sucks" who sat up front, tense and poised, ready to catapult their hands in the air when the teacher asked a question. She seldom did. In fact, she didn't volunteer anything unless she was asked. Yet when she was asked, she always seemed to know the answer. She didn't run around in the playground at recess but stood leaning with her back against the wall while the rest of us skipped and jumped, shouting and yelling.

She had long brown hair streaked with blonde, so that it looked almost grey. It was held back severely by a barrette. She had a slender body and a sort of well-bred look to her that separated her from the rest of the girls in our class. Even though she wasn't part of our group in any real way, she didn't seem bothered by that.

When I think about her now, I think of an "old soul," an observer who has already been around several times, seen it all before and is somehow weary. It wasn't that I disliked her, I don't think anyone did. We simply didn't know her. Didn't recognize her as one of us. She fell into some category that couldn't be coloured by our young prejudices.

Seeing her lying on the trolley in the hospital corridor, I remember now I wasn't terribly surprised. She smiled ever so faintly at me, neither particularly sad nor glad to see me. The impersonal surroundings somehow suited her. No room for emotions in these corridors: just white coats, stethoscopes and the suitable distance that most of the nursing staff brought to the job. Here, no one would invade Daphne's privacy. Here she would be safe from snoopers. Only her medical history would absorb these healers. She would be impervious even to me who longed suddenly to know more about her.

"You two know each other?" one of the nurses asked.

"She's in my class in school."

"That's nice. Friends then?"

Wasn't she someone I saw almost every day at school? That surely qualified for friendship?

"What's wrong with you?" I asked.

She shook her head. "I don't know."

"Haven't they told you?"

"No."

The nurse made a head-shaking motion in my direction and moved the trolley off towards one of the rooms.

"Can I go to see her?" I called after the nurse.

"We'll see."

I was at the roaming stage of my hospital stay, finally on the mend and terribly bored. I could tell from the tubes and bottles attached to Daphne that she was just beginning hers. I didn't like to ask the nurses if I could go into her room, but I hung around outside every day and saw her father and sister going to visit. I was curious why her mother never came.

"She's probably dead," Nurse Halpern said matter-of-factly when I asked. There seemed not an ounce of kindness in Halpern. She was all stiffness, starch from her brain to her toes.

It was shocking, this monumental bit of information about being motherless. It was a state I couldn't imagine and dreaded to even think about. I mulled it over in bed at night and brooded about the possibility of my mother being struck by a car or dying of some awful disease.

Usually I liked night time at the hospital best mostly because of Nurse Burns. She was plump and pink, softer than any of the other nurses. Her stocking seams were always slightly crooked and the toes of her white shoes scuffed as though she kicked footballs in her off-duty moments. Her hair often straggled out beneath her cap. She came at night when the other patients were asleep in the ward and brought me thinly sliced, buttered white bread as a special treat.

"*To fatten you up,*" she always whispered.

Now when she came I would ask her about Daphne. The report was always the same, "*As well as can be expected.*"

"Couldn't I share her room?" I asked one night. "It might cheer her up."

"Well, I don't know. I could ask the doctor to-morrow. Are you sure that's what you'd like?"

I nodded vigorously. "I'm her friend, you see."

It was an outright lie, but in comparison with the people in the other beds around me, it seemed almost to be a truth. There was an empty bed on either side of me and on one side a very sick girl who lay all day with curtains drawn around her bed. On the other side, a crazy woman who spent all day counting her change and accusing the nurses of stealing her money.

"Go to sleep like a good girl, and we'll see!"

The following afternoon, when the doctor had finished his rounds, one of the other nurses came to tell me the good news. I was to be moved to Daphne's room.

Later, I made my way down the corridor to her room and

pushed open the door. The curtain had been pulled around her bed and someone was in with her. I sat tentatively on the other bed and stared at my narrow feet and sparrow-like ankles. I waited patiently for the curtain to be drawn. I heard a groan from the bed and felt a moment of apprehension.

Some time later, when I seemed to have been sitting for an eternity, the curtain was drawn and a nurse came out carrying a basin and several towels.

"Well, here's your friend," she said brightly to Daphne. Daphne looked at me with an odd, surprised expression, as though she hadn't for a moment imagined she had a friend. Her skin which had always been pale, was now almost yellow. Her huge eyes, instead of being the greyish blue I remembered, were midnight blue and far too deep in her skull.

"Hallo!"

"How are you?" I asked, already uncertain I even wanted an answer.

"Fine." She heaved a heavy sigh and stared up at the bottles which hung above her bed.

When the nurse had left, I asked about the bottles.

"What are they for?"

"I don't know, but I think they will make me better."

"Good. I'm almost better," I said cheerfully, as though to reassure her it was something she could expect at any moment.

Her eyes closed and she seemed to drift off into sleep. I was suddenly not sure any more that this was what I wanted. At least on the common ward there had been bustle and noise of the nursing staff coming and going. Here, in the small room, with the one window so high that it was impossible to look out, I felt like I was in prison.

Worse still were the visits from her father and sister, who came and greeted me briefly, with terrible sad resignation, then closed me out as they drew the curtains around her bed. When my family came, they burst noisily into the room, all their happiness spilling out and filling the emptiness. Then, in deference to

Daphne, they would subdue the conversation. I could see Daphne turn her head away.

One day, after my parents left, I opened the parcel they had brought me. There were some comics in the package, and when I unfolded them a Mars bar fell out. There was a little note that said, *"For when you are better. Love, Rose."*

Rose was my cousin. She wouldn't have considered the cruelty of sending me something I wasn't allowed. The very sight of it made me ache. I fondled the brown wrapper on the chocolate, feeling the juices running in my mouth. I felt as though I could taste it already.

That night in bed I lay staring at the bar of chocolate. The entire bar would definitely not be good for me, but shared with Daphne, it would surely do no harm. I'd never seen them bring food to Daphne, and one of the nurses had told me that the bottles were in fact feeding her, but I rationalized that like Nurse Burns's treat of the bread and butter, half a bar of chocolate would act like a tonic.

Throwing back the covers, I eased my skinny legs over the edge of the bed and held out the half bar of chocolate towards her. She stared at it for several seconds as though it wasn't registering, and then her arm moved, the arm that held all the long tubes running like outer veins and arteries from the bottles. I saw what seemed like a dark stain on the top of her hand where a needle went into her flesh. She took the chocolate, staring at it for a moment.

"Thank you!" she whispered.

"I'm not allowed it either," I said, perching on the edge of the bed. "It tastes better when you're not allowed it," I added philosophically.

"I wish I'd known you a bit better." She turned her head in my direction.

"We know each other now. We can be friends when we go back to school," I rattled on brightly.

"Yes," she said uncertainly.

"I used to think you were a 'suck,'" I carried on, "then I saw you weren't."

"Did you?" She closed her eyes and I wondered whether she was in pain.

"Does it hurt?" I asked, not knowing what it was that should hurt.

"No!"

"Where were you before you came to school?"

"In England ... in London. I hated it there. My father moves all the time. We never stay anywhere more that two years."

"I couldn't imagine that. I've been here all my life."

"It's hard to get to know people ..." Her voice tailed off. "Sometimes I don't even want to get to know them because then I have to leave them ..."

"And your mother?" I asked tentatively.

"My mother left when I was small. I suppose she didn't like moving either."

"I'm really sorry."

"That's all right. I hardly remember her any more anyway. It doesn't matter."

Could it possibly not matter having a mother who ran away and left you all alone?

We talked quietly for a while longer as I nibbled on the Mars bar, trying to make each mouthful last as long as I possibly could. I thought I saw her eating hers, but now I can't be sure, and even now, though I try to bring back the moment, I really don't know whether she ate it or not.

In the middle of the night there was a great deal of commotion in the room. Doctors and nurses and then an orderly came and wheeled my bed out. I was deposited back on the main ward, my bed parked close beside another empty one. There seemed to be a terrible stillness in the ward, nobody stirred. The nurses who occasionally patrolled were all gone. Pulling the sheets up around me, I shivered. I felt more alone and more afraid than I'd ever felt in my life. I imagined the chocolate bar in my insides eroding whatever good had been done. Perhaps I would even die.

Tears oozed out and down my cheeks until my pillow was wet with evidence of my self-pity. Too tired and too despondent to turn the wet pillow over, I finally fell asleep, my cheek pressed against the dampness.

The next morning, I waited for somebody to tell me why I'd been moved. Perhaps Daphne had asked to be alone? That possibility crossed my mind. I remembered her standing with her arms behind her back, leaning against the brick wall at school. Perhaps she'd become so accustomed to being alone that she had hated me being there? Perhaps the doctor would tell me the reason for my removal? But he came and patted my head and said I would be going home in a day or two and made no mention of Daphne.

Later, when Nurse Halpern came to take my temperature, I asked about Daphne.

"She died last night," Nurse Halpern said without moving a muscle of her face. She lifted the thermometer out of the liquid, shook it with a sharp motion and stuck it into my mouth.

My teeth clenched around the thermometer and I heard it snap. Then everything exploded out from my mouth: bits and pieces of the thermometer, saliva, and tiny balls of mercury, scattering on the covers. Halpern grabbed the back of my neck and, lifting a glass of water, forced it to my mouth, telling me to spit everything out.

I will always remember the thin line of her mouth, lipless in her anger. I did what she asked, unashamedly spewing over her white uniform, tears cascading down my cheeks. I could hear a long wail coming from what seemed a great distance.

"Stop mewling!" Halpern's face twisted in anger.

I wanted to yell out that I had killed Daphne, but it seemed too important a thing to say right then — it somehow gave me a place in her death and it seemed better to wait until they came and told me that they'd found the Mars bar wrapper and knew what I'd done.

I lay motionless on the bed when Halpern and the orderly had gone and all the chards of glass had been cleaned up. They would come back and find me dead too. I crossed my arms over my breast and lay waiting for what I thought was the inevitable.

"You took my money." I opened my eyes. The crazy old woman was standing over me. "They took you away. I knew you'd taken my money. Where is it?" she hollered at me. "They'll put you in prison. That's what they'll do to you for stealing money."

I closed my eyes again. Prison. Yes, prison was what I deserved. I should have felt afraid or nervous about her and her threats, but deep down I knew I needed to be scolded. I wouldn't open my eyes, but I heard Halpern's voice and sensed the woman had been led away from my bed.

Then, a while later, I heard Halpern again.

"Are you all right?" she asked close to my face.

I kept my eyes tightly shut. I prayed she would go away, for I felt the well of tears again and knew that no matter how hard I pressed my eyelids shut, at any moment they would spill over. It seemed important that I shouldn't lose control again.

The Woman in the Mirror

Thank God for frozen phyllo pastry, Lynn thought as she separated the delicate sheets of dough. *Spanakopitta* would have been impossible under the circumstances. Six dozen down, three dozen tiny crab quiches, three dozen stuffed mushrooms and twenty dozen more to go. Lynn's eyes took in the shelves of hors d'oeuvre neatly lined up on the aluminum foil sheets.

The phone rang and Lynn put it on Conference. That had been one of the small efficiencies Jim had insisted on setting up for her. It meant she could keep right on working and talk without having to hold the receiver.

"Jen, is that you?"

"No, Mother, it's Lynn."

Her hand shook and one of the sheets of phyllo came apart. She laid it on the oiled baking sheet and pressed together the edges of the tear. When her mother phoned and called her by the wrong name, she was often tempted to accept the mistaken identity and pretend. It didn't seem to matter anyway, Jen and she were completely interchangeable in her mother's muddled mind.

"That woman's back in the apartment, dear, can you come and take her away? She doesn't say anything, just stands and stares at me. She needs a doctor, she's bleeding, just like before. I hate her. What's she come looking for? She has blood all over her arms, dear, I'm scared."

Lynn felt the throbbing at the side of her head again. Jen had started the lie that the woman in the mirror was looking out for her mother; then, when she hadn't accepted that, in despair they'd covered all the mirrors in her apartment with brown paper. "She doesn't like to see herself getting old. It's denial." Jen, with her degree in psychology, needed to classify everything.

Lynn had already gone to see her mother that morning. The first thing she'd noticed was the paper torn off all the mirrors. She hadn't been able to find her mother. Finally, she'd heard a whimper from under the bed. She was hiding from the woman, she told Lynn. Forgetting about Jen and the lie, with her arm around her mother, Lynn guided her gently to the mirror and tried to convince her she was looking at her own image.

"I don't want to look." Her mother averted her face. "I don't want to see the blood."

"There is no blood, look!" Lynn commanded.

Her mother turned her face slowly and fearfully. "Who are those women?" She stared into the mirror with a puzzled expression. Lynn put a hand on her chest. "That's me and that's you." She touched her mother. It seemed she was explaining it to herself at the same time. Her own sagging figure with the careworn face might be the confused one and the other tall, thin woman with the blank face could easily be the rational, sane one. In some ways it was unfair; it would have been more humane for the body to be a reflection of the mind. For an instant she perfectly understood her mother's confusion. She rubbed her mother's hand in sympathy. Only recently had she been able to touch her mother affectionately. Touching hadn't ever been a pattern. "Dysfunctional," Jen now tagged them. As though giving it a name somehow normalized their youth.

Lynn tried to remember how many layers of phyllo she had carefully brushed with oil. She listened to the sound of her mother's voice and imagined she was coating her own being with a protective film.

"Go next door, Mother! Ask Mrs. Pryzbinski in for coffee."

Mrs. Pryzbinski was an elderly widow who had idolized her mother. They had been Belle and Renée to each other before the Alzheimer's had started and relegated the friendship to some dead part of the cortex.

"Who's she?" her mother asked petulantly.

"Mother, I have thirty dozen hors d'oeuvre to get ready for a party. I have to go."

"You're having a party?"

Lynn sighed. There were moments when she felt her mother knew perfectly well what was going on but deliberately planned to frustrate her.

"Not my party. I'm making them for the Erlichmans."

"That's just like you. Like your Auntie Pauline ... a cooking fool she was. Two hundred and fifty pounds of lard, those idiot sisters of his. You're just like them."

Her father's sisters had always irritated the heck out of her mother. They had been the largest women imaginable but with hearts to go along with their size. Lynn took after her father's side of the family, tending towards chubbiness.

"*Genes will out!*" had been her mother's favourite cry when she measured Lynn for one of the creations she used to fashion for her daughter's less than perfect shape.

During Lynn's childhood, Renée Girand clothes had been a fabulous success throughout Canada. She'd been given the Order of Canada. Lynn and Jen had been the envy of every girl in high school for having such a mother. Renée Girand was hailed as a magician who understood the female body as no one else in North America. Ironically, her mother might have been intimate with all kinds of bodies, shapes, and sizes, and what suited best, but she had never possessed an iota of insight when it came to the mind and what people were thinking.

Her celebrity status died with her memory lapses, and the business slipped under the forgetful queen. A tailspin had ensued, until finally her mother had run through every asset, almost bankrupting the company. The only thing left at the end of it all had been the building which sold for a healthy profit. Lynn and Jen had managed to get a court order which allowed them to manage whatever was left of their mother's money. Now, if she sold the condo, they could easily find a home for her, but Jen demurred, calling it heartless.

"Hardened arteries at sixty. Pauline gone with angina and Evie had a stroke. You'll end up like that!" her mother warned. It was odd how her mother's memory held on to the old and most annoying litany.

"Mother, I've had enough. I'll call you later!"

Lynn hung up the telephone and felt a moment of irritation with Jim for having set her up with the phone in the first place. If she'd had to hold the ordinary phone, the conversation would have ended minutes before. Dear Jim who wanted nothing better than to make her life easy. He would have computerized her kitchen if she'd allowed him. Today, at this very moment in fact, if he asked her again to marry him, she might easily agree. Sometimes, late at night in bed, she tried to imagine what it would be like to have somebody care for her. It was a concept and nothing more. From early childhood it seemed she had looked after everyone else. The house, her father, Jen, and even at times, when she had been allowed, her mother.

Now, the catering had taken over her life completely. She told herself she had done with caretaking. There was something marvellously absorbing about the creation of food. It could wipe out anxieties. She knew how her mother must have felt in the old days creating her haute couture, the absorbtion with cut and colour and texture. How easy it must have been to block her family out of her life, address herself to a bolt of wonderful fabric and a drawing board with a pristine sheet of paper, waiting for inspiration to shape and form the bolt of cloth into something magical — and shape it she had with an amazing wizardry.

Another filmy layer of pastry tore in her hands and fell onto the other layers. She remembered too late that she had forgotten to oil-brush the top layer, and immediately the pastry stuck. Impatient now, and agitated, her fingers shook as she tried to detach the layer from the one beneath. It came away in her hand, bringing with it some of the pastry from the layers below: a failure of sorts, one half expected, like the many there had been over the years.

The family heirloom tablecloth had been just as delicate. Using the marvellous cutwork edge of the cloth as the hem for her doll's dress, she was positive she was doing a good job. Her father was enchanted with her childish efforts. Renée Girand outraged, not so much by the destruction of the cloth, as by the clumsy attempt to create something. She was eight years old then, barely able to sew, and each stitch was a minor triumph.

Her mother ripped the dress from the doll in anger and quickly disassembled her clumsy sewing.

She had only dim memories of the lesson that followed about style and cut. It had been meaningless to her childish ears. There was only an overwhelming sense of failure.

Lynn felt a quick rush of heat irradiate her body. It often came in unexpected surges now, unpredictable waves of discomfort that made her arm pits and solar plexus wet. "Change of life," the doctor had said. Such an odd, stupid term for what was happening to her. Nothing, it seemed, was changing about the way she lived. She had needed none of the inconveniences of menstruating in the first place, for she'd never married. There had been intermittent yearnings for motherhood, quickly dismissed when the realization came that she wouldn't be any good at it, no better than her mother.

"How did your mother handle 'the change'?" her doctor had asked. She was used to being questioned about her once-famous

187

mother and for a strange moment she thought he was talking about money. She gave a quick snort of laughter when she realized her mistake.

"*Fine!*" she lied. Just as her mother had always assumed her daughters didn't need explanations about the starting menstrual cycle, she also assumed that the other end of that cycle needed no illumination either. Whatever hormonal flushes or erratic behaviour she herself had gone through had been buried in between their father's desertion and the gradual decline of the business.

The phone rang again and she ignored it, furiously thinning the crab filling for the quiches. It seemed to ring interminably and then suddenly quit, leaving her ears echoing with the aftersound.

Her mother's memory loss was endearing when it began to happen. It gave her a vulnerability she had never shown before. She seemed more human, turning from Renée Girand into a mother. But things quickly got out of hand. The vulnerability had switched to helplessness. They were forced to pretend they were a family: mother and two daughters. Three strangers suddenly trapped in an uneasy comradeship without anyone having given them the code for communication.

She lifted a batch of quiches from the oven; the colour was exactly right, reheating would be no problem. Her fingers became steadier, the kitchen began to fill with rich smells and the colour of her creations. The phone rang again, and she leant over and switched on the radio, hoping to drown out the sound of the ringing. Somebody was being interviewed, something to do with airline safety. She knew the voice. It was Danny Armato. He was frequently interviewed on the topic. From plain civil servant to head of Safety Control for the federal government, he was practised at keeping himself in the news.

Danny and she had been in Grade Thirteen at Jarvis Collegiate together. Sleek and olive-skinned, he'd been born in a small town in southern Italy and had humble but aspiring parents who wanted the world for him. Most of the girls in class had been in love with Danny, including herself. She'd been flabbergasted when he'd asked her to the final school dance.

Her mother gave her dress for the dance priority in the workshop: an impossibly gorgeous creation, a shimmering blue-green silk taffeta, strapless, that showed off her good shoulders and slimmed down her waist. Danny came to pick her up, looking unbearably polished and handsome, wearing a rented white dinner jacket. Her mother, dressed as though she were his date, charmed him completely.

"Clever little girl," she whispered to Lynn in the kitchen while she got Danny his coke. The magic of the night vanished then, as Lynn puzzled over how and when exactly she had been clever. The mood turned to misery at the dance when he danced with almost every girl in the room except her, coming to her only for the last dance. She knew later it was her mother's cleverness, not hers, that had to be applauded.

He'd never taken her out again and eventually married a girl who had been a year behind them in school. She met them once in town with three beautiful children in tow, and felt a deep ache of regret when she saw how he looked at his wife.

The phone began to ring again. She removed the last tray of hors d'oeuvre from the oven. Still holding the oven mitt, she answered the phone.

"Come quick, dear! It's terrible."

It was Mrs. Pryzbinski's voice.

"What is it?"

"Just come!" The woman was crying uncontrollably.

When Lynn arrived at the apartment, the ambulance was already outside and clusters of neighbours gathered in hushed groups. Mrs. Pryzbinski met her in the hallway outside her mother's door. She could see the back of the ambulance men.

"Don't go in, dear!" Mrs. Pryzbinski grasped her arm.

She brushed the woman off and pushed into the apartment. Her mother was lying in the centre of the off-white carpeting. She had put on her favourite green silk dress. Her face was ivory white, except for streaks of blood. Her arms were extended backwards and long rivulets of blood streaked her arms like arteries. The carpet had soaked up blood in great wet patches. For one wild and absurd moment the image of a nouvelle cuisine platter came to mind. Everything perfectly framed according to colour. Renée Girand had arranged herself with artistry.

"Looks like she put her hands through the mirror. Her knuckles are shattered," one of the men bending over her said.

"Her hands are full of shards too," the other man said.

"You related?" the first one asked, looking up at her.

Lynn nodded dumbly.

"Severed an artery in her left wrist. Bled to death," he said, staring down again. "The police are on their way." He covered her with a blanket.

Lynn walked into the bedroom. The room seemed suddenly smaller. The mirror was now an empty frame, all the glass gone. Lynn looked down at the dressing table. All her mother's make-up was laid out like that of an actress. Her mother had prepared for her death, just as she had for her shows. At some point between Lynn's making of the spanakopitta and the crab quiches, her mother's arms had crashed through the dressing-table mirror.

Cats

October, 1993

Dear Marjorie:

Why do I only ever write to you when I'm totally ticked off about something? I guess because you're probably the only one who'll understand. God, I wish you were back in the office.

(Surprisingly, that's true. I mean Marjorie could drive me bananas at times, one of those people who had to tell you the entire story line from a movie she'd seen the night before, including the punch line, but basically good-hearted.)

Leonora is getting me down totally. I cannot stand that woman and she doesn't seem to know. It's funny really because I like most people. I've always made a big detour around the "clashers," you know the ones I mean: the ones who reach for something just as you do, or speak just as you're speaking. I've been moving around Leonora like that, but she doesn't seem to get the message.

I swear people are like cats. One circuit of a room and a cat can always scent out a hostile lap. People are just the same, or at least some people. They sense when you don't like them and they hang around trying to show you that they really are nice. As far as I'm concerned, they can stand on their heads, punch me, hug me, nothing changes. I know right from the beginning if I'm going to like a person.

(*Actually, now that I think about it, I didn't really like Marjorie from the beginning. I mean Marjorie could never answer a simple question with a "Yes" or "No." She had to go into every last detail of what happened. Like you'd ask, "Did anyone see my pen?" and Marjorie would launch into a complicated story about how the phone had rung suddenly and she couldn't find hers anywhere and how the guy on the end of the line had been impatient and she'd just had to borrow mine. I didn't care a darn. I mean, just give it back and cut the crap, but not Marjorie.*)

I tell you, Marjorie, it's impossible to avoid Leonora, she sits three desks away from me in the newsroom. She's one of those types who's gone back to basics. Remember Carswell in the Life Section who wrote about quilts and baskets? Like Carswell, only worse. Two years ago Leonora stopped wearing make-up, threw her mascara and blusher in the wastebasket and decided to go "au naturel." Now she shops at Evening Star. You know the kind of stuff, all Indian cotton and creases, dangly earrings made of tin? I swear to God she wears the same three outfits year in year out. She has this peasant blouse she pulls up to her neck in the winter, and in the summer she's a kind of Anna Magnani peasant, all off the shoulder. Her hair's frizzy, a bush in fact, and not just on her head but under her arms too, it's revolting.

People like her break me up. Sits on my desk morning, noon, and night and gives me all this stuff about her philosophy of life. She's a vegetarian ... "meat kills" all that crap, meanwhile she's smoking herself to death. You should hear what she goes on about. "You're sick if you let yourself be." You just want to come into the office with a cold, half dying and listen to her going on about having control of your life, not giving in to germs, etc.

I can hear you now, Marjorie, telling me to calm down, not let her get to me, but I'd like you to try it. The thing about her that kills me is that she's a real sham, especially when it comes to men. She's a blinker, Marjorie. Remember how we always used to have a laugh about the eyelash batters like Sue Anne? Believe me, Sue Anne is an amateur compared to this one. Not only that, she lisps when she's talking to men, like she's about six years of age again. They love it, dumb jerks. It's enough to make you puke just to watch it in action.

"You're jealous," I can hear you say, Marjorie, but I swear I'm not. Visualize this! You remember how Bill Merton, the editor of the Business Section always used to come in with his socks full of holes? Last week Leonora came in with a darning needle and wool and there she is sitting with her hand stuck up that creep's sweaty socks.

(Mind you, not that Marjorie wasn't a sucker when it came to men, too. There's this great independent career woman, terrific writer, who could turn marshmallow in front of the right man. Not that it did her much good. For some reason men didn't take to Marjorie. She came on far too strong. "Take me, I'm yours," kind of thing, scared the heck out of them.

Actually, I don't think Bill Merton's a creep. I've liked him from the first day I stepped into the newsroom, but there's no point letting Marjorie know that. She kind of uses things like this when you least expect it, preferably when someone else is around. I know there are a lot of ways of getting Bill's attention. For instance, taking his socks home and darning them or even doing them on the spot like Leonora did, but I just can't bring myself to do such a thing. I mean I wouldn't lower myself. You have to have some pride. If you don't have pride, you're dead. I don't know why all the guys I meet want to be mothered. It drives me crazy, but what's worse is that there's always someone like Leonora around to oblige. I mean you can't win. Another thing is, I can never lie to a man. I have to tell the truth, but truth is something they don't want to hear. At least Bill doesn't. You see, I've been out with him, so I know. He took me home to cook dinner for his two young sons, if you can call that "going out." He's been divorced for about three years. His wife ran away with a waiter ... a maître d' actually, but Bill always calls him "the waiter." After meeting the sons, I don't blame her for running away. Anyway, the only way I could even think about living with this guy is if his sons left home and that isn't likely to happen. They're monsters. The first thing they asked was, "Are you Dad's new broad?" Bill thought it was cute. I told him it was rude. He hasn't asked me out since. Leonora's been to his place ... cooked them all meatless lasagna. I've tasted Leonora's meatless lasagna. It's more than those brats deserve. Anyway, all I can do now is wait around for the sons to grow up. By then he'll be into younger women.)

The thing is, I feel guilty as hell about Leonora. Last year, when I ended up in hospital with the flu, guess who was the first one to visit me? Leonora. She turned up at the hospital with a pot of chrysanthemums. I've always hated chrysanths. They have that sort of strong, earthy smell, nothing you can classify as a perfume, just a smell of hot soil. It was typical in a way she should have chosen the one flower I hate.

I still remember I was burning up in that hospital bed, felt like dying, and there she was sitting on the bed, right on the sheets so that my toes were squashed flat, going on about the power of the mind and how sickness was a subconscious desire. When you're half-dead it's just what you want to hear: that you have no control over your life. In a way, though, I guess she was right. If I had control, she wouldn't be part of my life.

But how do you put someone like that off? Especially when they're always doing you good turns. She brings me homemade yogurt all the time, plain yogurt. I hate plain yogurt. I like the kind with all the gooey fruit at the bottom that you can mix in and pretend you're not eating yogurt. I've even told her I hate yogurt. Well, I suppose I didn't exactly tell her ... what I said was, I like the kind with fruit, but I don't think she heard me.

Something else she does that drives me bananas: she's always trying to make you feel like your values are all wrong. Last week, I remember, I was all excited I found this fabulous old basket, perfect to put my plants in, something to make the apartment look quaint.

"You're always buying things," she accused me. "I've given up all that kind of stockpiling." Well whoopdeedo! I mean what does she want, a medal? "My work is the only thing important to me." She stared up at the ceiling all dreamily. "I want to be able to pick up and move, maybe to Crete or Piraeus and not have to worry about possessions."

She didn't bother saying how she planned to live when she got there. For sure not on this performance poetry she writes. I didn't tell you about that, it's all sibilant s's and hisses. It's ghastly.

"I don't want to have anything tying me down, nothing to worry about. I mean I could just walk out of my apartment tomorrow and carry one knapsack on my back and I wouldn't have a thing to worry about."

Marjorie, I wanted to yell, "Go! Go! Good riddance." And what did I do? I smiled, for Pete's sake, I smiled. I couldn't think of one cutting thing to say. I suppose that's why I'm dumping on you now.

Sorry, pal, but at least I've got it off my chest. I wish you weren't so far away.

Remember the good times?

(Well, we did have some good times, Marjorie and me. I mean once you forgot about all the annoying things, she wasn't bad company.)

Anyway, toodleoo for now. Write soon!

Love

Sylvia

April, 1994

Dear Marjorie:

I don't know if you remember my mentioning Leonora to you? I think I wrote a few nasty things about her last year. Anyway, I feel really rotten about that because guess what? She's got cancer

195

and only has a few months to live. It's horrible. It's like with all that travelling-light stuff she gave us she knew she was going somewhere, but it sure as hell wasn't Crete.

She's been in hospital for a couple of months now and I visit her several times a week. She can't stand the hospital food, so I try and cook her up something, without meat of course, although I don't know what harm it would do her now.

I feel so sick and sad every time I look at her. She's sort of fading away on the pillows. What's worse than anything for her is that this is something she finally can't control. Oh, she talks a lot about how she's getting better and the challenge of it all, but you can see just looking in her eyes she knows she's dying.

The most awful thing of all was that she told me the other day how much she'd always admired me, especially for my honesty. Can you beat that? I feel like the lowest kind of maggot. I started crying, and then I knew I didn't hate her at all. I suppose I have been a bit jealous of her because she didn't mind showing herself as she was. I mean she had the confidence for that. Something else struck me about her too, that I wasn't right about people not liking her. Everyone likes her, not just the men, but the women too. Or maybe they are just pretending because she's dying. I've noticed that before. I guess it's got something to do with people not being able to stand their own guilt.

Well, anyway, the thing about Leonora is that she was generous. You see, already I'm talking about her as if she were dead. But if you had to visit her three times a week, Marjorie, you'd see she is dead. It wasn't really a case of darning Bill's socks because she wanted him. In fact, she told me the other day that she felt sorry for him because he had such a shaky personality. Can you beat that?

Life is so damned unfair sometimes. I almost wish it wasn't Leonora who was dying, that it was me, because I feel I deserve to die for writing all those things about her. Please burn the letter if you still have it.

I swear I would give anything to have her back, sitting on my

Cats

desk blowing smoke in my eyes, I would see her completely differently. Instead, the female who's taken over her job is a real cold fish. We always keep a pot of coffee on the go in the office. I swear she drinks it all herself. Every time I want a cup of coffee, there's none left. It's maddening. She also wears far too much perfume. It stinks up the entire room. She must think the perfume will convince people how sweet she is, but it doesn't work. I can tell nobody likes her.

September 30th, 1994

I didn't get the letter finished the other day because Leonora died. Her funeral was today. It was awful, everybody crying and I cried hardest of all. I swear, Marjorie, I felt like dying too. How can you go on when you realize that you can be so wrong about a person? What's even worse is that Leonora left me her notebook with all her latest poems, which means that she never really knew I hated her poetry. Here I am, the one who thinks it's so great to be honest, and a dying woman leaves *me*, the one who hates her poetry the worst, her latest poems!

October 8th, 1994

I'm having trouble finishing this letter. There are so many interruptions. I can't stand seeing this woman Myrna at Leonora's desk. She's one of these *filers*. Everyone's desk in the newsroom is a pigpen. Not Myrna's. She has pigeon holes, cardboard files, boxes with labels, baskets within baskets. If you want something, she can put her hand on it in a minute. She doesn't smoke either. In fact she's started a movement to ban smoking in the newsroom. I was the first one she tried to sign up. She takes her lunch everyday at the same time as me. She always wants to sit in the coffee shop with me. I don't know how to tell her I'd rather be on my own.

I swear to God, Marjorie, people are exactly like cats!
Write soon!
Love, Sylvia

Where Dreams Have Gone

Eveline sneezed into her gin. She always sneezed after rain and when the sun came out. Because of that sneeze, she could be blind and still be certain of one fact: that the sun was shining.

The courtyard was quite pretty-looking now. Forsythias, shimmering with raindrops, glinted pure gold in the late afternoon sunlight. Wayward beads of moisture scattered and sprinkled the guests as breezes lifted and shook the branches of the overhanging bushes. Becky stood unbride-like, mutely unhappy, outside the open French door. Eveline felt a moment of irritation with this favourite niece of hers. It was the least she could do to look happy for her own wedding. Becky hadn't inherited any of the family's good looks; both her brothers, although completely unalike, were knock-outs. Still, there was something endearing and sweet about Becky. She had always been Eveline's favourite. Usually she was the one most anxious to hear about her Auntie Eveline's exploits, the one who listened avidly and whose eyes took on that faraway look – not unlike the expression she had on her face now — when Eveline told some of her more fantastic, but utterly true stories. The boys always listened laconically, as though they only half believed what she told them. Becky's eyes were always wide. That was why she'd expected better things of her. Now here she was, disappointing Eveline by marrying this dull, but good-looking boy. He was knee-high to a grasshopper and talked incessantly as though in the belief that the quantity of his verbiage would make him interesting.

God knows why Martha had chosen to have the reception here. Becky wasn't the type to enjoy show. But Martha had wanted it at the Greenwood Inn. The Greenwood was a landmark in and around Belfast, even with all its pretensions, its worn-out furniture and only half-decent food.

Becky and "dull Malcolm" had been living together for five years. Everyone had concluded they would marry quietly. Not so. Martha had insisted the marriage be sanctified in style. The bill would be enormous, more than Martha could afford, but she would somehow manage. Martha had always been generous to a fault.

The strain of the wedding was obvious on Martha's face but Eveline refused to feel pity for her. Martha meant more to her than any other human being on the face of the earth, but she could at times be misguided. This particular production was one of those times. Another of those times had been her marriage to the oversexed Sandy. But no amount of argument could have talked her out of either mistake. Sandy's running off with another woman when the children were all teenagers had been a relief more than anything else. Martha had, from the beginning, been the chief breadwinner in the family anyway. She had always provided and was still providing.

It would have been nice if Becky could have looked beautiful for her wedding day, but the bridesmaids, Becky's best friends, Louise and Jeannie, stole all her thunder. Becky hadn't even had the sense to say no to their choice of dresses; Louise in amber chiffon that looked wonderful with her glossy chestnut hair; Jeannie in russet tones that perfectly suited her colouring. At the altar they had looked like two magnificent lions flanking some poor trapped meal.

Becky came over to Eveline and looped her arm through hers. "Well, Auntie Eveline, how's London?" They all thought she led a fantasy life in London and she'd never told them otherwise. This Irish lot needed their dreams, and who was she to disillusion them.

"Reminds me of your mother's twenty-first birthday. We had it here, you know. I was going with Derek McCardle then. Bastard! Got drunk as a lord, lost the damned car keys. I had to get a taxi home and pay. He couldn't find his wallet." She felt the warmth of Becky's arm around her. She loved this niece almost as much as her mother ... "Couldn't believe it when I wanted to call the whole thing off. Roses for two solid weeks ... long stemmed, one dozen, then two dozen ..."

Louise looked away ... *Was she rambling?*

"Ask your mother! She'll remember. He came one night and when I tried to close the door on him he twisted my arm, almost broke it. I kept screaming, under my breath of course, for your grandfather would have broken his neck."

Lying, always lying. Nothing would have woken up her father when he was full of booze, and he would have been full of it that night, just as always. There was no prince to rush to her rescue, never had been.

"Know what I did?"

"What?" Becky smiled across the length of the patio at her new husband. He didn't seem to notice. He had captured someone in conversation and was no doubt boring him to death. Becky's smile faded and the forlorn look returned.

"I took off." Eveline squeezed Becky's arm. "I flew off to London at the end of the two weeks. Not so much as a by your leave. Nothing! Gone. Got a job working for an German company that manufactured business machines, secretary to the president." *Had she told her this before? Probably, but then again maybe not.* "He wanted to marry me after a year. Wanted to ditch his wife, promised me the earth. Pathetic he was!" At times she persuaded herself that this was the truth. Maybe the only reason she'd never completely gotten over Gerhardt was because he had been unattainable.

Eveline watched Martha moving restlessly back and forth across the patio, doing her duties as hostess. Pulling with her person after person to introduce to the bridegroom's parents. God, even the awful Fergusons had been invited. They should have stayed long lost relatives. They'd come over to Belfast from Bristol for the wedding. Eveline had talked to them for ten minutes, enough time to hear the entire whine from Jean about the trip over. "The incivility of them. I told them, didn't I, George?" pronounced like Godge, over and over again. "Isn't that right, Godge?" and "Didn't I, Godge," as though she distrusted her own memory, and good old Godge only managed to look stunned, as if he'd been run over by a ten-ton lorry. But then who wouldn't have looked stunned in his position.

"It's too bad Robert couldn't come," Becky said sympathetically.

"Yes, too bad." *Robert was long gone, but she'd never bothered telling them. There had always been some man in her life and now wasn't the time to disappoint them. Robert, Angus, Harry, Sydney, Desmond, Jeremy, James, or was that the wrong order? What did it all matter anyway? None of them had been up to scratch, but even at their worst they were better than dull Malcolm, and she could have had any or all of them. Rings given, plans made, and then just before the altar ... she'd run away ... from what she'd never been certain. Still, there were no regrets. God forbid there were ever any regrets. She was better off on her own.*

She finished the gin and handed the glass to Becky. "Would you mind, luv?"

Becky took the glass docilely. She was used to doing things for people. It wouldn't strike her as odd that she was performing this duty at her own wedding. Eveline smiled a bright *"I'm all right"* smile towards Martha who was staring at her, and sauntered over to a waiter who was drying off the chairs with towels. "Could you bring me a G & T?" He looked up. It wouldn't do any harm to have a backup if Becky failed to return.

"G & T?"

"You are a waiter?"

"No, as a matter of fact I'm not."

How embarrassing. Things were definitely blurring now. She should have known, for didn't waiters wear white coats, not black? This one was more like a minister or priest. Had he been the minister then? God, she hated the whole bloody breed, no wonder she couldn't remember. Her father had always gone drinking with a priest, every night of the week, got stinking drunk with the same old reprobate priest. "Hello, Daddy. Can I get your slippers? How was work?" She'd met him at the door each night, perhaps trying out for a job she would never be any good at anyway. Nothing in return except a sullen face and a "go away" gesture. Daddy, I'm your little one, the one Mummy loved so much, the pretty one, the darling. Don't you see me any more, Daddy?

Round tables, eight to a table. Seated between someone who worked with Martha, a woman wearing a dress that resembled the wallpaper they'd once had in a bathroom. On her other side sat Martha's dentist. His eyes focused on Eveline's mouth. Did all dentists do that? He'd know which teeth had been capped, what kind of fillings she had, and what should be done about the small tooth that had always stuck out and over the four good front teeth.

In between inventory taking of her enamels, he was rambling on about relationships. Eveline smiled vaguely. There had to be at least a hundred people on the patio. A bobble of red, white, and blue hats, some of them as round as frisbees and just as darting, or was that her eyesight? Things were blurring again.

"I get these terrible neck aches," she heard herself explaining. "The only thing that makes me forget about them is gin." The one in the black jacket, who'd said he wasn't a waiter, set a glass in front of her. The wallpaper woman was interested in the neck aches. Eveline focused on the surface of her gin which looked greasy like a colourless oil slick.

"Have you tried traction?" the woman asked earnestly.

Soup, the colour of rust puddles and smelling like Oxo, wafted over her shoulder and was dumped on her plate. Its surface reflected her chin; for that matter, two chins. The pills had swollen her up of course — those damned pain pills that had made her gain thirty pounds in the last year. All water, all bloating, and still the creaking and clicking in her neck, like an old stubborn door hinge that had worn itself away.

"I heard this terrible scream. I didn't realize it was me." The woman took a quick sip from her wine glass. "Next thing I was in hospital. The doctor said, 'Unlucky you! this is something you'll have for the rest of your life,' the neck that is."

Eveline felt a bubble of laughter rising in her throat. Somewhere between her soup plate and her mouth, the spoon had slipped. She saw the brown stain on the front of her white dress.

"Soda water will do it," the dentist advised.

"Salt!" someone else suggested.

Dousing her napkin in the water glass, she scrubbed the offending spot. Martha was there suddenly, pulling her up, pulling her away and into the dark room where they had all waited for the rain to stop.

"For God's sake, not now!"

"Not now, what?"

"Can't you stop drinking until this is all over?"

Didn't Martha realize it was the pain in her neck that made her drink?

"Becky's anxious. You're spoiling it for everyone."

Martha's words swept over her, paralysing her. Martha and she had always had each other. That, at least, had been something dependable when everything else failed.

"I'm sorry, I'll leave."

Martha put her arms around her and drew her close. "Don't be silly. It wouldn't be a wedding without you here. Becky would hate it if you left." She held her out and stared at the stain. "Let's see if we can get that cleaned up." She bustled off.

Eveline caught sight of the bride and groom talking with

some of the guests. Rather, dull Malcolm was doing all the talking, probably one of his usual interminable speeches. His arm was around Becky's waist to prevent her escape. Thank God she'd never needed that! Thank God she'd never needed a man that badly! Thank God she was independent!

The room smelled no different from any of the Irish pubs you would encounter anywhere, and yet Martha would be paying an arm and a leg for all this.

In the corner, half-hidden by the cigarette-smoky curtains, she saw the little alcove. The curious little cloister where all those years ago .... She crossed the room and sat down on the worn seat. It felt like a confessional ... a place where things happened, where defences were suddenly lowered. The heavy smell of perfume, Worth's "Je Reviens," was warm and sweet in the air. *"No, verboten!" she laughed as she took Brian Spence's hand from her breast. He put his head down suddenly and kissed the white flesh just above the rim of her strapless dress. It was all wrong, he belonged to Martha. Not that he'd ever made any kind of declaration, but everyone assumed ... Besides, Martha was madly in love with him. How long since she'd realized that men came to her like cloth bonding to velcro? The heady power of doing so little and still luring them away from whatever other distractions had held them before. The problem was getting them unstuck, always had been.*

God, Brian Spence could kiss like nobody else! Every pore in her body had responded to that kiss. It had all been over for Martha then, but she'd used Brian for a little while and tossed him aside like all the others. What if she hadn't? The question imploded in her head and brought her back unpleasantly to the present. She might not have been the "odd" aunt, but the "dull" aunt, comfortably married to a fat gynaecologist, for that's what she'd heard he'd become.

Martha was back with a cloth and a bottle of soda water. Pulling at the front of Eveline's dress, she scrubbed as if she were cleaning a child's bib.

Martha had always been the responsible one. The one who had taken over when their mother had died. Martha insisted they be allowed to go to the funeral. "Women don't go to the graveyard," her Uncle Dick said. Martha ignored him, buttoned Eveline into her coat, put her hat on, and hustled her outside to wait for their father to take the car out of the garage.

"We're not staying behind with a lot of mewling women." When Father had tried to send them back inside, Martha's lips were tight, her small chin firm and resolved, "We're going to the funeral."

He stood looking at them helplessly, then looked up at the window where Theresa, the maid, stood with the curtain pulled back watching to see what was going to happen.

"Go see your mother off!" Theresa had urged. "It isn't natural not to see her off."

See her off to what? A question the funeral never answered. They waited while the spade loads of dirt were thrown on the coffin, and Martha sat in the back seat of the car on the way home dry-eyed and rigid, squeezing Eveline's hand in a vice-like grip.

"I'm sorry, Martha, really sorry." The stain was gone, but a greater, wider water stain now crossed her chest in a broad swathe.

"There's nothing to be sorry for," Martha said briskly.

"Brian. I'm sorry about Brian, I really am."

"Brian?" Martha frowned.

"Brian Spence. You thought he was great, do you remember?"

"Barely."

"Sure you do. I knew you liked him, and I shouldn't have let him."

"He's boring and fat now, so I didn't miss much!"

"'Any man's better than none!' Remember Auntie Maggie always saying that?"

Eveline giggled. "Uncle Artie never quite proved that, did he?"

"'The animals went in two by two.' Don't forget that girls," Martha said, standing up. Eveline caught her hand. "You shouldn't have done all this, you know." Eveline threw her arm wide to indicate what she meant. "What about something for yourself?"

Martha hesitated, the cloth dangling from her hand, and for a moment Eveline was scared that she was going to be angry with her, but instead she said, "This is for me."

"You approve of him?" Eveline asked, referring to the bridegroom. At the same time she let Martha's hand slip away.

"They're good friends, that's the main thing, isn't it?" Martha moved off, disappearing with the cloth towards the kitchens. Friendship was something Martha had never managed in her own marriage.

Eveline's hand smoothed out the fabric of her blouse. Her father would have turned in his grave if he'd known Martha would marry Sandy McAllister.

Deception! Lies again! The fact was her father had forgotten they existed. What if he had been around when she got engaged? Would it have registered? Probably not.

How many times had they been shunted off to relatives for holidays? He would be there to give a solemn and dramatic farewell. "You might not see me again, girls," was the frequent refrain. He suffered from so many ailments it was difficult to take any of his complaints seriously, but nevertheless that one sentence was enough to fill them with guilt and totally destroy their holiday.

Then he died on her fifteenth birthday. Just lay down on the bed and quietly left them. Asking not for Martha, not for Eveline to be near, but devout thick Theresa with her beads, to say "Hail Marys!" over him. His own Protestant religion could never deliver him from eternal damnation. With the Catholics he might, after all, have a chance.

They stood at the back of the room quietly waiting, hoping for a summons. There was a faint smell of dirty socks with a whiff of urine from the commode he used when he couldn't make it to the bathroom. The partially closed curtains let in the thinnest veil of light and you could see the specks of gold in the flecked wallpaper.

The huge mahogany wardrobe stood solid and oppressive, a wooden tomb, against the wall. Inside were remnants of her mother, pieces of shell left behind: hats on the top shelf, dresses on the rail, and on the bottom, rows of her shoes, as though waiting for her to come back and step into them. The dresser was well dusted for the occasion, their mother's silver brush-and-comb set polished to a bright shine, the initials G.J.B., her mother's initials before she'd taken on his name, clearly defined. Even from where they stood they heard the confession, heard how he felt he'd neglected their mother; how he'd locked her out in the cold one night when she'd gone to a friend's house. She'd spent the night in the car, freezing, but had forgiven him for his pettiness. He was jealous of her friendships. Jealous when he wasn't included. Father Mulalley employed placatory, meaningless phrases, the last stayed with Eveline forever. "Sure isn't it all God's will."

Martha said nothing about going to his funeral. She didn't run out to join the male relatives as they left for the church. Instead, Eveline had found her upstairs in the dark bedroom, grovelling in the great big wardrobe that smelled of mothballs, tears streaking down her cheeks, pushing her hands deep down into her mother's shoes as though she might find traces of her still there.

Eveline watched from the dressing table. Sitting on the little stool covered with faded green silk that her mother had always sat on while she fixed her hair in the mirror, Eveline fingered the silver brush that had been her mother's, running her fingers over the engraved initials, digging her nails into the fine grooves carved out of the silver, and waited for Martha's crying to stop.

Feeling a speck of moisture on her arm, Eveline looked down and saw a wet spot. She put a hand to her face, her cheeks were damp but, interestingly enough, she didn't feel any emotion that might go with tears. It was like the time Martha's oldest, David, had been married and she'd wet her pants. She giggled at the memory. There was no recollection of even having wanted to go to the bathroom. Odd how her body let her down at the most important moments, giving her no warning. She slipped sideways, her head catching on the curtain, oblivion washing over her in blessed relief.

The Family Historian

The teeth stared up at him from the drawer, macabre and awful with their solitary grimace: the gums the colour of bubble gum, teeth the shade of the faded ivory keys on their upright piano. Jeremy had no idea who they belonged to for neither his mother nor his father had false teeth.

Most things he found in the drawers were intriguing, but these he couldn't touch, for surely they would snap back at him, take a lump out of his hand, accuse him of being a sneak. On his bad days he accused himself of this, on his good days he dubbed himself the family historian. By poking and prying he would finally know what kept his mother and father together. Through closed doors at night when he was in bed and supposed to be sleeping he heard their raised voices, but only snatches of their arguments ever came through clearly. Unhelpful snatches that gave him no understanding of why they fought.

He sat down on the bed. He loved this room and its smell. One winter they had stored apples in a barrel here because it was the coldest place in the house. The scent still permeated the walls. In the good old days, when his father's business was doing well and they had money, it was the maid's room. Now it was used for storage. How the girl had stuck the cold was a mystery. The tiny gas heater would surely have been inadequate to warm the place up. On the wall over the bed hung a watercolour of a beach scene with two tiny figures in the foreground. It had been painted by one of his mother's relatives. His father had heaped some scorn on the tiny dimension of the two humans in the picture.

"*You know nothing about art,*" his mother had scoffed. "*Turner's figures were out of proportion too, but he was making a statement.*"

"*I can't paint! I can't paint!*" his father chanted and then exploded with laughter.

"*Philistine!*" his mother accused, but she smiled nevertheless, knowing he was more than half right. The painting had ended up in this room.

He thought nostalgically about the good days, when they'd all been happy, or almost happy. His father's business had been going great guns and there'd been money for almost everything they wanted; then his mother had been able to join in his father's jokes instead of reacting violently against them. Those days were long gone, and maybe it would have been better if they'd never had any of it, for it was all his mother could do now to keep herself silent about the failure.

Beside the false teeth, there was an old pair of suspenders, then cuff links of singular ugliness: huge silver things with a great glittering emerald set square in the middle of each. Uncle Bill had come from America and brought them as a gift. They'd been received with amazement. "*Like something a wide boy would wear,*" his mother said when Uncle Bill had gone. "*Maybe they're genuine,*" his father offered, peering at them closely.

"*Aye! Genuine glass,*" Mother said grimly. "*He's close as a hairpin, that one. More likely they were in a Christmas cracker.*"

"*Why don't you leave him be. At least he brought something,*" *which is more than can be said for your lot of parasites when they descend."* It had been one of the many arguments that erupted over simple things.

In a way his mother and father's quarrels were like the Bach fugues his piano teacher was doing his best to teach him: recurrent themes with varied rhythms and multi voices. The only difference being he didn't tire of Bach.

There was something wrapped in an old stretchy bandage. He unfolded it. Once, his father had hurt his knee and this was likely the dressing he'd worn for several weeks. Jeremy held it up to his nose and sniffed. It smelt faintly of the liniment his mother always recommended for all external physical ailments. He pressed the folds. There was something inside. Envelopes fell out. He looked at them curiously. Letters from a child maybe? They were addressed to his father in big printed capital letters that were at deliberately skewed angles from one another. Almost immediately he dismissed the idea they were the work of a child. It was as though a kind of evil emanated from the bundle.

He sat with the envelopes in his hand. This was the point where he could make the decision to ignore them. Leave well enough alone. But in the interest of his information gathering he knew suddenly he had to know what was inside the envelopes. He opened one of them. A shiver ran down his spine as he looked at the crazy combination of letters that someone had cut out of newsprint and pasted onto a sheet of paper.

"WILLIAM

DID YOU KNOW THAT MARGARET HAS A LOVER? ASK HER SEE WHAT SHE SAYS. I KNOW I SEE THEM TOGETHER.

A WELL-WISHER"

Jeremy felt ice cold. He opened the others with no care as to how the letters should go back inside the various envelopes. He spread them around him on the bed.

"WILLIAM

ASK HER WHAT SHE DOES WITH HER LOVER WHEN YOU'RE AWAY.

A WELL-WISHER."

Was this then what all the fighting was about, or was it just a symptom? Surely this was some kind of joke? Malicious, but nevertheless crazy. His mother with a lover? He knew it wasn't possible, but he couldn't imagine anyone might hate her enough to do such a thing, or maybe love her enough to cause a marriage break-up. That was also a possibility.

The black, ugly cut-out letters jumped out at him. That's what he got for prying. More than he'd bargained for. More punishment than he'd ever thought he might receive. He held one of the letters up to the light, hoping it might tell him something. Odd that his father had bundled them into his old bandage, also odd that he'd kept them at all. They were all undated and the postal date was undecipherable.

He put them back in the envelopes randomly and wrapped the whole package up again. He felt like dashing down to the garden and burying them. They had raised too many questions, questions that he knew wouldn't be answered.

He put everything back in the drawer and went slowly downstairs. His mother was in the garden. She was wearing an old beaten-up cloth hat with a dipping brim and was listlessly pulling up weeds in the flower bed. She liked to garden. It seemed to give her some comfort. In the old days Billy Templeton would have taken care of all that, but there wasn't enough money to pay Billy any more. Jeremy felt guilty that she should be working while he had been just passing time. He walked to her and she straightened up, letting out a little groan as she put a hand to her back.

"Get a trowel and lend a hand here!" Wisps of her hair hung down on either side of her face, giving her a forlorn look. She was wearing a flowery summer dress that opened up down the front and showed a little bit of cleavage. He felt his face flush as he drew his eyes away from the space between her breasts. He tried to stop thinking about what was in the letters. Perhaps it had all happened when he was small and his father had been away at the war. Maybe she thought his father wasn't coming back.

He felt angry with her suddenly. Nobody ever made him feel as angry as his mother could, without him ever knowing why. Other times he felt helpless with love for her. She'd been in hospital once and he hadn't been allowed to go and see her. He had been five or six at the time. Without her everything had lost its colour. A monochrome world replaced the usual one. He'd felt ill with fear at the thought of losing her. His father had talked about God a lot. That was something he didn't quite understand now, for his father's link with God was tenuous at best. Certainly, it never manifested itself in any outpourings on Sundays, but then maybe it was a one-to-one relationship with God. "We must ask God to look after Mummy, make her better."

Jeremy devised a mantra directed straight at God. "Please make Mummy better and I won't eat dessert for the rest of my life. Please make Mummy better and I'll never make her cross with me again. Please make Mummy better and I will be a good boy for ever and ever." God answered his prayers, and for the longest time Jeremy had been true to his promises, no dessert, no bad behaviour, but his goodness had eventually worn off.

"What were you doing?" his mother asked as she stood up to rest.

"Looking for an old notebook," he lied easily.

"What was so important about it?"

"I wrote a poem years ago. I wanted to find it again."

His mother's face was suddenly transformed. He'd always known how to please her. It delighted her to think that he took an interest in poetry. Years before, he'd found an old leather-bound, gold-tooled volume of poetry in her dresser drawer: a book with a little frond of red silk markers, like threads of blood, marking off the poems she obviously liked best. She was especially fond of Shakespeare's sonnets: "Farewell, thou art too dear for my possessing ..." That she had underlined in pencil. Perhaps in memory of some lover. He stared at her pale, freckled arms. Had those arms been around someone other than his father? The thought was unbearable.

"Stop daydreaming!" his mother commanded. "Dig deeper. No use pulling out the tops, the roots always come back."

They worked away silently side by side. Little rivulets of sweat trickled down his mother's neck. Every so often she would take her gardening glove off and wipe the sweat away. "God, how I hate this heat," she muttered once.

He finally found a rhythm and began to actually enjoy the job. The shock of finding the letters was dissipating slightly. After all, how long had they been there?

"I'll make a big jug of lemonade when we've finished this bed." She spoke to him as though he were little again. She often did that. Sometimes he resented it. At other times it gave him a warm feeling. He sat back in the grass, his knees suddenly aching from the hunkered-down position. He stared at the webby patch of his mother's elbow, maybe the only ugly part of her, as her arm worked with the trowel. One day she might look like that all over. The thought was unbearable.

"I'll make the lemonade," he said quickly.

She turned to him, surprised. "You could." She sounded doubtful, but then she laughed. "Why don't you do that. Use the lemons on the counter."

"Don't give me instructions, Mother!"

"Right! Sorry. No instructions."

He stood in the kitchen, helpless for a moment. He hadn't the faintest idea how to make lemonade, but he would improvise. Lemons, naturally. He lifted a couple from the bowl and stood weighing them in his hand, rubbing a finger along the almost greasy surface. Why were they like that, he wondered idly? Did they come glossy off the trees, or was this something shopkeepers did to make them look more attractive?

That day they'd bought lemons and oranges on the way

back from town. It had seemed such an odd thing to do on such an extraordinary day. Funny how he remembered every minute of that afternoon. His mother had worn her odd severe burgundy hat that made her look like someone else altogether. She had been terribly serious and preoccupied. All the way to town in the bus, she had hardly spoken and he'd had the feeling he got when they sometimes went to church on Sundays: that it wasn't right to talk or even whisper, so he hadn't said a word, just stared out of the window and wondered why they were going to town on such a miserable, wet and windy day. He had his wellingtons on, but she wore her best shoes.

On the street her umbrella kept catching the wind and blowing inside out. They were both soaked. They walked to one of the buildings near City Hall. They hadn't brought any bread for the pigeons the way they usually did when they went to town. Perhaps they were even going to the dentist and she hadn't bothered mentioning it.

"Are we going to the dentist, Mummy?"

"No, of course not. What made you think that?"

They waited in the hallway for a moment while his mother shook off the umbrella, propped it against a wall and consulted a piece of paper she had in her hand. Then they got into a rickety old lift that creaked from floor to floor. He could look down the sides and see the cage climb laboriously.

The office they went to was just like the dentist's, only there was nobody waiting, just an empty room with a big desk and no magazines like at the dentist's. They could see through to the other room where a man sat behind a desk. He got up when they entered and came out.

"Do you want to leave your little boy here," the man suggested. "Sorry my secretary's sick today."

His mother shook her head. "No, he can come in with me."

The man looked doubtful. His mother gripped his hand so tightly it almost hurt. He sensed she was nervous and her grasp made him feel as though he was big, not just six years old, and that he was protecting her from something. Perhaps even the man — although he didn't look particularly dangerous. He had a great, droopy moustache that he kept scratching with his fingers, and droopy eyebrows that sprang out in different directions from his brow.

He remembered little about the room. He had been mesmerized by a dirty-looking lion with a head that bobbed when you touched it, that sat on the edge of the desk. The man set it going and Jeremy was mesmerized by the movement. Whenever it slowed down, he flicked at it again, as though to divert Jeremy's attention from the conversation. It did to some extent, for he could only remember bits and pieces of what was said, and not much of it made much sense at the time. At one point the man said, "You suspect he has another woman?"

His mother nodded. "I've written all the details down."

"You want to know everything?"

She hesitated. "Yes, everything."

Then they talked about money and his mother promised to give the man a certain amount each day. When they were finished, they went to a café for tea and a milkshake. "You're a big boy, Jeremy, and you can keep a secret, right?"

He nodded. "Don't tell anyone where we were today. This is our private secret. Especially not Daddy."

"Especially not Daddy," Jeremy recited, feeling proud to be trusted this way.

"Nobody. You must never tell anyone."

"Not even Granny?"

"Not even Granny."

This was strange, for there was seldom anything Granny and Mummy didn't talk about. Since he was a very tiny child he'd felt excluded from their conversations, sent to the kitchen to get some milk or allowed to play in his grandmother's attic which was another treasure trove of historical information. So inviting was the attic that he was content to let them talk. Somehow he felt he might find out more from the huge trunk under the eaves than from anything that was being said. The trunk, like the drawers, turned up more mysteries. Once he'd found a lock of beautiful chestnut-coloured hair, wrapped in a fine cotton handkerchief. It was tied with a blue ribbon and had lost very little of its sheen.

"So where's the lemonade?" Mother's voice interrupted his reverie.

"I've squeezed the lemons." Jeremy showed her the pitcher with a pathetically small amount of lemon juice on the bottom.

"That's all? How many lemons?"

"Six."

"And this is all the juice?"

"Who did the curl of hair belong to?" Jeremy asked later as they sat across from one another at the kitchen table drinking the lemonade his mother had finally finished making.

"What curl?"

"In Gran's trunk."

"What?"

She puzzled for a while over the question and then was diverted before she could answer by the telephone ringing.

Jeremy finished the lemonade and went outside. The conversation would be a long one as it always was. His mother never had short telephone conversations. Clutching the cord like a lifeline, or some kind of connection that could keep her alive, she would get lost in another world. Early on in life, he'd learned he could do almost anything while she was on the telephone and she wouldn't notice.

It was going to be a long, boring summer. Most of Jeremy's friends had left the city for the seaside. He knew they couldn't afford to go anywhere, so he'd been vague when people asked about his holidays. "We might go overseas," he'd lied.

He lay back in the deckchair and stared up at the dripping eavestrough. It had rained the night before and there was still the steady drip drip of water that told of clogged eaves and work that needed to be done on the house. He knew he should take over where his mother had left off weeding the flower bed, but he felt no inclination.

His mother came swinging out of the house suddenly, her face radiant. He was mesmerized by the sudden change. She bent and clutched at his arms, half pulling him out of the deckchair. She hugged him and swung him around.

"Jer, it's all going to be better."

All. Did she mean their life? Did she mean the summer?

He tried to extricate himself from her embrace. He smelt a faint body odour mixed with the flowery perfume she used. Up close he could see the tiny red broken blood vessels at the side of her nose. His grandfather had those lines, but that had been from too much drink. His mother didn't drink, or at least, if she did, in modest quantities. The lines therefore were some handed-down trait that he might be unlucky enough to inherit. Did one inherit unhappiness too, he wondered, willing himself not to be infected by her mood?

"Daddy has a new partner who's going to inject some money into the business, bring some of his own clients. Oh, Jer, everything's going to be different." She set him free and twirled around happily, her print dress flying out around her.

Money then. It was money that was the cause of unhappiness?

"Will that make everything all right?" he asked uncertainly.

"What do you mean?" She stopped dead in her tracks.

"I don't know ..." His voice tailed away.

"Our little squabbles?" Her voice had a slightly coquettish quality. It made him want to slap her. He'd heard her use that tone on his father many times when she wanted her own way. His father seemed to like it, Jeremy didn't.

She put an arm around his waist. "Money makes everything easier." He was at eye level with her now. He refused to look at her and pulled away from her arm.

"Let's make Daddy something really special for dinner. The runner beans are ready and we could have chicken. Why don't you go pick them, Jeremy, and I'll prepare the chicken." He wanted to protest, but with a jaunty step she disappeared into the house.

Later, as he was cutting the beans with the scissors she'd given him, he asked her, "When did we lose our money?" She looked around at him. "What do you mean?"

"How old was I when Dad's business wasn't so good any more?"

She stopped what she was doing, her hands still in the basin of bread that she'd been working into crumbs. "I don't know. Five years maybe. Perhaps only four."

"So everything was fine when I was little?"

"You're not exactly an old man now, Jeremy. Thirteen is hardly old age."

Jeremy felt a sinking feeling in the pit of his stomach. He cut a clump of beans on the diagonal as she'd instructed. So violent was his motion that the scissors almost cut his hand, only the rounded end of the scissors saved him from a more serious injury. He had pierced the skin, but there was no sign of blood. He looked at the scissors, "*Rounded edges, a little blunt, but rounded edges so that you won't cut yourself.*" That's what she'd said when they had played together at the table. A pile of magazines and newspapers covered the tabletop. "*Find a's, Jer. Lots of a's, then we'll do b's.*"

"Are these the scissors we used to cut things out with?" Jeremy stared at the scissors.

"Cut things out with?" She turned, looking blank.

"Yes. I think I remember cutting things out with these scissors. Right here at this table."

"What things?"

"From newspapers and magazines. Letters. Why did we cut letters?"

She turned around and wiped her hands on her apron. She was frowning as though some unpleasant memory had been touched off.

"Have you finished those yet?"

"Why did we?"

"Jeremy, Jeremy, questions, questions. How do I remember

why? Probably to help you learn your alphabet." She smiled brightly as though her humour had been restored. "Yes, I remember now. To help you recognize the letters of the alphabet."

"What did we do with them?"

"Here, let me help you." She got another pair of scissors from the drawer and sat down opposite him.

"You asked earlier about the lock of hair in the trunk. That was your grandmother's sister's hair. She died of pneumonia when she was very young. Granny was very fond of her. Her name was Miranda. Granny always says her name was too fancy, too exotic ... Granny always says just like some of those beautiful tropical flowers, she bloomed bright and beautiful, but died quickly and early ..."

Jeremy heard his mother's voice without really taking in what she was saying. Would it always be like this, he wondered? His mother answering questions late and never the right ones. He lined the beans up according to size and then pressed them all together and dropped them into the bowl. His mother's voice went on and on, and he tried to slice into the beans as the cadence of his mother's voice rose and then fell again. He was cutting up her sentences, storing them away as part of his history of the family. One day he would have it all, would have all the sections, all the pieces. In the meantime, he was the recorder.

Forgive Me, Father

It was the brandy and soda that cemented the friendship. A man who drank brandy and soda was a man after his own heart. Never mind the dog collar, the smoky odour of incense, nor the slightly furtive air of someone who might have sins to hide. He would do.

Other things brought them together night after night in the Malone Bar, but what they were was hard to say. They spoke in bare monosyllables at first.

"Right are you?"

"Feeling the weather?" "Knee bothering you? Sure isn't it the damp." Little inconsequential pleasantries exchanged in passing or as they sometimes sat side by side. The discussion that made them friends had taken place on the eve of the Orange Day Parade. They'd both sucked up the brandies, storing them for the next day when the pubs would be closed.

"Bloody-mindedness! That's all it is."

"What would that be?" Father McGann asked, the familiar

facial expression relaxing after the long day's deprivation. Surely to God, alcohol couldn't be faulted or the drinker be blamed for enjoying the flood of well-being brought on by that first taste.

"The glorious bloody Twelfth! Sorry, Father. Excuse the "bloody"! They should forget about damned King Billy. Get on with it!" Cecil said vehemently.

"Didn't I think you were a Protestant." Father McGann half turned in his seat.

"Am't I one. That doesn't mean I approve of them. They should erase history as a subject in the schools. Isn't it only a bloody trouble maker."

"Now they could hardly do that," Gerry McGann said. "Wouldn't we then have no reason to do anything."

"We only do things because of history? Is that what you're saying?"

It was the first real conversation they'd had, and both men got so caught up in the discussion that their glasses were empty for more than five minutes before they thought of getting refills.

Johnny Gault, the bartender, looked on and eavesdropped. Johnny knew too much. It was what kept Cecil making the rounds: the Malone Bar one night, Dogherty's the next, Mooney's, the Botanic, one for each night of the week. It was only by chance he discovered Father McGann had a rotation too when he ran into him at Dogherty's one night. Since then, they hadn't needed to exchange a word of explanation. Each knew the other's line of thought. Now, before they left one another, they agreed on which pub it was to be the next night.

Each night as he tried to remember the pub rotation, Cecil swore a little to himself. Too bad drink couldn't be dispensed the way those headache medicines worked, little capsules exploding at intermittent intervals over a twenty-four-hour period: little jolts that would make memory uncertain, keep sadnesses at bay.

"Cochrane's Saddlery & Leather Goods" was Cecil's business. Davy Cochrane, his father, was well known and well respected in Belfast, a man as unbending as his collars and smooth as the serge in his good blue suits. A man so upright that the bloody pews in church weren't stiff enough for his back. A man proud he'd never had to put his signature to a contract, never had to go to the bank for a loan and never welshed on any verbal assurance. "Don't I have a contract with God," was his solid claim when anyone asked for something written on a piece of paper. The reply always gave Cecil a pain in the arse.

Gerry McGann's background was as different as could be. "Bog Irish," Cecil's father would have labelled him had they met, but that would never happen. There was a level of sophistication missing from Gerry, but it was precisely his simplicity that appealed to Cecil. There was no put-on, no pretend that he was more than he was. If he had been the slightest bit more self-effacing, he would have been an irritating companion, but as it was, he was a comfort to Cecil. A friend whom at some point he might confide in.

As a middle child of twelve children, Gerry had run around in his bare feet in County Donegal where he'd been born. "Soles like good leather," he told Cecil, pointing at his feet. Cecil grinned at the thought. He almost wanted to ask Gerry to take his shoes off and show him. To Cecil's mother, shoes had been the most important thing. Because of some strange obsession about fit and quality for a growing child, Cecil constantly had to put his feet in those X-ray machines to make certain his shoes really fitted. Cecil described his mother's obsession to Gerry.

"Sure weren't those machines you put your feet in to see X-rays harmful to the health."

"You mean I might get cancer in my feet when I'm an old man?"

Gerry smiled. "Better than in your nuts where must aul' sods get it." Cecil admired the slight vulgarity, it counteracted the whiff of religion.

At times Cecil had difficulty understanding some of the things Gerry McGann said. There was a sort of fatality about his line of thought that was bothersome. Perhaps it was bothersome because, underneath, Cecil had a feeling that the control he thought he might have over his own life was strangely eroded. Partly that had to do with Fern being gone. Partly to do with the way she had died.

One night when he'd come home from the shop, she'd been waiting for him, seated at the kitchen table. Her long slim fingers restless against the formica table top, tip-tapping as though to allay the seriousness of the topic.

"I have to have an operation." She stared not at him, but at the ceiling. He sat down opposite her. Never in all the years of their marriage had she ever talked about her health. In fact, he had come to think of her apparently visible fragility as being something of a fraud. He was the one who got colds and coughs. She somehow managed to avoid all illness.

"The doctor says I have a growth on my ovary."

"How can that be?"

She shook her head. "I've not been feeling well. Been having pains."

"Why didn't you say something?"

"What was there to say?"

"I could maybe have helped."

"Have my pain for me?" She laughed. "What a double burden."

He didn't know what she meant. He went to her and took her in his arms. "You'll be all right, though. The doctor said you'd be all right?"

She smiled. "I'll be all right."

How much more confident he would have been if the old family doctor, Dr. Walker, had still been around. For all his washing of hands, Dr. Walker had died of sepsis five years earlier. He'd nicked his hands while operating and lived for only a week afterwards.

With much anxiety Cecil paid a visit to Dr. Walker's successor, Grant Bartlett. Grant was a short, blustery fellow with bandy legs whose body gave off a whiff of ether and cachous. Cecil always thought of Humpty Dumpty when he saw him. He tried to visualize him managing in his surgery. His stomach would surely get in the way of the table. Cecil had little experience of his doctoring, but Grant Bartlett was pleasant enough and reassuring about the operation.

"Routine! Routine! A large cyst on the ovary. She'll feel better when it's over."

"What if it's something else."

"You mean cancer?"

"Right."

"Even if it is, get it early enough, no problem."

"Who'll do the operation?"

"I will. Done a hundred, no problem."

The morning of the operation, after delivering Fern to the hospital, he'd gone to seek out Grant Bartlett. He found him between morning rounds and pre-surgery. Grant had produced a bottle of whisky from the drawer in his desk and poured a quick nip for both of them. He said it was his custom, that it steadied his hands.

Fern died three days after surgery. Grant Bartlett had somehow nicked her bowel and paralysed it. "Complications" was the official statement on the plain white sheet of hospital stationery.

Gerry, beside him, raised his hand and called for more brandies. "I've somehow made you gloomy. I beg your pardon."

"Don't be so bloody ...." words failed Cecil. What he wanted to say was obsequious, but he knew it would give too much offense.

"I'm uncomfortable with the swearing," Gerry admitted. "... but if it's something you have to do ... then that's it, isn't it."

At that moment Cecil hated his hypocrisy. Gerry McGann could give as good as he got when it came to coarseness.

"I don't *have* to do anything. It means bugger all," Cecil said. They were reaching a level in their conversation where they were far less guarded, but neither of them would ever reach the insult stage. It was as though a curtain dropped when they loosened up too much.

"My father never liked Fern," Cecil said suddenly.

"Fern?"

"My wife, who died."

"I'm sorry. I didn't know."

Cecil had fallen in love with Fern quickly, before he'd even spoken to her. It somehow seemed as though Fern needed nurturing, needed love. Fern worked at Sommerville's, the piano shop. She had been hired mostly because of her piano playing, and it was hearing her playing that had drawn Cecil into the shop one day.

Music had never been part of his life. His parents seldom listened to the radio and they certainly had no record player. He watched her extraordinary large hands moving over the keys, and for one bizarre moment he imagined her as a tiny baby fresh out of the womb. He saw her hands as large fronds that must have covered her face, covered her entire body perhaps. He laughed suddenly and she looked up surprised.

"Is something wrong? Did I play a wrong note?"

"If you had, I wouldn't have known."

"So I look funny then?"

"You look earnest."

He never did explain what had gone through his mind. She went back to what she was doing, but it was plain she was disturbed by his standing there. It had seemed perfectly natural to ask her out. There had been no hesitation on her part.

"Fern never took to my father either." Cecil took a large draught of his whisky.

The first day they'd met, his father had wanted to know why she stared at him so. Perhaps Fern had gazed at him for a few seconds too long, but that was her way of getting some kind of reading. His father needed to be stared at for a long time before one might guess what was beneath the surface and even then he doubted most people saw beyond the celluloid exterior.

"He hates me," Fern had said, smiling a soft little smile

as though the knowledge gave her no pain. "He thinks he's lost his influence."

"That's ridiculous."

"No, it's not really. Your father likes owning things and people. Too bad he doesn't understand about the impermanence of things." She didn't explain what she meant.

"Do you like your father?" Gerry asked, breaking the long silence.

"No, I don't suppose I do, but he's the only one I have left."

Davy Cochrane had fallen head over heels in love with a woman ten years older than himself. Minnie, his beloved, had only produced one child and this one, Cecil, came so late in life that any hope for a second one had been more or less abandoned. Minnie died when Cecil was fourteen. Just at the point when it became obvious to everyone that Davy Cochrane had married a much older woman.

If there had been other children, the whole path of Cecil's life might have been different. Early on, it was made plain that Cecil would take over his father's business. From the age of ten he'd been taught how to show a good saddle, how to tell a customer the difference between good and inferior workmanship. Right from the beginning he'd failed to understand his father's preoccupation with the business.

It was the only saddlery business in Belfast, so even when times were bad, the well-heeled still beat a path to Davy's door. He felt honoured to know Lord Connaught, Sir Stephen Leggett, a slew of luminaries from the riding world. Cecil was always proudly introduced to them as the son and heir. It sounded pompous when his father made the announcement, and Cecil inwardly blushed for shame. Was he then to spend his life dodging in and out the lines of hanging saddles? Selling leather seats for the bums of Ireland's so-called royalty?

His mother had known how he felt about following in his father's footsteps, but she'd already failed his father by not producing another offspring; it would have been more than her life was worth to take Cecil's side.

From the time he was six, Cecil had known what he wanted to do with his life. He'd been sick with mumps and Dr. Walker had come with thermometer and relief, and even though he'd felt deathly ill, somehow the doctor's presence had given him infinite comfort. He would survive not because of any natural recuperative power, but because of Dr. Walker's touch. The doctor was a big, gentle man with bushy sideburns and a fixation about washing his hands both before and after he touched a patient. Just the touch of those well-cleansed hands was all Cecil needed in order to know that he would, in fact, be perfectly all right. He resolved then and there that he would be a doctor when he grew up. In his hands he would hold the power to heal people. He lay feverish and delusional, dreaming of laying his hands on people and not only curing their bodies but willing them to inner peace.

"Did you always want to be a priest?" Cecil asked Gerry.

"A priest? Not at all. Wasn't it a way out somehow ... a way out of poverty ... a way out of Donegal ... a way out ..." He stopped, not finishing his train of thought.

Rejoicing. What rejoicing there had been when Gerry announced he was going to the seminary to study for the priesthood. What shock they all would have felt if they'd known it was Father Mullan of the fair complexion and blue eyes who had drawn him in. Father Mullan, all steely, fair, and hard-muscled, who had drawn him inexorably into both his arms and the arms of the church. What would they have said? What would this man say if he told him what made him do the rounds of the pubs every night?

"Into the nothingness of this life?" Cecil stared into his drink, finishing McGann's sentence for him.

It didn't seem to be what Gerry McGann had in mind. He frowned. "Sure isn't there plenty there. There are days when I know I'm really useful ..."

"And the other days?"

"And you ... We've never talked about you."

"I wanted to be a doctor."

228

"What happened?

"Nothing happened. The business was there to be run and I was set for it, no discussion."

He had told Fern almost right away of his own desires, and she had seemed bemused by his dilemma.

"Just tell your father."

"It would kill him."

"Nonsense, he'll survive."

But he hadn't been able to bring up the subject. It became even harder when his father offered to buy a house for them. He'd never asked for it or even wanted it. Fern was quite content with the small flat. She gave piano lessons at home, and her students found the flat convenient, close to the bus route as it was.

"Use the money to go to university."

"I couldn't do that. He was specific."

"You be specific," she said gently. "You only have one life. Live it now."

His father had found the house for them. Around the corner from where he'd always lived. It was a lovely house, and though they'd reluctantly gone to look at it, they had both fallen in love not just with the house but with the garden as well.

They'd moved in, and neither of them had brought up the topic of his doing medicine again. When he thought back now, he couldn't quite remember when he'd started making the trip to Jameson's or the Botanic, or how many times a week he stopped in on his way home from work. Not that Fern ever said anything. She often had pupils early evening, and when he got home, the sound of faltering music almost reassured him that his small digressions were neither noticed nor faulted.

When she didn't have pupils, she was playing the piano herself and didn't even raise her head. He felt cut off when she didn't respond to him. He was used to her pre-occupation when she was playing though. She went off into another world. There had to be a key to entering that world but he had never discovered it in the fifteen years of their marriage.

As time went on, she was often lying down in a darkened room when he got home. His supper was usually in the oven, gone flaccid and unappetizing. He had little taste for it anyway. More often than not, it went into the rubbish bin, untouched.

"You have children?" Gerry asked. Perhaps it was a question posed in the hope of making the conversation lighter, more joyous. It had the opposite effect.

The only real illness Cecil had ever had, mumps, the illness that had inspired his desire to be a doctor, had made him sterile. When he was finally told, he'd accepted it philosophically; it had seemed a fair exchange. He'd felt very little emotion one way or the other. If he had been able to produce a child, he would have imposed nothing on that child, overcompensating, no doubt, for his own father's dominating ways. He rationalized that he would probably have been a rotten father.

On that very first day of their courtship Cecil told Fern that he could never have children. It was tantamount to declaring his intentions. She didn't hesitate either. She told him she didn't want children, never had. Apparently, she had always been told she was too frail to ever think of giving birth. Were they not a matched pair? It seemed like fate.

Fern had been aptly named. There was something ephemeral and wispy about her. She had been a premature child, a six-month baby, weighing only a pound and a half. Her parents had intended calling her Margaret, but when they had taken their first look at her, "Fern" had immediately come into their minds.

What grew in Fern's womb had certainly not been serious enough to kill her. Cecil went into shock. His father had rallied, almost too supportive and willing to gloss over the hospital report. Cecil brooded about the shared drink. Remembered over and over Grant's assertion that one whisky steadied his hand. Was it possible? Had he inadvertently caused his own wife's death? He was tormented and there wasn't anyone he could tell. Nobody would understand. Had it perhaps not been Bartlett's first drink of the day? Was it something he should have reported? In reporting it, he would condemn himself.

After the funeral he moved around the house that had never really been his and felt like an alien inside the walls. He listened for sounds of the piano. Expected to hear Fern's soft voice from behind the door; sat and watched for the door to open and one of her pupils to step out. He collected her music in a bundle, running his hands over the sheets, looking at the notes, at the clefs and breves, and ached with a longing that it could all start again and that he could inch his way into her world instead of shutting himself out as he'd always done. He might have learned to read music. Then again, Fern might not have wanted that. Perhaps they'd respected one another's privacy too much. Her mother and father came and collected her music and Cecil offered them the piano. In a way he wanted it out of the house.

His father pressured him to come home. "Sell the house and move in with me again."

Cecil had no intention of ever doing such a thing, but to say no right away would keep the question coming up over and over. If he stalled, his father would give him time and perhaps eventually forget about it altogether.

In one way Cecil would have gladly sold the house. The light, flowery perfume Fern had always worn rose up to disturb and prick his conscience when he went into drawers and cupboards. He fancied he still smelt her scent on the pillows he laid his face against each night. He woke up often imagining her soft body beside his. He sometimes thought he heard her footstep on the stairs. One night he dreamt she was knocking at the window of the bedroom. When he opened it, she stepped in, smiling, and said, "Oh, this is what the house is like. I've often passed here and wondered what was inside."

"And what exactly makes you feel useful?" Cecil asked. He hated to think of that dream. Hated to remember Fern's face at the window. He couldn't expunge the vision of her face which seemed to tell him that she'd never known much about him because he hadn't really ever admitted her into his private world.

"The confessional," Gerry said thoughtfully. "It's a revelation to hear what goes on in the minds of people." He took a deep drink from the brandy glass.

"Do Protestants ever come to Confession?" Cecil asked.

"Protestants?" Gerry looked at his companion. "Why would they?"

"And you? Who do you tell your confessions to?"

"Other priests."

"And you tell all?"

Was there a flush that rose to Gerry's face? The room was too dim to know for sure, but Cecil was certain he'd caused some discomfort. "So you have sins that you can't tell to anyone?"

"Which of us hasn't?"

Weeks later, right before Christmas, on a night when Belfast had a sudden light snowfall that clothed the city and wiped it momentarily clean, making it beautiful, Cecil and Gerry met in the Botanic Inn. Both had snowflakes still on their shoulders. Both were filled with a kind of wonder. Neither of them made any move to shake off the snow from their shoulders. If they could have preserved it, they would.

For a brief instant Cecil thought about ordering a Coke or a ginger beer. But that urge passed quickly as Johnny Gault slung the brandy across the counter and he saw the beautiful golden glow of it shimmer in the bottom of the brandy glass. Sure wasn't it every bit as beautiful as the glisten of the snow and wouldn't it disappear from his stomach almost as quickly as the snow would melt on the street.

"It's a brave night!" Gerry said, sliding into the booth opposite Cecil.

"It is. Bloody great!"

They talked of inconsequential things as they always did, but tonight it was different. There were longer pauses. There was expectation of some sort in the air. Both sensed that there was something unusual about the evening, not just because of the snow or because of Christmas which was fast approaching.

"Protestants aren't supposed go to confession, but there's nothing to stop me telling you here and now," Cecil said after the third brandy.

"Telling me what?" Gerry McGann braced himself. He wasn't used to anybody telling him anything of import outside the confessional. He suddenly felt like running. Was something about to change? Could this make a difference to the friendship?

"The morning Fern was operated on, I had a drink with the doctor." Gerry swallowed hard. "He bloody botched the operation. He bloody well did. So it was all my fault."

Gerry McGann looked up nervously. It seemed a tear glittered at the corner of his friend's eye. He signalled to Johnny to bring more drinks.

"He probably would have had the drink whether you were there or not." Did his voice sound convincing? Was he sure himself? Was it not bloody reprehensible to have done such a thing? But then he was used to not judging, so what made him so ready to judge now.

"That's not the point. Like we were bloody celebrating something. Like it was before a horse race or toasting an engagement." Cecil wiped a hand across his eyes. "I can't stop thinking about it. I can't ever forgive myself." He looked up. "Not just that. I was here night after night and she never said a thing."

"What drove you here?"

"What drove me here?" He looked away. "I couldn't stand the days. It was the days I couldn't stand, and every time I went home I thought she was blaming me for something. Maybe thought I wasn't enough of a man to stand up to my father, and you see she was right. I knew she was right. Every night I came here I always told myself it wasn't too late. I was sure I'd somehow get up the courage and go tell him to stuff it. Just stuff it! It's my life. It's my life." Tears were flowing freely now. Gerry's hand loosened around his brandy glass and he moved it towards Cecil's hand as it lay now on the table.

"Some nights I felt full of it."

"Full of it?"

"Courage. I'd leave here sure I'd tell him in the morning. That's what I'd do. I would tell him in the morning." Cecil pulled a handkerchief from his pocket and mopped his reddened face. "Then in the morning I'd go in and there was no way."

Gerry's hand collided with Cecil's as Cecil put his handkerchief back in his pocket. He hadn't managed to touch it, but he felt a great warmth enveloping him. This was what true friendship was all about. This was true sharing.

"I'd no calling," Gerry heard himself say. "The only thing I had was the certainty that I was like no one else, and the church seemed the only place to go."

He wasn't sure whether his words were penetrating. Cecil appeared sunk in gloom. He did look at him, but blankly, in an uncomprehending way. Somehow the brandy had destroyed the order of things. Later, years later, he would blame it on the brandy. He would blame it simply on the wrong order of telling. He should have waited, should have paused and listened instead of dashing like a lunatic into the relating of his own experiences.

Long after, Gerry couldn't remember the words he'd used to explain what Father Mullan had done to him. Couldn't remember whether he'd explained that he'd been a willing participant. He couldn't even remember how Cecil and he had parted. All he remembered was the expression on Cecil's face, the drawing back, the look of horror.

"Jesus! I'm talking about death, and you're talking about some perverted, disgusting groping." Then the examination of the hand Gerry had touched just for an instant. He'd looked at it as though it was in some way contaminated?

Bloody hell! No, he wouldn't swear, not even in his head. Hadn't he stated clearly that he was uncomfortable with swearing? Although what the fuck difference it made now he didn't know.

They sat winded, facing one another, as if somebody had walloped them both in the chops. Stone-cold sober, it suddenly seemed, and if Gerry could have erased the night from the records he would have. Maybe they said good night to one another. Maybe they didn't. The only sure thing was that, as they went out the door, the cleanness of everything was gone. All the beauty had disappeared. The cars had turned the white road into grey slush, and the snow on the pavement was eroding in holes bored by the spatters from passing traffic. A car send a shower of slush and slop over both men as they turned away from one another and made off in opposite directions. Neither of them paused to look down or to stare with disgust in the direction of the offending vehicle. They might not even have noticed.

A Missing Rib

"Never leave her!" Mary's long-dead mother's voice is sharp in her ear even now. "Wheel her to school and don't leave her. You are lucky to have your legs. Don't ever forget that!"

"Eileen can look after herself." Her father had always known the competent one. "Don't baby her. She's a survivor."

Everything in the apartment is a reminder that Eileen has indeed survived.

The apartment is in the best location in town. The furnishings expensively done by a decorator, lampshades matching curtains, paintings that might well have been cut from swatches of the sofa material and framed, nothing jarring or disjointed. There is no clue as to the owner's personality or wishes.

The building, like all high rises, seems to feed from the lungs of the inhabitants rather than from fresh air. Even through the heavy perfume of the flowers, no doubt sent by Eileen's partners in the agency, Mary feels she is breathing in other people's breath. The air is so dry that it might be from the tomb of Tutankhamen.

Despite her father's claim that Eileen was a survivor, he left everything to Eileen in his will. Ironic, too, that she had done far better than Mary. Eileen was a brilliant copy writer and the prized partner in Vyfield & Carpenter, Toronto's premier ad agency. Mary, a respected editor in Winnipeg, is much in demand but always working for a pittance. Should one equate money with success? some voice from the past asks. Yes. Yes. Money is power.

Somewhere, some floors up, or down, a pneumatic drill vibrates, penetrating the walls of the apartment, humming in the air, destroying any sense of peace or harmony. Notices in the lobby warn that parking-garage repairs are under way. Every time she comes home to Toronto, the entire city seems to throb with drills. Why couldn't the city have been built for longtime wear? What is it about the place that demands perpetual care? Perhaps if she came in the winter, things would be different.

How diminished Eileen is without her wheelchair. In the chair, she is an undeniable presence, never slumping, never feeling sorry for herself, always respected. She knows Eileen is aware of her being there. She assumes now, as always, that Mary has come out of pity, when in fact she has come partly to save herself. She needs distance and time from her own life, and Eileen is her excuse.

Eileen's eyes open and she stares at Mary, at the involuntary tears squeezing out of her eyes. Not what Mary has planned. There is no corresponding pity to go with the tears, so how have they arrived? Her eyes are watering, that's all. It has been a tiresome day, with the flight delayed three hours.

"Hi!" Eileen's hand is dry and scaly. The nurse is all business, competent with needles, efficient with thermometers and clearing of the lungs, but not the kind to smooth cream on the hands or comb her hair or give Eileen any real comfort. How quickly Mary finds herself falling into the old role, the one she had promised herself to forget forever. She would deal with Eileen's affairs but would not assume the role of nurse. Taking cream from her handbag she smooths it onto Eileen's hands. The body contact brings fresh tears. There Eileen lies dying. Taking with her Mary's rib. Mary had been born with one rib missing, Eileen with one extra.

"You're tired?" Eileen asks. As usual she doesn't wait for a reply, but in the next breath asks for water. As Mary feeds her water, she knows she's being observed closely. Eileen detests pity.

"Don't know how she stands it." Nurse Ballard, busy with medicine and syringes, refers to the vibrations. She pauses for a moment at the huge plate-glass window, an octopus of tubing dripping from her hands. "I'll show you what to do in the night. Your sister said there would be no need for a night nurse when you came."

"My sister is wrong." How firm and sure her own voice sounds. She is able to speak up, for Eileen's eyes are now closed. "I'm no nurse. I've come to help, but I can't possibly do any of these things." On this at least she could stand firm. Eileen had money. Let her pay for nurses.

An enormous crash galvanizes them for a second. Nurse Ballard goes to the window again. "Good gracious. What on earth is happening? It's bedlam."

The building might be in jeopardy, but Mary isn't to be sidetracked. "I'd like to arrange for a night nurse. She had a night nurse until today?"

"Oh yes, but whether we can book her now is another question. I'll contact her if you wish."

"Please."

Mary continues to sit by the bed, in no rush to go and unpack. She wants her mind to be occupied with practical things so that she doesn't have to think, but images keep intruding into her consciousness. Images of Jennie and scenes of devastation and ruin from earthquake. Then cosier scenes of Graham in some kind of sexual conjunction with Vera. She muses on the name Vera. What an odd name for someone born in the fifties. Reminiscent of forties movies with counterspies, espionage agents, femmes fatales who worked for foreign governments.

How straight and honest Graham had been. He felt this compulsion to sleep with Vera but wanted Mary to know first. He couldn't stand anything underhanded. It was noble of him in some way, but the pain was intense, and at the moment of telling she would have exchanged him without question for someone sly and secretive.

Fool! Eileen would have had that word for her. What would *she* have done in the circumstances? Cajoled, raged, blackmailed, any number of paths but the one Mary had taken: retreat. But then again, running to the aid of a dying sister could hardly be called retreat.

She still has to work out in her head whether she is truly devastated by Graham's admission. He had cradled her in his arms when he made his confession. "I do love you, darling, but this is something I can't avoid." Of course he could have avoided it. One avoids walking into traffic, stepping over cliffs, one avoids giving pain as much as possible, one avoids breaking one's marriage vows, or was she hopelessly out of date, hopelessly naive, hopelessly idiotic?

There had been an earthquake in Japan only recently. Surely that meant that Jennie, their one and only darling child, was not likely to be in danger? She calls once a week and assures them everything is wonderful, but still Mary wakes in the night wet with sweat, sometimes digging in rubble to find Jennie's body. In one dream she swims over crumbled skyscrapers looking for Jennie. Every night a different dream, always searching for Jennie after a disaster.

"Reba will come tonight, but she's booked for tomorrow night," the nurse's voice breaks into Mary's fearful musings. Reprieve. She doesn't have to know about draining Eileen's lungs, doesn't have to administer injections. That's all that matters.

Mary sees her out the door, glad when her chatter is gone. Only the rattle of Eileen's uneven breath reminds her of what is supposed to be the true purpose of her visit: to give comfort to the dying.

"Mary! Mary!" The voice is feeble, coming only faintly through the vibrations of the workmen rebuilding the garage.

"Sit!" she commands Mary. Doesn't she notice that Mary still wears her jacket, that she is, if not travel weary, life weary? Of course not. Leaving this world is an all-encompassing business. All else must stand still and wait. But the workmen haven't heard, Eileen; they press on, undaunted. Mary wants to draw attention to that, to make her feel the vibrations, but is quiet, dutifully sitting by the bed and taking Eileen's hand, re-connecting herself to the old Eileen. The one she'd once loved and admired and served.

"Something's wrong?" Eileen asks. *Of course something is wrong. You are dying. Taking that extra rib. The one that should be mine.*

"I'm tired."

"I know, but something else."

She could lie, prevaricate, waste time, but Eileen would ferret it out.

"I see," is all she says when Mary blurts out her story. "And what are you going to do about it?"

"I have no idea."

"Do you still love him?"

"I'm not sure."

"So you were happy to run away and avoid it all?"

"I've come because of you."

She says nothing, just stares at Mary — *through* her to be more precise, the way she always could. Mary feels real tears squeezing out now. Honest-to-God ones of self pity and helplessness.

"Divorce him!" Eileen's voice comes in a kind of hiss of disapproval. "That's your problem, Mary: you need people too much. Tell him to piss off and take his pleasure. Have some self-respect!"

It was a commodity she knew she'd long been missing. Possibly Eileen is right. Divorce, the only answer, but Graham is her best friend. Does one divorce one's best friend, or simply wait around for circumstances to change?

"I've always wondered about passion," Eileen whispers. "Not about feeling it, about satisfying it. Tell me about that!" She presses her hand urgently. Embarrassment and panic overtake Mary. Can one deprive a dying person of the right to know? Is there anything in the vocabulary to describe what she once felt for Graham? Even now she can only think in the past tense. Yet images are surfacing. She doesn't want to have that happen, because in place of herself, she sees Vera. She can only imagine Vera experiencing the pleasures.

"Please!"

If Eileen realizes she's making her suffer, she doesn't show it. Her needs are more important than anyone else's at this particular moment. The rest of the world will have a shot at repairing itself, she will not.

Mary hears her own voice as if from a great distance. After a while, so faithfully is she managing to relate the sensations and exquisite precision of what had been a wonderful sexual relationship, that her body burns, as though reliving the moments. Eileen turns her face away. Perhaps she is getting more than she bargained for. Sex isn't something they have ever talked about. She doesn't understand her sudden eloquence.

The light is finally fading when she finishes. She is certain Eileen is still awake, for who could possibly sleep through such a storm. Mary feels totally drained. Only the knock at the door rouses her from her strange torpor. Eileen's head is turned away. She shows no reaction to the door.

Reba, the night nurse, is a huge black woman with straightened hair, tinted reddish.

"You're the sister," she says, making Mary sound like someone from a religious order.

"I am."

"Nice to know you." She holds out a large hand with puffy, smooth fingers. Her grasp is crushing. This woman would be able to lift Eileen with one hand. She can see her on Sundays in the front row of a Baptist Church, leading the congregation in vibrant renditions of spirituals.

"She sleepin'?" she asks in a lovely Jamaican lilt.

Mary nods, knowing perfectly well that there is no way that Eileen might have dozed off during her truthful reportage. She feels uneasy about what she has spewed out in answer to Eileen's request. What was she trying to do? Revive her own interest in continuing the marriage or point out to Eileen what she had missed? In honesty, probably both.

Reba lifts Eileen's bedsheets and sticks her nose under to sniff. "Changed her, did she?"

Mary has no idea what the Ballard woman had done. Reba gives Mary a questioning look. Shouldn't a sister know something like that? Shouldn't a sister care? She sweeps past her in a swish of meshing thighs, leaving a heavy smell of rose-petals in the air. "Mercredi! Mercredi!" she tut-tuts. Before very long, Mary becomes used to Reba and her "Mercredi! Mercredi!" cry, which seems to substitute for stronger expressions while still giving her some satisfaction.

It is a tortured night, for after the recounting of passion to Eileen, so fresh is her love for Graham, so intensely painful are all the emotions, that she feels suicidal. Reaching out for Graham constantly, she gropes only with space.

The emptiness that overwhelms her in the morning is worse than anything she has experienced so far. The peculiar sensation in her throat is the feeling one gets just before throwing up. Thank God there is plenty to do. Reba sees to that.

Eileen's breakfast is prepared with exact specifications from Reba: half a grapefruit removed from the rind, a quarter of a dish of oatmeal porridge, one slice of brown toast, and strong coffee. Nothing tempts her own appetite. Her once healthy eating habits are a thing of the past. She sips coffee and it tastes sour and distasteful.

Eileen, propped up in bed seems scrubbed and pink. Healthier looking than the previous evening. Reba is humming to herself and rearranging things on the bedside table when Mary comes in with Eileen's breakfast.

"How are you this morning?"

"Well scrubbed. Reba wants to make sure I go to my maker with clean feet."

"Mercredi! Mercredi" Reba shakes her head. "Dirty feet don't get over de threshold."

How easy their banter is. No denials, no pretend. Reba has no doubt described what Eileen can expect in the next world. They both know where Eileen is going and chatter about the ground rules. Mary can't do that.

Mercifully, the workmen have either not started their awful racket or they have finished the job. Early in the day, the phone calls start. Sammy, who won't be able to make a visit that night but wants just a word with Eileen. Andrew, who will be by later with some Thai food. Is that actually permitted? Thai food for someone dying? Judith, just to say "Hi!"; she will come at the weekend. They all sound desperately rushed, as though they are speaking on car phones. How easily Eileen makes friends.

It is a relief to step outside the condominium later in the morning, to make a trip and get supplies. Since there is no car, she is forced to buy things from the local delis and grocery stores. She flinches at the prices that she would never dream of paying in Winnipeg, but Eileen gave her money and, as though mind reading, warned her not to be shocked and not to be stingy.

She feels strange and out of sync walking down the street. People sweep past, jogging her arms but never making eye contact. Usually in pairs, they talk intensely and fast, in odd juxtaposition to the slow moving traffic. Mary turns away from the indifferent faces and gazes up at the townhouse shops. One enters boutiques by either going up a few steps or down. They are the kinds of places she feels uncomfortable even browsing in. She imagines the salesgirls pricing her clothes, shunning her for a lack of flare, writing her off as a potential customer.

Jags and Porsches cruise slowly, windows open, gold-watched

wrists resting on the door. Her mother in her Englishy way would have called some of the drivers "spivs." A word that used to send Eileen and her into rifts of laughter. A lovely word, with a kind of dangerous connotation. She'd had a boyfriend once whom her mother referred to as "that spiv." Danny had been sleek, dark, and Greek, but quiet as a lamb and with none of the shady associations the word "spiv" evoked.

Nobody rushes to serve her when she walks into a small deli that displays a dazzling range of cooked salads: slithery squid in tomato dressing, artichokes in yellowish oil, vivid asparagus arranged with lemon slices. Exotic-looking breads and aromatic coffees are behind the counter. Displayed on glass shelves are Belgium chocolates and tiny baskets filled with glass bottles of caviar and canned quail. Eileen wants a special walnut bread that is sold here and needs more coffee, a house blend that seems to Mary way over-priced.

She takes her time examining a wall freezer of various pastas, marvelling at the shapes: some like yellow plastic bows, others like frills. Bending to peer at the sauces in little see-through containers, she hears a voice beside her.

"You have to be Eileen's twin?"

She looks up in surprise into a face staring at her intently. "Andrew Wright," he says, holding out his hand. "I think I spoke to you on the phone this morning."

Hypnotists have eyes like this: grey blue and ringed by such dark lashes that the white of the eye seems bluish.

"Sorry, I'm being rude, but it's so odd to see someone so like Eileen standing there. You look a little lost. Is there something I can do to help?"

"I am a little lost. It all seems a bit much."

"Yes, it is, bloody expensive. I expect your prices are a bit more modest out west?"

He makes it sound as though she's come from the boonies. She's noticed before that Torontonians always speak of points west as though of strange outposts that only idiots could inhabit.

"Not really," she lies. "It's just that I'm trying to find my way around. I have all Eileen's instructions and a list as long as my arm of things she needs."

"If I can help?"

"No. It's fine. I have time."

Do people actually go to work in khaki shirts and shorts, she wonders? His hair is wildly curly, beginning to grey, and just long enough to place him not in a conventional office but rather in some outside adventure. Perhaps in the deepest jungles of Africa, studying gorillas in their habitat or searching for hidden cities. He has the slight stoop of the tall man. It is hard to place him as far as age, but she guesses around fifty, give or take a couple of years.

"How is she?"

"Putting on a brave face."

"She's one terrific woman." He touches Mary's arm. "Anyway, I'll let you get on with it. See you later ... with the Thai food, remember?"

"Right." Mary watches him go. It pleases her that he'd called Eileen a woman and not a "lady," as a million other men might have done.

Later, sitting in one of the open-air cafés, surrounded by her shopping, she can't remember whether cappuccino is the milky one or the sludge that comes in a demi-tasse. Eileen would know. She'll have to take her chances. She orders bravely and is thrilled when it arrives with frothing milk. She makes a mental note not to forget. She would like to sit here all day just watching the passing crowd, making up stories about the more interesting ones, trying to block out all thoughts of Graham, but guilt about leaving Eileen for so long makes her lap up the remains of the wonderful coffee and pay the bill.

She might just as easily have stayed, for when she gets back, Eileen is sleeping and has been for several hours — the usual uneasy, rasping sleep that one senses isn't replenishing her but is mercifully taking her outside of pain. Sitting beside her on the bed, Mary stares at her face. Her own face, but yellow and thinner. For just an instant she feels a twinge of hurt at Andrew Wright recognizing her, even comparing her to the figure in front of her in bed. But there are the unmistakeable features. The hair fuzzed and curled slightly on the forehead, exactly the same colour and texture as her own. The mouth with the slightly puffy bottom lip and the tiny dent in the centre that is such a give-away. The neck overly long for the rest of the body. On Eileen it was ringed; perhaps from too many years in the wheelchair her entire frame had sunk perceptibly, the neck too, folding slightly in on itself. Her own neck is still white and slender. She's always been proud of her neck. How odd to be sitting beside Eileen making silly comparisons that make her come out somewhat better, more attractive.

"You should do something else," Nurse Ballard says. Mary has no inclination to ask her for her first name — whereas with Reba, to call her anything more formal would be ridiculous. What else could she be doing? Mary wonders. There is nothing in the apartment that seems to need reorganization; everything is neat and in its place. She could read a book or write something, but neither appeals to her.

"You are prepared, I hope?" Nurse Ballard stares at her. For one irrational moment Mary thinks she's referring to her marriage. But then horror overtakes her. Somewhere in the past there was such a conversation, and it had been in a hospital room when their father lay dying. The doctor had discussed the impending death as though her father couldn't hear. They'd all stood and listened, too stunned to warn him off.

Mary holds up a silencing hand, pointing to the door. She allows Nurse Ballard to follow her out. "Don't ever discuss it in there," she says fiercely, once they are in the hallway.

"She's asleep!" Nurse Ballard says defensively.

"We don't know that for sure. I won't have it discussed in the room." She's surprised by her own vehemence, but she doesn't care.

"She talks about it herself."

"That's fine, but we won't."

247

Nurse Ballard shrugs and, turning, goes back into the bedroom. For an instant she feels foolish. After all, she has heard Reba and Eileen talk sensibly about death.

All afternoon she sits in the living room writing in a notebook taken from the kitchen shelf. It is pristine as though waiting for some kind of outpouring. She writes:

"*Dear Graham:*

Take Vera! Be my guest. I'm not coming back and I hope you will be very happy. No, I don't hope that. I hope Vera is a tart and hurts you as much as you have hurt me. I hope you live the rest of your life in deep regret (and sorrow). Also, that she proves fecund and gives you six children. I would like to see you with the children you never wanted and deprived me of. May they be a royal pain in the butt to you and detest you in your old age – as I shall do.

Mary"

"*Graham:*

(Scrap the "Dear," he was not her "dear" any longer.) I find life without you rich and full. I realize now that I have been living behind shutters for too long. Feel no guilt! In fact, be proud of yourself, you have set me free."

Free for what? she wonders, studying the word that had written itself on the page. It is a proper word, somehow suiting the connotation with the two vowels at the end. On the tongue it slides out in a wonderful singing sound. It doesn't correspond in the least with what she is feeling.

"*Dear Graham:*

I am dying. You have caused me irrevocable damage. I feel dead inside. I feel betrayed. I feel angry. I feel hostile. I feel lost.

Truthfully,

Mary"

There it is. This is the one she should send. She tears out all three sheets of paper and scrunches them in a ball, throwing them into the garbage. Fingering the surface of a grape that sits in a bowl on the table, she tries plucking it from the stem. She realizes suddenly that it's plastic. How odd, when it looks so real. The greyish purple sheen makes it look straight from the vine. Long ago, she and Eileen had talked about their detestation of artificial fruit and flowers. What had made Eileen change her mind?

Nurse Ballard comes into the kitchen and fills the kettle with water. She casts a quick, resentful look in Mary's direction.

"Your sister's awake."

"Right." Mary looks up.

The days pass slowly. People coming and going from the apartment, some giving Eileen energy, some tiring her out. She is brightest when Andrew shows up. She talks about him a lot and Mary guesses she's more than a little in love with him. All the men who come to visit appear to have been through several marriages; Andrew is recovering from a failed relationship. He was married and divorced when he was very young. He seems not to want to take the step again.

Eileen comes to life and radiates energy. Mary feels tiny and colourless as she always has. It takes her back to their school days when she wheeled Eileen to school. They'd always been joined by kids from different classes who all knew Eileen and loved her company, so that the wheelchair was soon surrounded by people jostling just to say a word or give a greeting. Like the Pied Piper, they always arrived at the school yard with an entourage of mesmerized people. None of it had to do with the kids feeling sorry for Eileen. She wouldn't have stood for it and they sensed that. Sometimes Mary felt as though all her own energy drained out right through the handles of the wheelchair she was pushing, so that she

249

became invisible, a kind of zombie whose function it was in life to hang on to the chair. It was no different now. Although she was no longer attached to the chair, her energy disappeared when she was in Eileen's presence.

Flying out to join Graham in Winnipeg had been the most frightening thing that had ever happened to her, but somehow, in order to save herself, she knew she had to make the move. Her parents had been shocked. Eileen was understanding, which had made her feel even more like a heel. The sense of freedom she'd felt that day on the plane to Winnipeg had been overwhelming. It was as though her chest had been cut open and her heart and lungs were allowed to expand. She could breathe again. Could finally live. She was actually a person, a human being with her own life, her own energy. Now she had to remind herself of that again. She had to fight against the memories.

Sometimes Andrew comes into the kitchen where she sits reading a book and brings her some of the supper he's brought for Eileen. She usually opens a bottle of wine and they drink it companionably. He makes her think less about Graham, and for that she is grateful. He is interested in her life in Winnipeg and she finds herself telling him more than she intends.

"Your husband, what does he do?"

He sleeps with another woman. He holds me in his arms and swears he loves me and takes another woman to his bed. No, that isn't what she tells. She lies a little about Graham, all the time half wondering if perhaps Eileen has told him the truth. It pains her to think of them both in the room feeling sorry for her. Labelling her as a pathetic individual who lacks the guts to make decisions.

For some odd reason she looks at his thighs when he sits opposite her at the table. Lovely thighs, strong and muscular and far more powerful than Graham's. On every visit he wears shorts, and she longs to tell him to cover himself up. Sometimes she feels like laying her hand on him. He is no longer young, but he has the kind of face that is both thoughtful and sorrowful. At one time he must have suffered just as she's suffering now, but she can't hope to talk about that with him. He is first and foremost Eileen's friend.

Eileen dies ten days after Mary's arrival. It is totally unexpected in a way, for she had been full of spirit when Andrew left that night. So much so that Mary felt she and Andrew were both there on a false mission. Sometime in the night, while Reba makes herself a cup of tea in the kitchen, the rattling, laboured breathing stops and Eileen finally finds peace.

Reba wakes Mary at 7.00 A.M. to pass on the news. She lies rigid in the bed, paralyzed by grief. She is slow to go to Eileen's room and surprised when she finally does. It doesn't seem like Eileen lying there. The face is waxen and unreal and reminds her of her own at the most futile times in her life when she has felt powerless and without personality. She has never been religious, suddenly the idea of the spirit makes more sense. For this is not the Eileen she knows. That person has flown in the night and left an empty shell behind.

She phones Andrew right away. He arrives at the apartment transformed into a city person, wearing grey flannels and a blazer. When he hugs her, she finally breaks down and sobs. He holds her and murmurs words about allowing herself the freedom to cry, and she wants to tell him that she isn't crying for Eileen but for her own rebirth, but it's all too confusing. Following him into Eileen's room she feels an overwhelming sorrow. Standing side by side with Andrew, they cry together. He wipes his own eyes and hands her the handkerchief. She blurts onto its dampness, mingling their tears.

"Will your husband come?" he asks.

"No." She shakes her head. She couldn't bear Graham's arms around her. She knows that now.

"Let me make the funeral arrangements," Andrew offers right away.

"Yes, but that's not fair. Still, I haven't a clue what to do. If you could help ..."

"Of course."

The funeral home where Andrew takes her is sepulchrally

quiet, everyone moving on slippered feet, self-effacing and colourless. It is also a reminder of her own complete aloneness. Before she dies, she will leave instructions for her ashes to be scattered.

Eileen had told Andrew she wanted to be cremated. There was to be no open casket, or visitation to the funeral home prior to the funeral; she'd been specific about that. Andrew goes back with her to the apartment and together they go through Eileen's address book, marking off the names of the people he believes they should call. They divide the list.

She's surprised how much Andrew knows about Eileen's life.

"She was lucky to have you," Mary offers.

"I was lucky to have her as a friend."

At the apartment people come and go — friends she's never even heard Eileen mention and the richness of Eileen's life keeps unfolding, reminding her of the drabness of her own.

They expect her to be exactly like Eileen. Most of them remark on how wonderful it is to meet her and comment on her likeness to Eileen. She finds herself expanding under their eyes, turning into what she feels they expect her to be. Andrew watches her. Only he might know her for what she truly is. He has seen her in action when Eileen was around. Meanwhile, she fields telephone calls from Graham who is solicitous and somehow doubts she can manage without him.

She finds an envelope addressed to her and reads a curt little businesslike note from Eileen giving her the address of her lawyer and advising her that everything has been left to her. What everything amounts to she is still unsure, but in her methodical way, Eileen has listed her bank, her investment company, and the deed to the apartment. That, it seems, she owns outright. Through all of Eileen's illness Mary has never really thought about this part of it.

It is pouring rain the day of the funeral. The streets steam with humidity, giving an other-worldly feel to the events. The cars seem to float as though on grey clouds. When they step out of the car eventually, a warm, gusty wind has come up, lifting people's skirts, shaking the trees. Andrew carries an enormous, striped, red-and-white umbrella. There is to be nothing sombre about this gathering. Most of those huddled outside the funeral home are clustered under multi-coloured umbrellas: a gathering of exotic butterflies, clotted together by a gust of wind.

She learns from the many people that Eileen has talked often about despising mourning. Sammy, her partner in the agency, even wears an extraordinary shirt covered in parakeets.

"Eileen always said this was the shirt I had to wear at her funeral," he says with a grin.

There is a kind of forced gaiety to the service. Sombre funeral-parlour employees stand at a respectable distance and obviously wonder about the collection of oddly dressed mourners. Mary's own subdued, grey, nunlike dress feels totally wrong. People come and press her hand, no doubt wondering about a sister who knows so little about her twin that she has chosen to wear grey.

They are ready to forgive, though. "You're so like her," one woman gushes, clasping Mary in her arms.

Andrew manages everything in his methodical way, even arranging for a caterer to provide food back at the apartment. It is an odd sensation stepping into the apartment only to find it taken over by three efficient women who appear to have found everything they need in the kitchen to serve the food. Mary feels like an intruder. One of the women asks her impatiently to move away from the refrigerator.

"This is my place," Mary says in a distressingly thin voice.

"Sorry, Miss, I didn't realize ..." The voice tails off and for an instant the woman stands helpless.

"No, no. I'll get out of your way. You seem to have found everything." She tries to repress a feeling of impotence which intensifies when she sees the hoard of people that turns up at the door. Had they really all been to the funeral? She no longer remembers. She finds herself wandering, standing at people's elbows silently until they turn and when they see the resemblance to Eileen, include her in their conversations. A total sense of unreality takes over. As more wine is drunk, voices become louder, laughter more sustained. For a moment she imagines she is Eileen, looking down on the party from a distance, virtually out of body. She feels a hand on her arm and hears Andrew's voice in her ear.

"Holding up okay?"

She nods.

When she is finally alone in the apartment, there is nothing left to remind her, aside from a couple of bouquets of flowers, that anything has happened. The women have come and gone, washing every last dish, cleaning out every ashtray, neatly packaging and labelling the food before putting it in the refrigerator. She feels a great emptiness. She still has to tackle Eileen's wardrobe, clear out her clothes. That she dreads. She stands staring into Eileen's closet. Everything has been arranged at a level where Eileen could reach. There is an elaborate pulley system that hauls down an upper rack of clothes.

Blouses and sweaters are predominant. Everything is extraordinarily neat. Shoes are slotted into special built-in boxes. Mary picks up a pair of shoes. They look brand new. Of course, they've always looked that way. She sits on the edge of the bed and tries them on. Eileen and she had perhaps started off life with the same sized feet, but her own have grown and expanded, spread every so slightly, so that the shoes are tight and uncomfortable.

The telephone rings. It will be Graham again. She allows it to ring, not rushing to pick it up.

"Hello, Mum."

"Jennifer?"

"I'm sorry. Dad just told me. Are you all right?"

"Yes. "

"Was it all awful?"

"No. Actually, it wasn't. She went very peacefully and we had a sort of party today. They all say she wanted that."

"Sorry I'm not there."

"Thanks, darling."

"Why didn't Dad join you?"

Because he's busy, darling. Because he's a big shit. Because he's going through a mid-life crisis. Because he wants to have his cake and eat it too. Because he's a child with a child's appetites.

"He's busy at work. Besides, I have plenty of Eileen's friends to help." She knows it sounds lame. The silence at the other end of the line is longer than can be accounted for by delayed reception. It isn't fair to cause Jennifer to worry, but the excuse is the best she can manage.

"Is there much to do?"

"Yes, lots. Dad never was very good at that kind of thing. Now what about you? Are things any better?"

Last time they had spoken, Jennifer was living in Osaka with a rather rigid Japanese couple who wanted to keep tabs on her every movement. Seeing themselves perhaps as surrogate parents, they had imposed curfews. While she had sympathized with her daughter over the restrictions, she'd privately been glad. It comforted her to know that someone cared.

"I'm sharing this place now with a couple of other teachers. It's not terribly private, but it's a million times better."

While they talk, Mary thinks about how she will deal with Jennifer if she decides to stay on in Toronto. It's the first time the thought of staying occurs to her, but it wouldn't be such an illogical move. She may feel strange and disoriented in the city now, but that would fade. It isn't as though she knows nothing about Toronto. It had, after all, been her home at one time. She can rationalize staying by claiming she has to clear up all the business associated with Eileen's death. She won't have to explain to Jennifer what is going on at home.

"Listen, darling, write to me here for a while. There are a million things to be arranged and cleared up. I can't imagine being able to get rid of the apartment for a while. Real estate is moving slowly right now."

"Can't someone handle all that for you?"

"I would rather do it myself. Besides, it's a break for me."

"Is everything all right?"

"Of course. Why shouldn't it be?"

"Well, Daddy not being there. I just wondered."

"He wanted to come. It was my idea that he shouldn't."

She knows it doesn't sound convincing. Jennifer is used to her mother and father working as a team. Is her voice perhaps too cheerful, are her assurances too glib?

Later, just as she is about to go to bed, Graham calls.

"Hello, darling! You all right?"

"Yes. I'm fine."

"How was it?"

"I think it was a party Eileen might have wanted to attend."

"She would have liked that."

"Yes."

"How long will it take to get everything cleared up?"

Is there a hopeful note in his voice? Is Vera perhaps curled up against him, maybe even listening in on the conversation?

"I have no idea."

"Listen, if there are any problems, just fax me. She has a fax, doesn't she?"

"Yes. What kind of problems?"

"Legal things that you might need advice on ... that kind of thing."

It's odd how Graham now holds back from asking the question that she knows is foremost in his mind. How much exactly had Eileen left. A kind of formality has suddenly crept into their dealings. No doubt this comes from his feelings of guilt.

She surprises herself by sleeping well, a quiet and dreamless sleep. The following morning, dressed in one of Eileen's more exotically coloured robes, she eats some of the leftovers from the refrigerator: smoked-salmon canapés, and even though they are slightly soggy, it feels decadent and appropriate. The coffee that she's learned to brew according to Eileen's instructions is also perfect.

Later in the day Andrew calls. She hasn't realized that it is

Friday, almost the weekend. The days of the week have seemed singularly unimportant of late. Her normal routine all destroyed, she has allowed time to wash over her without any accounting or note. Her watch has been barely looked at in the last couple of days.

Andrew wants to come and take her out to lunch; she declines without knowing why. She explains her refusal away by claiming to have much to do, including a visit to the lawyer's office. She tries to ignore the overly long pause at his end when she says this. She suspects he has been thoroughly enjoying her "helpless female" role, the one she has so readily fallen into. In that regard he is no different from Graham.

Clearing away her breakfast dishes, she makes a mental note that the kitchen counters will have to be heightened. Obviously the interior of the apartment had been put together with specific instructions from Eileen. She would break her back if she had to work at any of them. They were definitely for a wheelchair user. They all had overhangs, too. Opening the cupboards, she inspects their insides. The bottom cupboards are all narrow because of the overhang. She could easily alter their size.

Later she dumps the sofa cushions in a pile on the floor and bundles them in a large, ugly, multi-coloured sheet she finds in the linen closet. She hates decorator cushions of this sort. They have to be disposed of in some way. With a shock she realizes that she is actually planning to live here. Even when she spoke to Jennifer, she talked in temporary terms, but now she knows there is nothing to stop her from staying on indefinitely. It would be an out for Graham. It would remove her from the awfulness of knowing all about his comings and goings in Winnipeg, and the guessing as to when he was with Vera.

She keeps herself busy doing simple chores like clearing out kitchen drawers. She feels a distaste for tackling Eileen's clothes as yet. At one point she realizes she is freezing cold, but can't find a thermostat to turn down the air-conditioning. It is amazing how emotionless one feels in a chill. She compares how she felt in Winnipeg before leaving home. The weather was relentlessly hot and they had never had their house air-conditioned. She was constantly in a swelter of ache and pain, everything somehow magnified in the heat. Way back when they'd been first married, it had been the beginning of August, and all their lovemaking had taken place in lashings of sweat, everything magnified and sweeter in the musk and warmth of their little apartment under the eaves in the River Avenue house; squirrels skittering across the attic above them, adding somehow to the excitement and total euphoria brought on by prolonged and ecstatic lovemaking. She wondered if Graham remembered those days. Perhaps he was trying to relive them now with a different heroine.

Later, stepping out into the shimmer of Yorkville is like stepping onto a bank of steaming sauna coals. The air feels tropical, heavy with dampness. She is sure a mist rises from her body as hot air meets cold skin.

The lawyer's office is just around the corner. Her ears are assaulted by the din of voices and traffic. Could she get used to this? Does she want to get used to it? She isn't certain of anything any more; only the sense of being an alien stays with her.

Elliot Miskey, Eileen's lawyer, is little and round with a completely bald head, its surface shining as though French-polished. He is immaculately clad in cream linen slacks and a beige silk shirt, but in keeping with his Yorkville setting, he has no tie — the perfect lawyer for his more than perfect clients. His office is decorated in oyster tones, the carpet a terracotta shade, thick and spongy underfoot. One could easily drown in such a carpet.

There is to be no reading of the will. He brings a young man into the room whom he claims Eileen appointed as her executor, and hands the sheaf of papers over silently, sitting back to watch Mary as she begins to read.

She reads the attached note first.

Dear Mary:

Rid of me at last. What a relief that must be. No, don't deny it. I've always known I've been a kind of ugly shadow in your life ...

Mary looks up. The envelope had been sealed, but she wonders if either of the men in the room have seen the letter. She looks down at it again.

... One good thing ... this should at last make you independent. Show Graham the door! You might not always have known it, but he hasn't been the perfect husband ...

Mary's stomach is turning over. She'd never talked to Eileen about Graham. Until the event of Vera, as far as she knew he had always been faithful, but now the seeds of doubt are sewn.

Eileen must have considered that it might cause her pain to read this? Her eyes mist over and she folds the note up. Setting it under the other papers, she opens the will. It is full of legalese, and, folding that too, she looks up at Elliot Miskey, giving a little helpless shrug. He hands over some documents. Eileen's bank statement. An account of her share holdings. "Brian here has made a kind of summary for you on the last page."

Mary turns quickly to the last page. The figures blur before her eyes. Is it even possible? She is rich. If she wants, she can sit back and do nothing for the rest of her life. How much of the money came from her father she isn't sure, but obviously Eileen has either been a good money manager or had good advice.

"A considerable sum," Elliot said, smiling.

"Yes. I don't know what to say."

"There will of course be death duties ... but your sister did take the precaution of putting many of her securities in both your names. Also, her apartment was in both your names, so you might be able to avoid some of these."

She walks back to the apartment in a daze. Elliot has put the papers in a thick large envelope and she feels the bulk of it under her arm. Her feet seem heavy. A kind of acid produces a tiny pain in her stomach.

Back in the apartment, she goes to Eileen's room and, opening the clothes cupboard, she begins pulling everything off the hangers and throwing the clothes in a heap on the floor. A kind of frenzy builds in her until she is almost panting. She has no idea what fuels the rage, but she is shocked when she surveys the empty hangers swinging in the cupboard and the riot of colour on the floor.

Next, she pulls out the boxes at the end of the cupboard. Most seem to contain photographs, all meticulously labelled: the years carefully noted. In a frenzy she dumps the content of several boxes on top of the clothes. None of the photos have been saved in albums; they're held in piles by rubber bands.

A pile marked "Graduation 1975" catches her attention. Pulling the elastic off, the photographs fall to the floor. Hunkering on her knees, she begins to pick them up. There is Eileen, mortar-board and gown, a huge bouquet of flowers on her lap and their mother and father standing proudly on either side. Mary is slightly outside the grouping. Neither parent looks at her. They are both intently focused on Eileen. Had that worried her? She doesn't remember any more. It probably didn't register, for it had ever been the same.

Mary puts the photo down and picks up another one. A different location this time, but again, she is slightly outside the threesome. Looking down, her eyes focus on a photo of Graham, also in cap and gown. She pushes the photograph aside, and there are more of Graham. There is one of him standing in the middle, Eileen on one side in her wheelchair and Graham with one hand on her shoulder and the other hooked in Mary's arm. Mary picks up the photograph and examines it more closely. There is an odd look on Eileen's face, almost a look of fear. She is sure she has this photograph at home somewhere, it is vaguely familiar, but she has never really looked at Eileen properly before.

Why were there so many photographs of Graham? He had

of course been part of the family for a long while, always careful to include Eileen in many of their activities, but Mary had never had the feeling that Eileen particularly valued the friendship. She had been rude about him when he'd accepted the job in Winnipeg and even more scathing when Mary had decided to join him there. *"He's far too charming, Mary,"* had been her only comment when the engagement was announced. *"He'll make you suffer."*

Mary picks up a photograph of Graham alone. He is sitting on the grass in what looks like their garden. He is wearing shorts and has obviously been caught in mid-sentence. He looks as though he is delivering instructions about how to hold the camera. Turning the photograph over, she sees printed in large letters: MINE. Had she printed that herself and somehow left the photograph behind? Not that she could remember. What did it mean?

She undid the elastic bands from some of the other bundles from around that time. There are an extraordinary number of photographs of Graham, but not just Graham alone — Graham with either Mary, or her mother or father, or Eileen. She studies the ones of Graham with Eileen. There is no doubt Eileen looks supremely happy in those. Was it possible that Eileen had been in love with Graham and she'd not even been aware of that? It didn't seem likely, for no matter what man, or woman for that matter, had been around, Eileen had always sparkled. She had always managed to be the centre of attention. Mary remembers now how she had assumed that Graham was more attracted to Eileen than to herself.

Graham was one of her father's top students, one he'd chosen to work on his special projects. For a long time she believed he came to the house only to talk to her father about one of their endless experiments. Graham usually managed to wangle an invitation to dinner from her mother, and then it had always been a kind of triad at the dining table — her father, Eileen, and Graham.

The night she'd discovered his interest in her had been pure magic. Her mother had sprained her ankle and Mary was doing most of the cooking. Graham had taken off his jacket, come into the kitchen, rolled up his sleeves and pitched in to help.

It was only the two of them in the kitchen that day, and she'd felt enveloped by his presence. Graham had always been like that, larger than life, more intense than anyone she'd ever known. At times his vitality was almost frightening. He seemed to keep bumping into her, and she'd chided him gently for being more of a nuisance than a help.

"You look so sweet and all fussed," he said at one point. "Just relax. It will all be fine, and what if it isn't? It's just family."

He seemed to be including himself in their family. The very idea made her feel hot all over. He intended to marry Eileen. That was it. She stopped what she was doing and stared at him. He had his hands in the salad bowl and was tossing the salad with his hands. Somehow, it seemed like an extraordinarily sensual thing to be doing. He looked up and saw her watching. "I always do it this way. Don't you?"

"No. I hadn't thought of it."

"Best way." He grinned and held out a finger. "Want to taste the dressing?"

She felt herself blush. "I know what it tastes like."

"No, you don't. I added a few things." He still held his hand out, and before she knew what she was doing, she moved to him and holding his hand, licked his finger. He closed his eyes and put his head back. "Lovely." Before she could move away, he put his arms around her and keeping his actual hands off her body, he kissed her directly on the mouth. She felt her lips opening under his. It was the most delicious kiss. "There, I've been wanting to do that for months."

She stood perfectly still, too startled to say anything.

"I'm sorry. Have I offended you?"

"No, it was lovely. I thought you came because of Eileen."

"Wrong, because of you."

An unbelievable happiness radiated through her body. Right there in the kitchen they arranged to meet outside the house.

It was weeks before she found the courage to break the news

to the family that she was seeing him on her own. Eileen said nothing, merely wheeled herself out of the room. Perhaps, like Mary, she had considered him her suitor. It was the only thing that spoiled her happiness at that moment. From then on, Eileen managed to arrange to be somewhere else when Graham came to the house. Mary rationalized her absence with the thought that Eileen was practising for the inevitable, the time when she would be alone and have to look after herself.

Surrounded by the photographs, she is all at once overwhelmed with sadness. Behind each image there is a story, a hidden story of wants and desires that could never be met. It isn't necessary to study the dates on the back of each one to know which were taken before she and Graham had become an item and which were taken after. All the anger she has been feeling at the letter the lawyer gave her, dissipates. She cries a torrent and this time they are genuine tears for Eileen.

That night in bed, she falls asleep exhausted, and close to morning comes an erotic dream — a dream so real, she awakes in a sweat of passion, expecting to see Graham beside her. This time there is no pain, as there had been so many of the previous days when she awoke filled with the terrible ache of betrayal, alone in the bed. It is curious how Eileen alive, and now Eileen dead, forced her to conjure up memories of that passion in such exquisite recall. There has to be some meaning to that.

Her body cools. Her pulse returns slowly to normal. She feels philosophical and calm, as peaceful as after satisfactory lovemaking. She turns towards the window and watches the creeping light of dawn erase the night's menace.